PRAISE FOR SAFFRON DREAMS

"Set in post-9/11 America, *Saffron Dreams* tells the moving story of Arissa Il-lahi, a Muslim Pakistani-American, as she struggles to fulfill her different roles as daughter, wife and mother, confronting conflicting cultural expectations and Islamophobia. Eloquently written, a must-read for anyone interested in explor-ing the lived experiences of Muslim women in the United States."
—ALI ASANI, PHD, PROFESSOR OF THE PRACTICE OF INDO-MUSLIM LANGUAGES AND CULTURES, HARVARD UNIVERSITY

"There are books that are beautiful simply because they are so positive and pleas-ant. And there are those that manage to be beautiful in spite of the pain and the suffering and the heartbreak contained within. Shaila Abdullah's *Saffron Dreams* is both. Her writing is mesmerizing. On one hand it feels like a classically cut diamond – precise, sparkling, blindingly beautiful, but also incredibly sharp. On the other hand her writing reminds me of a dish I've often had traveling in In-dia—a *thali*....It was comforting, it was funny, it was spicy; and then heartbreak-ing, full of despair, filled with hope, amazingly fresh and vibrant and satisfying. Following Arissa's story makes the reader realize how little most of us know and understand the world of Muslims, and how incredibly wrong so many of our perceptions are."
—OLIVERA BAUMGARTNER-JACKSON, READER VIEWS

"A much-needed perspective in the void of the American Muslim experience, *Saffron Dreams* is an unflinching look at the societal pressures of widowhood, the role that art can play in the healing process, and the impact of media bias and stereotyping on the Muslim American community in the aftermath of the 2001 terrorist attacks."
—SANDHYA NANKANI, LITERARY SAFARI

"Shaila Abdullah's *Saffron Dreams* is a fascinating look at how events can quickly change a life forever. One focus I found interesting was looking at the tragedy of 9/11 through the eyes of an American immigrant....The thread of Muslim beliefs in a modern world, and especially how women balance ancient and modern traditions, is a fresh, different viewpoint. Finally, the self-affirmation that we can handle whatever life throws at us is valuable."

—SANDIE KIRKLAND, REBECCASREADS

"A poignant story that affirms the redemptive power of storytelling. Abdullah gracefully maneuvers between sentiment and domesticity rewarding us with her insight."

—SEFI ATTA, AWARD-WINNING AUTHOR OF *EVERYTHING GOOD WILL COME*

"Word artist Abdullah, through rich description and evocative detail, shares her characters' love story, how it develops and endures through conflict, chaos, and terrorism. The extraordinary power of this book is not to be missed by the serious or casual reader, for it proves that we are all one in our most elemental human needs and emotions."

—SHIRLEY M. HORD, PHD, SCHOLAR LAUREATE, NATIONAL STAFF DEVELOPMENT COUNCIL

"*Saffron Dreams* is an intimate portrait of a young Pakistani widow in New York, coping with the transformation of her life and identity wrought by 9/11. Grief, memory, dreams, and relationships dance sensuously in her awareness alongside the rich flavors, aromas, and colors of her domestic reality, as Abdullah skillfully draws us in for a closer view."

—STEPHANIE GUNNING, COAUTHOR OF *WILL POWER AND CREATING YOUR BIRTH PLAN*

"In this engrossing and beautifully written novel, the author shows how losses can actually strengthen and provide a sense of meaning and purpose. The birth of a child with severe disabilities, in contrast to the devastating loss of a spouse enable us to see the beauty in creation that is sometimes missed in the glow of perfection. This is not a story of happy but rather of hopeful endings. Our lives are uncertain, but with hope and courage bitterness can be replaced by an appreciation for what is present."

—TIMOTHY S. HARTSHORNE, PHD, PROFESSOR OF PSYCHOLOGY, CENTRAL MICHIGAN UNIVERSITY, PARENT OF A CHILD WITH CHARGE SYNDROME

"Exquisite. That best describes the book, *Saffron Dreams*. The story is from a woman's perspective with true pain, ambition, desperation, duty, and love all mixed together....The care of the characters, complete with flaws exposed, makes this a reflective and insightful read for everyone."

—TERI DAVIS, BESTSELLERSWORLD.COM

"*Saffron Dreams* captures the tone and emotions of the early twenty-first century, while leaving the reader much to think about in terms of what it means to be an American, what the future of America may be, and the hope that exists in future generations.

—TYLER TICHELAAR, PHD, AUTHOR OF *THE MARQUETTE TRILOGY*

"*Saffron Dreams* is a literary masterpiece that lifts the spirit and twists the heart."

—BOB RICH, PHD, EDITOR FOR LOVING HEALING PRESS

"*Saffron Dreams*—besides being a powerful and compelling story of love and loss—captures that fine dance between cultural diversity and common humanity, the complicated steps of which we are all trying to learn."

—JO VIRGIL, VICE-PRESIDENT OF THE WRITERS' LEAGUE OF TEXAS AND A COMMUNITY RELATIONS MANAGER FOR BARNES & NOBLE

"A tender, erotic, and poignant novel. It weaves the clashes of self, family, culture, and country into a tapestry in which soul-searing loss is a recurring, multicolored thread."

—LOREN WOODSON, AUTHOR OF *THE PASSION OF MARYAM*

"*Saffron Dreams* is a chiaroscuro study in which Arissa, a Muslim woman living in the U.S., struggles to fulfill her dreams regardless of how the world violently reshapes them through the September 11th tragedy. Most importantly, this story is about the healing power of love that arrives in surprising shapes and tones.

—DIANE J. HERNANDEZ, 2007 PRESIDENT, WRITERS' LEAGUE OF TEXAS

"Timely, poignant and heartrending, *Saffron Dreams* captures the essence of a Pakistani woman's life after the throes of 9/11 when her husband dies in the tower destruction. Racial tension and disturbing displacement prevail as Shaila Abdullah weaves a plot that is so real the reader will feel every sentiment and relate to the mixed emotions."

—IRENE WATSON, AUTHOR OF *THE SITTING SWING: FINDING WISDOM TO KNOW THE DIFFERENCE*

Saffron Dreams

A Novel

By Shaila Abdullah

MODERN HISTORY PRESS

BOOK #5 IN THE REFLECTIONS OF AMERICA SERIES

Library of Congress Cataloging-in-Publication Data
Abdullah, Shaila, 1971-
Saffron dreams / Shaila Abdullah.
p. cm. -- (Reflections of America series ; bk. 5)
ISBN-13: 978-1-932690-72-9 (alk. paper)
ISBN-10: 1-932690-72-7 (alk. paper)
ISBN-13: 978-1-932690-73-6 (pbk. : alk. paper)
ISBN-10: 1-932690-73-5 (pbk. : alk. paper)
1. Widows--Fiction. 2. Muslim women--Fiction. 3. Unfinished books--Fiction.
4. Pakistanis--United States--Fiction. 5. Fiction--Authorship--Fiction.
6. Victims of terrorism--Fiction. 7. September 11 Terrorist Attacks, 2001--Fiction.
I. Title.
PS3601.B43S24 2009
813'.6--dc22
2008033774

Book design by Shaila Abdullah

Distributed by: Ingram Book Group

Published by:
Modern History Press
5145 Pontiac Trail
Ann Arbor, MI 48105
USA

URL: www.ModernHistoryPress.com
Email: info@ModernHistoryPress.com
Toll-free: 888 761 6268
Fax: 734 663 6861

ACKNOWLEDGMENTS

At the culmination of this three-year long journey, I would like to express gratitude to all those who helped me through major milestones. I thank my family for their support and their unwavering faith in me, especially my 5-year old daughter, Aanyah. Thanks to the following people who stepped in at various junctures to support this work:

Ali Asani	Irene Watson	Martha Boethel
Bob Rich	Jo Virgil	Olivera Baumgartner-Jackson
Chuck Reese	Katie Susil	Sefi Atta
Debbie Matasker	Leslee Tessmann	Shirley Hord
Debbie Ritenour	Leslie Blair	Stephanie Gunning
Diane Hernandez	Lin Harris	Timothy Hartshorne
Hobson Foundation	Loren Woodson	

And of course Victor Volkman of Loving Healing Press, without whom *Saffron Dreams* would still be just a dream.

They say that you no longer fly
Across the land in twilight's glow
That you no longer wander by
The lotus pools that dimly show
Below the whispering trees, and oh!
They say you never haunt the streams
And woodlands! But they do not know
The world is wrapped in saffron dreams.

David Russell
Ballade to Romance

ONE

November 2001
New York

I decided to carry out the first task on my list when fall was about to lose its hue.

All around me were walls of fog; it was just as well. This year the trees of the mid-Hudson Valley were reluctant to shed their leaves. A few fallen ones—the glowing golds, the bloodlike reds, the brazen browns, and the somber yellows—crackled under my feet, crisp and lifeless but not without a voice. There is an old saying that it will be a bad winter if the trees decide to hold on to their leaves.

I wanted to take this journey myself. Unseen. Unchallenged. The air outside was thick, buttressed by my decision, sparse in joy but swollen with complexities. It comforted me; tingled the soles of my feet. The feeling of heaviness that had been lingering for days was gone. I would have danced had I not been on a mission. I delighted in how clean my insides felt, like they had just been laundered and wrung dry, soapy smell suspended in the air. Invisible molecules tickled my nostrils and I sneezed at the thought.

I stopped by a toy store, its shutters down, occupants fast asleep. As I pressed my nose against the window, I marveled at the simple joys of childhood. My breath came in short waves and misted the window, creating tiny smoky bubbles of all sizes and shapes. I imagined being a toy horse, galloping on bound legs, destination firmly defined, thrilled with providence in my naiveté.

The subway ride was a quiet time for reflection with very few early commuters. I got off as if floating on air, tightening my *hijab* or veil around the back of my head. It had to be hysteria, this feeling within me of floating on air. A sharp change in the jet stream will channel numerous storm systems into the Atlantic, the meteorologist had predicted. One was raging within me as I walked westward from Canal to West Street. I felt a restless quest to outrun my fate, grind it beneath my feet.

Pier 34 was abandoned when I reached its southern tip. I faced it with a welcoming smile.

It had the lure of a mother's breast for me, the air throbbing in suckling anticipation. I leaned my protruding belly against the barrier that divided me from the deep stillness below. Another step and my body could easily plummet into the murky depths. I was afraid to touch my abdomen; I wanted to leave its resident out of this. He should never feel responsible for what I was about to do. My mind was full of the possibilities of what life would have been if the towers hadn't crashed.

The wounded skyline in the distance had its edges softened by the early morning fog. Even the air approached the buildings carefully, with reverence. So much was lost. A cool breeze was blowing, providing a hint of the approaching winter. For a brief sickening moment, I debated on which should go—the veil or me.

I slid the hijab from around my neck. The wind felt chilly on my bare head. It was a new sensation. *You can do anything you set your mind to, Arissa Illahi,* a voice from the past whispered to me.

In a few hours, it would be another normal day. Was there such a thing anymore? I appreciated the predawn quietness and looked down at the river with meditated concentration. They said that a new layer of sediment composed of ash and dust had formed a permanent footprint on the river bed after the towers had collapsed. Undisturbed, it had become a constant geological reminder of the tragedy, now etched in history.

The wind tore the veil from my hand, making my task easier. I grasped the cold railing with one hand and swatted at the fleeting piece of my life with the other as the wind picked up speed. It teasingly brought the veil closer to my face. I could have grabbed it. Instead, I let it sail down toward the depths, its grave.

I did not feel a sense of betrayal as I walked away from the pier, letting the wind dance with my hair for the first time. I pulled a few strands out of my eyes and looked back. The sun had just started to peek at the horizon, bleeding its crimson hue. It was a matter of perspective—to an onlooker I had removed my veil, but from where I stood, I had merely shifted it from my head to my heart.

"*Khuda Hafiz,*" I breathed.

Who was I bidding farewell to? I wondered: the age-old tradition or the husband I had kept alive in my heart?

TWO

October 2006
Houston

A housekeeper's nightmare.

An artist's haven.

There was no other way to describe my turpentine-reeking workroom.

For the longest time, I thought my life was like the canvas of a barmy artist who knew when to begin a project but not when to stop.

I looked at the tubes of color around me. They spoke volumes about my house management skills. They were all over the floor, squished, twisted, folded back, some oozing paint, others with rainbow-colored thumb imprints. I plastered the colors all over the canvas with no subject matter in mind, and gradually frenzy overpowered me. The brush in my hand took on a life of its own, and I bent to its whim. The frantic slish-slosh on canvas was deafening in the quiet room; the errant brush had its own mood. I looked at the hopeful blues on the canvas that with repeated strokes had turned the brilliant orange to sad murky brown. In the end, the hodgepodge of colors that dripped off the canvas all bled into one: scorching black, the only color I wanted to forget.

In all fairness, colors define me. Red reminds me of my marriage, the color of the heady, fragrant *mehndi* or henna, intricately tattooed on my palms in the ways of tradition; the crimson shimmering wedding dress called *sharara* I wore the day I married Faizan; yellow, the color of *ubtan*, a paste I applied religiously to my face twenty days before my wedding in the hopes of getting the coveted bridal glow; and orange, the color of saffron, dusty powder that with the right touch added flair to any dish. It was also the color that Faizan dreamed of having on the cover of his unfinished book, a project he thought would make him a famous writer one day.

But black reminds me of all that is sad and wrong in my life. Ironically, in this country, it validates my state of being a widow. It is also the color of my hijab—the dividing line between my life with Faizan and the one without him. How different lives are from continent to continent. White, the bridal color in the West, is the color a widow is expected to wear in the East, the color the body is shrouded in before being buried in the earth.

The brush fell from my guilty hands, landing on the floor with a tired thud. I stepped back as if struck and looked at the picture in mad fixation. Staring back at me from the canvas, behind the dull last strokes that failed to hide the subject, were entwined towers engulfed in reddish blue smoke. And in the midst of the smoldering slivers was the face of a forlorn and lost child.

My journey spans half a decade, from the biggest loss of my life to where I am now. It is a tale of grief and happiness, of control and losing control, of barriers and openings, of prejudices and acceptance, of holding on and letting go. It is about turning my heart inside out, mending it, and putting it right back in as it is about looking at life from the perspective of someone trapped in time. Finally, it's about filling shoes bigger than mine—and filling two with only one leg to stand on. This is the leg that over and over again will weaken with the weight it's expected to carry, falter, but eventually mend and march over the terrains of time.

I got home and put the groceries on the counter. I always have a list of tasks mapped out in perfect order for the evening. *Start a Soup.* I put a pot of water on the stove to start a vegetable soup for Raian. *Change.* I rescued a turnip that had rolled off the counter, and then slipped off my shoes, not bothering to untie them. The wide boots had grown used to being put on and taken off that way, their contours neatly shaped for a comfortable fit. I decided to change later. *Fix Tea.* I threw a teabag in a cup and put it in the microwave. Raian disappeared into the living room, and the different-colored lights emitting from the room confirmed that he had turned on the TV. He didn't turn up the volume; sound was useless to him. He coughed, and with an easy maternal instinct, I made a mental note to give him some medicine before bed.

There were three messages on the answering machine and I intuitively knew who they were from. I deleted all three in quick succession without hearing them—Ami, Zaki, Ami.

The kitchen felt a little cold as I walked back in to dice some shallots, turnips, and zucchini. I scooped them up and added them to the boiling pot. A crushed clove of garlic went in next, and I took slow sips of my tea as I studied the vegetables squirming inside the pot. *Start your dinner.* That one didn't matter much. Since Ma and Baba—my parents-in-law—had left, even Rice-A-Roni worked. I decided on some Chicken Helper. The freezer door pulled open with a sigh, and in the humming of the interior, I forgot why I had opened it in the first place. The rumbling in my stomach alerted me to the basic needs of survival as a small Ziploc bag at the far end of the shelf caught my eye. It contained shish kabobs that Ma had frozen before leaving. *Would they still be edible after six months?* I decided to take my chances. I tossed the kabobs in the microwave, watching the turntable swirl the plate. I missed my mother-in-law's elaborate home-cooked meals. In the five years that she and Baba had lived with us, there was a soothing discipline to dinner. Plenty of thought and planning went into what was presented on the table. A full meal consisted of a curry or stew, rice, and piping hot flour *chappatis*. Sometimes Ma had the fresh yogurt drink, *lassi*, on the side, or round fritters dipped in a yogurt and chili dip that transported me back home. Onion and cucumber salad garnished with cilantro was a must. Ma's pickled mangoes were a feast for the senses, and although her stuffed flour chilies with cumin powder burned your mouth, they were a great combination with the lentil curry. And her saffron-flavored rice pudding could shame even the old cook back home.

Saffron. It reminded me of an unfinished project that was much closer to completion than it was a year ago. I left my culinary project bubbling and walked into the den to turn on the computer. I lost the minutes and then the hours as I swam in a sea of words, oblivious to the world around me. The squeal of the smoke detector jolted me into action. I raced past my son, who had neither the sensory cues of smell nor sound to be alarmed by the commotion. He had missed his dinnertime but had not felt the pangs of hunger.

In that moment, I felt terrified for him and for the rest of his life.

The water in the soup had disappeared and the pot was burning with the shriveled turnips and zucchini stuck to its bottom. The shish kabobs in the microwave were hard as rocks. I poured the contents of the pot into the sink and slid the kabobs in the trash can. When I put a fresh pot of water on the stove, I decided to set an egg timer. It was time to check on Raian.

He was sprawled across the floor, the eye patch covering his left eye making him look like a pirate, one of the many gifts of his syndrome. Every day for a few hours, we put a patch over his good eye to exercise his lazy eye. Oblivious to the TV running in the background, he was studying an arc of rainbow colors draped across his arm—a direct result of sunlight filtering through the window. He swatted at it with his other hand and then crawled around in a circle trying to escape from it. I watched his captivating dance in fascination; he immersed himself in the light one instant and tore away from it the next—the dance that life played with him on a daily basis that he had by now orchestrated to perfection.

The light was his to tango, not his to hold; illumination, he had learned, wasn't the victory.

I looked at him with love-stricken eyes. How flawed he was to the rest of the world, but how very perfect to me.

Saffron, crocus veil, the flower with the three red stigmas.

It was 1 a.m., and I had been unsuccessful in shutting my brain off to get some sleep. Some images refused to let me be. They wanted to be released and live on paper. I approached the canvas in that state of mind.

I folded back the sleeve of my olive shirt kameez and laid some strands of saffron on the back of my left hand. Like eager devotees, they molded to its contour. For three thousand years, the purple saffron or *zafaran* flower, had sprouted in the dry summer across the Himalayan valley, the monsoons nourishing the crop. The plant is said to be named after the mythological Crocus, who after being rebuffed by his beloved was transformed into this flower, weeping blood red tears for ages to come. It was said that Cleopatra used saffron in her baths so that lovemaking would be more pleasurable. I imagined the strands to be a lover's fingers, and my hand shook a little. I dipped a long brush in some water and sprinkled it on the unruly strands with my free hand. Slowly they started to bleed orange tears that dripped off both sides of my hand. They say if rain arrives after it has flowered, the saffron flower dies suddenly. I watched the colors on my hand and with renewed determination turned to the canvas and started painting. I mixed a few tubes—red, yellow, and a touch of black—and referenced the orange on the back of my hand a few times as I tried to match the color. I painted in layers following the traditional rule of oil painting. Starting lean, I applied fatter coats by adding more medium as I went. The paint is less likely to crack as it dries with that method. I couldn't let a dream crack, not an important one anyway. I worked diligently and furiously as the hours ticked away. Around four in the morning, I stepped back in satisfaction and studied the orange sky on the canvas—the color of saffron, just how Faizan had wanted it.

I went to the bureau and kissed a folded veil that lay on top, a reminder of my past and a symbol of what I had given up. Faizan had harbored a reverence for the veil—to him it defined a woman. I always felt a twinge of guilt when I looked at that piece of cloth. Shaking that thought, I crashed on the bed, surprisingly exhausted from the night's work. Dreams are never easy to create; they take a lot out of you. Tomorrow I will paint in the two boys, the stigmas of saffron, I decided. That would be the cover of *Soul Searcher*.

I felt lightheaded in a fulfilled kind of way, tracing a shape on the other side of the bed. I still slept on one side of it, a curious habit that never left me, considering that I had been the only occupant for the past five years.

Sweet dreams, I whispered to the night air.

The curtains on the window rustled in response. I rolled over onto my side and hugged my pillow. The gentle hands of predawn passed over me, pressing my eyelids shut. I obeyed and let myself be led into the world of dreams.

THREE

May 1989
Karachi

Early evening cast its long shadows as I came out of my room, almost tumbling over Mai Jan. She was mopping the floor on her haunches with an agitated expression, her sari *pallu* tucked in her waist.

"*Choti Bibi*, watch where you are going!" Mai Jan's voice was a little harsh for her stature, and I glared at her without answering. At fourteen, I didn't think I needed instruction on how to go about my own house.

For years, I had seen Mai Jan come to our house daily at the first light of dawn to do what we deemed beneath our stature to do—clean up after us, launder our soiled clothes, wash our dirty dishes, and cook for us. The days she didn't show up, the dishes piled high, and we ran around dirty, unwashed, with stinky knickers, sweaty undershirts, food stains and the day's grime coloring our shirtfronts, hair unruly and uncombed. Ami pretended not to notice. On such mornings, she sat in her room, painting her toenails, Lata Mangeshkar blaring out of the radio, curtains drawn. *Us Basti Ko Jaane Waale, Leta Ja Paigaam Mera.* O Traveler, take my message to the village.

We were chased away when we tried to peek in Ami's room. She almost always had a headache that she was nursing and didn't want to be bothered. Usually when Azad Baba, our old driver, came back after dropping Abu off to the office, he came inside the kitchen to fix us *parathas* for breakfast—square, fat pieces of dough powdered heavily with flour so they wouldn't stick to the pan. He deep-fried them in canola to mouthwatering perfection and then slid the oily, slithering masses straight from the pan onto our plates, the steam partially hiding us from each other's view. The first mouthful would always burn and numb our tongues. Azad Baba always cautioned us. We never listened.

Where is Ami? I wondered. I was having my period and there were no sanitary pads in the house. As usual she had probably used the last one up and not bothered to restock. I headed to her room in a huff.

I didn't know about periods when they first started a year ago, not until I woke up one morning and my bed sheet had bright red spots that matched those in my underwear. I ran to Mai Jan sobbing, since Ami was not around. The old maid could not believe that Ami had kept such an important fact of life from me; God knew awkwardness could not have been the reason. In a dark corner of the kitchen, Mai Jan showed me how to loop the old fashioned bulky pad and wear it with woven string that we used to secure our loose trousers. Shaken and traumatized, I took the instructions but could not believe that I had to do *that* the rest of my life. I was certain my duck-like posterior hid nothing from others. I was certain people whispered behind my back, *she's menstruating, she's unclean.* Later when I washed my soiled linens under running water, I was so disturbed I wanted to injure somebody. But I didn't. I had read somewhere that you can't pray when you are having your monthly "problems." That wasn't an issue in our household. No one prayed there except Azad Baba.

"*Bibi*," Mai Jan called out to me as I headed in the direction of Ami's room. Her voice had an urgency to it. "Don't go in there."

"And why not?" I said rudely. "Why don't you mind your own business?"

Mai Jan wiped her nose with her pallu and sulked, tucking the cloth back around her waist. She was sweating profusely, her hair bunched in a damp, untidy coil on top of her head. The mole at the tip of her nose seemed gigantic today. She was looking at me blankly. I could tell she was fishing for a good reason.

"*Woh ji,* I just cleaned that area. It's still wet," she offered lamely.

"So what? I'll be careful." I got on my tiptoes and moved forward so as not to leave smudges.

"*Choti Bibi,* no." Her mole mocked me but I refused to be distracted.

Ami's door was half ajar, and I could hear a conversation within. *Oh, Abu is home, too,* I thought to myself. Maybe the discussion about pads would need to wait.

I glanced inside, opening my mouth to call out to Ami, and then stopped and swallowed hard. The man sitting on the bed with his back toward me wasn't Abu. He was leaner and taller, not balding like Abu. A plume of thick white smoke emerged over his shirtless back and like a halo circled his head before disappearing into the whirling ceiling fan above. He turned around and smiled. Eyes glazed and eyebrows furrowed together, he had the satisfied look of a cat that had eaten its catch; it was Uncle Jalal, Abu's chess buddy.

I heard the angry rustle of Ami's nightgown as she came toward the door and wordlessly shut it in my face. The draft from it sailed into my heart. I stood frozen, unable to move.

"I told you not to go in there," Mai Jan said from the other end of the room, a slight mirth in her voice at the treatment meted out to me by my own mother.

This is how a family unravels in a matter of minutes: through careless acts of meaningless alliance.

I often wondered if Abu knew about Ami's relationship with Uncle Jalal. There was no threat of the laws of the land among the elite class, although such an alliance anywhere else in the country was punishable by law. I had seen Uncle Jalal a couple of times after that event but never again in a compromised setting. He would be on his way out when I arrived from school with my siblings, Zoha and Sian. My brother always sulked around him and moved away when Uncle Jalal wanted to tousle his hair, averting his droopy and bloodshot eyes. I was never sure what Ami saw in Uncle Jalal, notorious in society for his drinking and occasional drug habits. He wasn't handsome; of course, I thought Abu was the best thing that had happened to mankind. I was a bit skewed in my analysis of my father.

The thing with Uncle Jalal, Ami told me years later, was never real or substantial to her. He was a necessary distraction she needed at the time.

When I was little and still thought the world of Ami, I would sneak into her room when she was taking a nap and pull out her *sarees* and try them on. My favorite was an orange organza saree with a red-sequined border. I remembered draping it around my waist and slipping on her high-heeled gold sandals on many restless afternoons. I enjoyed parading around the room like Ami and puckered my face at the mirror like I had seen her do when she applied lipstick. Later, I would fold the saree and stomp on it to get the poofiness out, watching as it deflated sadly before I put it back on the rack. Years later, I looked on in horror as she cut that saree to make a shirt that she then decided looked awful on her. I never saw it again.

Ami watched us closely when we left the house or accompanied her on her shopping expeditions and admonished us if we strayed too far. She said there were bad people around, people who carried you away and did unspeakable things to you if you were not careful or vigilant. She never answered me when I asked what those things were. In the society we lived in, knowledge comes from unspoken sources: snatches of news clippings, books no one expects us to discover, whispered grown-up conversations. *Sex,* I would say to myself when no one was around. It had a husky and penetrating sound to it. It made me feel unclean inside when I said it, but it also gave me a rush. It was the foreign literature that taught me the intricacies of sex and defined the unspoken, unwanted word called *rape.*

I could never understand what made people bad. Leaders, a childhood friend told me once, make society rotten and unsafe. Bad people were mostly poor, I learned later from overheard conversations. Middle-class folks were mostly okay. Many rich people were corrupt. We were an exception, Ami informed us, an unseen crown on our heads that rendered us superior. Uncle Jalal was an exception as well, Ami explained to me. We grew up with stereotypes fed into our brains, dictating the way we operated in our daily lives. When I walked in the market with Ami, I always eyed poor men with grimy clothing suspiciously, certain they would reach out to cup my breast or touch my behind. I walked with a crooked elbow jutting out to shield my body, my purse.

Eventually, I discovered, it is our own who harm us the most.

What can I say about the mother who abandoned us four times over a period of two decades? Abu had checked out long ago from his marriage. I saw it in his eyes, in the smiles that he did not give to his wife, in the questions that he did not answer for her. Instead, the air filled quickly with thick hurtful breathing when they were together, the unanswered questions conveying more than words could: bitterness, disappointments, and a drawn-out sadness. Like a dismal cloak, those emotions landed on us. I tried to gather most of it toward me, wishing to spare my siblings the worst.

"Your mother never learned to love. It took me years to understand that," Abu said to me years later. "Even on the day of our wedding, I had a sinking feeling that I had captured a *koyal* bird in a cage, bound her in a relationship that her heart had not accepted. She was born to be a free spirit. You cannot assign roles to such a person."

Abu had accepted that fact and moved on. I never did, not until I lost Faizan and understood what a free spirit really meant. Not until I met another mother who nurtured my wounded soul and allowed me to forgive myself. Forgive Ami. Forgive the world.

FOUR

May 1993

Ami's backless *choli* was an instant hit at Sabeen and Sarfaraz Khans' wedding anniversary party the year I turned eighteen. She was back in our lives for a short while and I watched Abu painstakingly try to cater to her every mood in an effort to get her to stay.

Ami emerged from her room, the pallu of her black crushed silk saree draped around her body. As soon as she turned, Abu frowned in disapproval at the exposed skin but said nothing. I felt a bit ridiculous in my own sage green low-necked *salwar kameez* with beaded edges that Ami had insisted I wear. I kept my exposed cleavage covered with the dark long-trimmed *dupatta*. We all knew why I was invited. Parties were a great place to arrange matches. While the singles roamed around, adults fitted them like puzzles and decided the course of their lives. It disgusted me. I was too independent-minded to succumb to such matches, or so I believed then. It was useless to argue with Ami; if things didn't go her way, she pouted for days. I had agreed to wear lipstick at Ami's persistence. After repeated strokes, almost bruising my lips with the plum-colored lipstick, she then proceeded to powder my cheeks when I decided I was done.

"That's enough, Ami." I eased out of the chair. I knew Abu didn't care much for makeup.

Ami shrugged and examined her own reflection in the mirror. She fluffed her hair and smiled in satisfaction.

The Khans' mansion was filled to the brim with the elite of society: glittering and heavily made-up women wearing dazzling jewelry, sporting the latest fashions, trying out fancy English accents when they had not yet perfected the grammar, while men huddled together in circles, comparing sales figures, watches and cars. An ever-growing mass of unrelated and indifferent uncles and aunts, titles imposed on them by society, approached me at intervals to peck me on my cheek. I looked around for Abu and found him sitting on a couch at the end of the hall. Earlier he had been in an animated discussion with some of his friends about politics, a subject he could discuss for hours on end. There was a general uneasiness among the public since the new prime minister had been ousted within months of coming to power. That year had been a political disaster for Pakistan. Both the prime minister and the president resigned from their offices citing serious differences. Even the central and provincial assemblies were dissolved. Abu had great faith in the interim Prime Minister, Moin Qureshi, and was impressed by his determination to check the plague of corruption that had been growing in the governing bodies. Abu's hope of such a person taking over the country and turning it around was futile; Qureshi's tenure lasted only 90 days.

"Politics today has gone to the dogs, Tehsin Saheb," Uncle Athar was telling Abu, taking a slow drag off the cigar in his hand. He was a pediatric surgeon at the hospital where Abu worked. "The governing bodies have wiped the country clean. Totally absorbed in their own personal gain. How can a nation grow in such a climate?"

"The whole country is rooted in bureaucracy," Abu observed, shaking his head. "Until that's taken care of, our progress is questionable. You can't even get a simple identity card without bribing someone."

"I waited twenty months to get a new phone line," offered Uncle Zahoor, a mutual friend whose profession I could never remember. "Twenty months, can you believe it? Even a baby is born quicker."

"Can't match that even if you count from the actual conception," Uncle Waqar interjected. He had thick, tightly permed hair that made him look like a hedgehog. "You might have better luck in that time period, Zahoor. Maybe you could end up with a son that you always wanted."

The men guffawed at that comment, and Uncle Zahoor looked mildly offended. He had four daughters and each year tried his luck at having a son and failed. So far his wife had been pregnant four of the five years they had been married.

I started to lose interest in the discussion and looked around. The single young women at the party looked like they were straight off the runway and paid to parade at the party. Like moths, they flocked together with no room for expansion and eyed me with disdain. Suddenly my 4,000-rupees suit lost its class. I had not seen many eligible bachelors that night, and I didn't see the sense of being dragged to a party where the primary purpose of my attendance was not being fulfilled. The only young men I saw were already with women or pretended to be.

"*Are Saheb*, corruption breeds corruption," said Uncle Waqar, "What can the public do when they can't even get basic necessities? It is simple. Without bribing, you will be in a hell hole and who wants to be there?"

"Did you look at the list Qureshi published of the defaulters of tax and bank loans?" Abu responded. "They say Rana and Jabbar are on it, too."

The men in the group exchanged uneasy looks.

"He's trying to expose the scams of the old governments," Abu continued. "I am not surprised that there are many affluent people on that list. Some that we even see here at this gathering today."

At that, a few disentangled themselves from the group and walked away to seek other, more uplifting conversations, far removed from actual reality. A handful of others simply slipped away.

"I think his idea of making the State Bank of Pakistan an autonomous body will go a long way," Abu said to Uncle Athar, his only audience by then, who nodded and was relieved when his wife called out to him. He hurriedly excused himself and left Abu's side.

Meanwhile, Ami flitted around from one group to another like a winged creature, creating a stir wherever she moved, oblivious to Abu's incisive conversation. Men ogled her *choli*, swooned over her, and even made suggestive jokes in groups. She seemed to enjoy it all until a hand swung her around and planted a kiss on her cheek in the ways of high-society—Uncle Jalal. *Fantastic,* I thought, and rolled my eyes. I sat down beside Abu, and he smiled at me, setting down his Coke on the side table—the womanlike contours of the bottle making it seem like a woman abandoned.

"Having fun?" he asked.

"Oh, is that what this is supposed to be?" I feigned surprise, and he laughed, hugging me close. That was the exact response he was looking for. I glanced briefly at Ami, now working the floor escorted by Uncle Jalal, who had his hand on her bare back. Every so often I saw that hand travel a little too low, and she seemed not to mind. I was surprised by how well they fitted together. They were both social butterflies, eager to be admired, thriving on attention. Abu probably just dampened Ami's style with his political talk.

"Come, let me show you something," Abu said after awhile, following my gaze and briefly looking at Ami and her beau. I wished his embarrassment was a tangible stain that I could scrub away. He stood up, taking my hand. I followed him to the Khans' library and almost forgot to breathe. It was no less than a museum of books. Two corners of the large ballroom-sized room were filled with bookshelves up to the ceiling, sections devoted to various subjects, even a music library at the far corner with headsets and a large collection of old records. There were three large mahogany tables with leather-backed chairs around each and a giant spinning globe in the very center of the room on an ivory bureau, an intricately hand-spun Afghan rug underneath. But the thing that caught my eye was a woodcut engraving on the adjacent wall. I inched in closer. It was an interesting composition of a city being trampled by a devil.

"It's New York," Abu commented, taking off his glasses and scratching behind his ear. "See the signature? It was created by Albert Abramovitz, the greatest engraver of all times."

There were more details below the artist's signature.

Mefisto, New York. 1932.

"Virtually all of the work Abramovitz created was socially and politically oriented," Abu explained.

I was mesmerized by the composition and its subtle details. There he was, Satan in a loincloth with a menacing expression on his face, crouching on a tall building and balancing his other foot on a smaller one. He had an arm raised in the air, watching, waiting to strike. I felt a chill run down my spine. The scene was of night, a clueless, unaware city lit up for its final destruction. Somehow I couldn't pull myself away.

Abu motioned me to follow as he walked over to a bureau and bent down to open the last drawer in a familiar manner. I realized with an ache that that room had probably been his refuge at many Khan parties when Ami was busy charming the crowd. Abu drew out a scroll map and laid it out on one of the tables, his forehead lined in concentration.

We stood with our heads bowed low over the map of the world in front of us. My eyes went over to the West, scanning it for New York. What had motivated Abramovitz to do a rendering of a city's destruction? I couldn't shake the thought. Abu's words brought me back to our side of the world.

"This is where your grandfather was born." He pointed to a tiny speck north of Karachi. "Khairpur."

The two ends of the map rolled down on both sides of the table and curled up. We studied the map, totally absorbed. "See how Pakistan looks," Abu pointed out. "Like a mango squeezed of its pulp, misshaped and misproportioned. Elongated and lost. Our poor country."

I peered closely and couldn't help agreeing. The marked lines defining the contours of the land looked like a piece of gum stretched in one direction to its maximum length. Pakistan was a shy, squirming bride next to India, which spread its corners all around, looking for opportunities to advance, captivate and mesmerize. Bangladesh, a teardrop of India, was caught in years of natural disasters, as if paying for the price of some transgression almost in a karmic way. It wasn't apparent looking at history what it was paying for, but someone knew.

We heard a laugh; it sounded like the tinkling of ice cubes in a glass. Ami's voice. We both looked up. Ami and Uncle Jalal had wandered inside the library, not knowing we were there. Uncle Jalal had his arms around her and had pushed her against the wall. He looked like he was about to kiss her.

"Hello, Jalal." Abu's voice thundered inside the library with choked-back anger. "Amazing how you stand out wherever you go, isn't it?"

Ami jumped and slipped out of Uncle Jalal's embrace.

"Did it occur to you that you might have gone too far?" Abu's question seemed to be directed toward both of them.

Uncle Jalal rested his elbow on the wall and turned around with a smile, not bothering to answer. It was almost as if he was unperturbed by Abu's presence. Could it be too much alcohol in his system?

"How are you, Tehsin? Arissa?" he acknowledged. "Reading as usual, I see."

Abu didn't reply and turned to Ami instead. She looked at him scared, tongue-tied. There was a deadly look on Abu's face, and it seemed that it took all of his willpower not to physically harm her.

"Arissa and I are going home," he said to her, his Adam's apple bobbing up and down, his tone definitive. I was certain Ami knew that she had pushed his very last button, and there was no turning back. "Seems like you are enjoying this party, so I won't inconvenience you. I am certain Jalal would be happy to drop you home."

With that Abu turned and escorted me out, his hand firmly holding my forearm. There was a tiny bruise on my arm when I sat down beside him in the car. We didn't talk the entire ride back, but I knew that that night would radically change our lives. I concentrated on the graffiti I saw along the way, starkly eerie in the dark, blocking out the apprehension for our future. DEATH TO NONBELIEVERS, one read. JIYE BHUTTO, read another. The final one, on a brick wall in the area we had nicknamed *Khuda Ki Basti,* or the village of God, where teeming masses of squatted and illegal dwellings sat right before we turned the lane into our picturesque neighborhood, admonished DO NOT URINATE. Below it ran a mocking tell-tale trail left by a brave soul.

"Your mother has left."

The unnerving words echoed across the dining room and like a leech drained the surroundings of all air. The ear-piercing silence that followed became an incessant buzzing that wouldn't go away. Like a bone, the joke we were laughing at minutes earlier got caught in our throats. Zoha's hand, which had just lifted a spoon to bring it to her mouth, came to halt midair, and I saw her lower lip tremble. It could only mean one thing. I curled my fingers over her arm and gently but firmly guided the spoon into her mouth. She began to chew her cornflakes slowly as tears ran down her cheeks. Sian, 14 at the time, laid his spoon on the table on the side of his plate, wiped his face clean with a napkin, and escaped to his room without a word.

I glanced over at Abu, who had just delivered the hurtful news, and our gazes locked. There was a plea in his voice meant for me, and I understood it in more ways than I cared to. You perfect that art of deciphering the unspoken words when you live in the Amaan household and confront a situation over and over again.

That morning, Abu's glance meant that I was to dutifully assume Ami's duties and become emotionally present for my siblings. It also meant that I should take charge of the help in the house, the driver, the gardener, Mai Jan, etc. It wouldn't be that hard. Ami had perfected the role of a lazy commander. Out in the real world of working folks, the help were almost always on their own since Ami was never good at supervising. Even when one of the newly hired help, Shama, the maid assigned to do laundry in the house, started stealing, Ami was oblivious to the entire thing. I was the one who caught her red-handed, fingers deep in Ami's bedside drawer, drawing out a wad of cash that Ami had carelessly left there.

"She hates us, doesn't she?" Zoha asked me once.

"No, she doesn't." I carefully weighed my words. "She just doesn't know how to love us."

Hate. Such a strong word, but it was also a mother's final parting gift to us, the knowledge that she despised us, me most of all.

"I wish I never had you, Arissa!" Ami had said, tears streaming down her face as she dragged her suitcase out the door. "It's because of you that your Abu and I were never happy together!"

And there it was: my baggage for many years.

FIVE

June 1996

The mango season arrives in Karachi with an explosion of the senses. The summer that Zoha got married, it had an enormous appeal for all of us.

The scent of its arrival permeated the four walls of the house, and a waft of it found its way to the upper floor. The entire house was alive with the aroma of *Sindri*, the plump yellow mango with a soft, luscious interior and an unforgiving center. Azad Baba got only the export quality for us. Not a scar or mark appeared on the coat of these mangoes. The ones that got squished or marred were separated and distributed among the help in the house. Only the perfect ones were reserved for us, and we didn't even feel like royalty most days. Azad Baba brought the mangoes in the house in wooden crates with lids, nails sticking out on all sides. In our hurry to get to them, we often nicked ourselves on those nails.

The mangoes were cut finely to put into the fruit custard that was to be served on the day of Zoha's mehndi ceremony. The green ones were separated for pickling. Mango pulp was used to make fresh juice for Zoha every day, while she was doused in ubtan daily to achieve a fairer skin. Not that she needed any help. She had taken after Ami, with her clear, pale skin that contrasted well with her wild, mesmerizing eyes, and the knowledge of her many assets and the effect they had on others. I was the plain one in the family; I had inherited Abu's dark complexion and his wide-set eyes. I thought of my straight long hair as a chief attribute and had nurtured it for years by applying a generous amount of coconut oil every two days.

Zoha's match was arranged by a matchmaker whom we loved to hate. Her name was Tehmina Bua and she staggered her heavy bent body in right after the festival of *Eid* that year with a huge black *burqa* cloak over her. The cloak carried the odor of having been worn an entire month without being washed and I had the urge to snatch it from her and dunk it in ten cups of detergent. How hard is it to maintain proper hygiene? I found it irksome. She was a matchmaker and bore an expression of forced jubilation that was both comical and annoying at the same time. Her visits only meant one thing. *Kisi ki shamat aai he*, Zoha and I joked. Somebody would be hitched up in the age-old tradition of arranged marriage, a science perfected over centuries. Although Abu was very open to the idea of us finding our own life mates, Tehmina Bua's visits were still tolerated in our house, so as not to create any bad sentiments within the community. It was ironic that both Zoha and I ended up having arranged marriages through her connections.

Bua constantly chewed betel leaf *paan* and brought with her a little attaché case that was a virtual paan assembling factory with its red Areca palm mixture, anise, lime paste, catechu, and crushed cardamom seeds. In one sitting, she could make and devour as many as five, and she never bothered to offer any to her attentive and at times irate audience.

"*Buri adat he*," she would declare, cursing her habit, peering at us over her glasses, her eyes underlined by two stacked pouches of loose skin. "Better to stay away."

Sian, our younger brother, had a theory about that habit. He believed Tehmina Bua added a few shots of tobacco to her paan to make them more flavorful. We were suspicious of a small mysteriously unlabelled container inside her mini paan shop. As we were trained to do, Zoha and I brought in a tray of treats when she arrived—some *nan khattais*, soft

crunchy cookies with a dab of jelly and pistachio center, and on hot Karachi days, two tall glasses of Shehzad mango squash with a few cubes of ice
in each glass. On days the temperature soared really high, we purposely
forgot to put ice in her drink, much to her chagrin.

"What will you girls do when you go to your own homes? Your *sa-
sural? Hain?*" she reprimanded us. "Mothers-in-laws have little patience
for such forgetfulness. Better eat some almonds daily. It will make you
more alert, *han.*"

And we covered our mouths with our dupattas to keep from laughing
as we escaped to our rooms.

That day, Tehmina Bua's cheeks looked puffed as if she was holding a
very important secret captive in her mouth. It was that or the paan. She
sat across from Abu and plunged right in. "Bhai Saheb, these kinds of
matters are best discussed among women, but with Saira Bibi gone—"

Her voice trailed off meaningfully and Abu looked irritated at the
inference. Ami's frequent absence in our lives, especially at pivotal junctures, provided ready fodder for the gossip mill in the neighborhood.

Tehmina Bua looked at me and frowned as I sat across from her after
serving her instead of leaving the room as Zoha did. She downed the
contents of her glass in one slurpy gulp, still staring at me. She perhaps
considered it objectionable for me to be in the same room where marriage proposals were going to be evaluated for me. Little did she know
that in a confidential chat that I had had with Abu a few months earlier,
I had convinced him that I wasn't keen on getting married any time
soon. My work as a freelance writer for *Sahara,* a new fashion magazine, kept me busy, and Abu agreed, with much cajoling from me, that
I needed to build my career. I also asked him to consider proposals for
Zoha if she were willing. She had just finished her bachelor's in com-
merce and lacked the ambition and drive to either study further or get
a job somewhere. Not that she needed to get a job. Abu's salary as a
cardiologist and his many assets brought in enough to keep our home
running smoothly.

"Saira is indisposed at the moment," Abu said, clearing his throat and declining his squash. "You can talk to me. What is it that you want to say?"

"What to say, Tehsin Bhai? You have a house full of girls," Tehmina Bua said sadly, raising her hand heavenward in a dramatic gesture. *"Allah ki den hai."*

I felt annoyed. We all knew what she meant—that girls are a burden to the family until they are married off. No wonder the woman rubbed me the wrong way, although she seemed to be doing a great service to mankind in an environment where it was not easy for singles to meet and fall in love. Not that most families wanted that. Most were content with the well-oiled vehicle of arranged marriage, which gave them perfect control over their children's destinies.

"There is a proposal from a very good family. *Amrikan* returned. Has his own shop selling prescription glasses. Very nice family. About 20 to 25 years old."

When Bua said a prospective suitor was 20 to 25 old, it was safe to add another ten years to his age. Car mechanics became engineers when she read their CVs, psychologists became doctors, and pharmacy assistants miraculously became owners of pharmacies. A suitor who took a single trip to the United States would suddenly emerge as an import-export businessman with widespread connections abroad. Yet Bua's claim that she was responsible for 250 happy unions to date was unchallenged in the community.

"What about his education?" Abu asked as he folded his arms over his chest.

This question always stumped Tehmina Bua and was one she rarely had a clear answer for. She glanced at Abu stupidly at first and then slapped her hand to her forehead in exaggerated frustration. *"Le,* I forgot to ask them that," she said, shaking her head. "I am sure he must be intermediate, at least," she added with pride. In her days, two years of college was considered a remarkable feat.

"In that case, let them know that we are not interested," Abu said without missing a beat.

Good for you, Abu. I smiled inwardly.

"What?" Tehmina Bua opened her mouth in surprise, looking at Abu and then at me. "Let me find out. In this modern age, he might have done full years of college. Who knows?" She held up her hand before Abu could speak. "No, don't give me your answer right now. Think about it. I'll come again next week and bring more information for you, *theek hai*?"

"We need the boy to at least have a higher degree of some sort," Abu reiterated. "Zoha is a college graduate. Without a proper education, I won't consider any proposal for her."

"Oh, for now I was talking only about Arissa," Bua said hurriedly, stuffing a paan deep inside her throat, exposing her four golden teeth.

"No, *we* are talking about Zoha," Abu corrected her.

Tehimna Bua opened and closed her mouth like a fish, looking from Abu to me and back to him. I smiled at her sweetly.

"But isn't Arissa older?" She seemed flustered. Her plans had gone awry.

"Yes, Tehmina Bua," Abu stated impatiently, "but not all events have to follow that order. Zoha is the one we are thinking of at present. Do you have any objection to that?"

The way he asked, it left no room for Bua to question the family's decision. Abu winked at me, and I smiled.

"In that case, I'll have to consult the family again." Bua's voice was quieter now, enthusiasm leeched out of it. Abu's pager rang, and that was the end of the meeting. He stood up, and Tehmina Bua lurched to her feet.

"Next time, I will bring pictures," she said quickly, thinking that a pretty face would somehow make up for a lack of education.

Abu nodded.

I showed Tehmina Bua out, keeping a safe distance so I didn't have to wrinkle my nose at the dirty dishcloth smell that radiated from her.

"*Bayti*, do think about what your Abu is saying," she tried to reason with me as I walked her to the door. "Youth is a fast-fading flower. It's hard to find a suitable match for girls when they get in their 30s."

"I'll try to remember that, Tehmina Bua," I said with forced cheerfulness. "But for now, I am just not interested."

It turned out that Tehmina Bua had found a perfect match for Zoha. The young man had finished his MBA from the University of Maryland and had returned to Karachi to run the family business of selling prescription glasses and contacts.

Ami missed Zoha's wedding, which was no surprise to anyone. By then she had moved to Boston where her brother lived, and her only contacts with us were rushed calls every festival of Eid when she tried to talk to each one of us for a generous two minutes before hanging up. She had moved on, and in some ways so had we.

SIX

July 1995
New York

"This one ends badly."

I turned around to see who had the unknown voice with the familiar accent. A man in an olive crewneck T-shirt stood watching me with a smug smile on his face. He seemed to be from some part of South Asia. I had arrived from Karachi to visit Uncle Rizvi because I was particularly restive that summer and yearning for a change of environment. Sensing that, Abu had suggested the trip as a twentieth birthday present. I saw no reason to decline such a tempting offer. I was particularly close to my uncle because of shared interests in art. That summer, Uncle Rizvi had accepted a job as a pediatric surgeon in Houston at the Children's Hospital and was moving in a few weeks. One reason for my visit was also to assist their family in packing and to spend their last summer in New York with them.

"I don't remember asking," I said as I smiled and turned my attention back to *A Fine Balance,* flipping the page. I was on page 34. The fat book was a little unsteady in my hands, and I laid it flat on the table. Visiting the Mid-Manhattan Library in the afternoons was my little treat that I looked forward to with childish abandon. The venue was my favorite with two of its five floors devoted to a collection of almost 130,000 literature and language books.

"You'll never learn if you don't ask." He shrugged and walked over to one of the nearby shelves. If I were back in Pakistan, he would have appeared quite forward for approaching a woman who was a stranger.

"I don't agree," I said without looking up. "I got most of my learning done through tacit observation."

He came around and stood directly in my line of vision, a stack of books in his arms, an astonished look on his face. He was a little fairer than most men from that part of the world, taller than my father, who is considered a giant at 6 feet 4 inches. "You never asked questions? That's impossible."

"Not really." I removed my sunglasses from my head and put them on the table. They had started to hurt the back of my ears. "I was one of those kids who sat at the very back of the class and knew all the answers but prayed that she never got called on."

"I've never known anyone like that." He pulled back a chair and sat uninvited across from me. He was still perplexed. His English had the slightest lilt of an accent that seemed to be on the verge of dropping off. Perhaps he had been an inhabitant of this land for awhile. There was an odd bluish mark on his chin, shaped like a crescent.

"Maybe it's because you talk too much and the quiet kids preferred to keep their distance," I declared bravely, speaking directly to his scar. What did I have to lose?

I was amazed when he threw back his head and laughed openly. He had a great laugh—unabashed, hearty, and full-throttled—but it made me uneasy since we were inside a library. His teeth were perfectly aligned, something I never had. My childhood was full of visits to the orthodontist, and I grew up dreading going to the dentist. The many braces I'd worn during my gawky teenage years did little to improve the natural flaw of design. *If I am born with it, I can live with it!* I'd decided when I was old enough to make my own decisions. The last young dentist I visited, who

I could tell had a particular fondness for me, led me out to the waiting room on what we mutually decided would be my last day of getting such futile treatments.

"Take a look at my patients in the waiting room on your way out." His whisper seemed to caress my ears, and I flinched. "And be grateful for what you have." He held my hand in a final handshake and seemed reluctant to let go.

"Go home and take a long, hard look at yourself in the mirror," he continued. "You will be pleasantly surprised. Our flaws are what make us unique. Yours makes you beautiful."

He seemed nice but didn't pull at my heartstrings. Nevertheless, I was grateful for his words and recalled them often at low points in my life. *Our flaws are what make us unique.* Mine must make me go off the charts. I had so many.

"What you need are books with nice endings," the stranger continued, flipping through the stack of books he had collected from the shelf. "Like this one." He handed me a copy of *The Chili Queen* by Sandra Dallas.

I took the book from his hand and glanced at it. "You don't like books with sad endings?"

"Those are the only kinds of books I like," he said as he sat back, crossed his arms behind his head, and studied me closely. He seemed to be in good shape, with strong biceps and a muscular chest. "But you don't look like the kind of person who should read them."

"Why?"

"Because you seem to be more on the emotional side," he explained. "You probably think about those endings for a long time afterward."

Right on the mark, I thought. I was intrigued by his accurate perception.

"For instance," he continued, coming close to the table again and leafing through some books that he had brought over. "These are classics if you are looking at quality multicultural novels. Most of the books from our part of the world are sad. That's what makes them interesting to read.

That and the perspective of a foreign land with a very different way of life. Our authors' attempt to capture that for a broader Western market lends a new dimension to it. For the most part, the outlook these authors present is almost always somber."

He handed me some books, one after the other, and I dutifully took them from his hands. *God of Small Things, Sister of My Heart, Cracking India.* Most I had read, maybe even a couple of times. I tried to recall my reactions to each.

"What's the saddest book you've ever read that also hit home?" I asked after awhile.

"*Moth Smoke.*" He handed me the last book in his hand. He had strong, sturdy hands. I fingered the teal cover and flipped the book open. "Then you are from Pakistan."

"Precisely!"

"What's the one book that you would call a must-read?" I was getting interested in this conversation.

"I haven't come across one. The only one I can think of is a work in progress by a new author," he answered simply.

"Who?" I was hooked.

"Me."

I was amazed by his aggrandized self-advertising, but he offered me no chance to counter that last comment.

"I would love to chat further, but I need to leave. I have to pick up a friend for lunch."

With that he walked out. I glanced at my watch and felt irritated and slightly used. I liked to control the time and duration of a conversation. I had lost control over both, plus I was late myself for lunch with Aunt Jamila, who had cooked my favorite *haleem*, a tasty wheat and lentil goob with cubes of stew meat. I always took time to admire the art on the library walls, which featured artists from different parts of the world but there was no time for that today. I briefly glanced at the photomontages of Pradeep Dalal on my way out. The autobiographical work seemed to focus on the artist's life in India and had a dash of nostalgia about elements sorely missed once away. Downstairs, I checked out Jhumpa Lahiri's *Interpreter of Maladies* for the second time in two weeks.

It wasn't until I reached my aunt's place that I realized that I hadn't even asked the stranger his name.

I thought of him as I stood at the subway station on my next trip to the library. I was a little annoyed with myself for taking the time to dress up that morning. I had painted my lips twice so the red was darker than I usually wore it. I glanced down at my brown crotchet-trim blouse, the one I had bought a week ago at Abercrombie & Fitch on a whim. It had banded puff sleeves that gave it a nice chic look. It had cost a small fortune but I thought it looked good against my dark complexion.

I was appreciative of the bustling, rushed feeling in the air as I climbed up the subway stairs to enter the city. New York, a city that walks. People walking with a purpose, never running, minding the space around one another, occasionally getting into sidewalk rage, but for the most part maintaining that unique New Yorker demeanor that is focused and primed but reserved. For me, New York held so much promise, opportunities bursting at the seams. There was a sea of faces around me, but they all looked past me. I was not the one they sought; they were not the ones I was looking for. As soon as I started to walk toward Fifth Avenue, tiny drops of rain dribbled down from the sky. I raised my cupped hands and tried to catch the gleeful, jumping droplets, catching pedestrians off-guard with my sudden halt. Rain, I loved rain. The air had so much promise. At once, vibrant umbrellas sprouted up on all sides; everyone seemed prepared but me. I saw the silent acknowledgment in the eyes of New Yorkers that at once declared me an outsider.

I entered a little park by the station and sat down on a bench near a homeless woman in tatters—her entire life inside ethylene. She was wrinkled and weathered, her hair in tangles. She had close to twenty well-worn grocery bags stacked inside a shopping cart parked near her. I smiled at her, and she frowned in return. Undeterred, I leaned back and closed my eyes, savoring the sounds of children at play, shouting, squealing as only the very young would. They enjoyed the rain in their uninhibited way, dodging their parents' efforts to gather them and head home before the weather grew worse. I had no such qualms; I was neither mother nor child. I sat in the pelting rain, and all else melted around me. The place felt like home, but it wasn't.

When I opened my eyes, the homeless woman was moving away. I called out to her on a whim and stood up to slip my blouse over my head. Straightening the thin white shirt underneath, I offered the sweater to her and she took it from my hands wordlessly, scratching the side of her head. I was amused when she sniffed it and offered me a toothless grin. Somewhere a cardinal sent out an aggressive "peetoo, peetoo" call, and we both looked up. The bird had flown away.

When I looked back down, she, too, had left.

As I stood up to leave, the homeless woman startled me by approaching from behind a tree. I nearly collided with her. The blouse that I had given her was tied around her waist.

"Some folks come bearing gifts," she said, her voice raspy, her face inches away from mine. "You came to the world with losses, you wretched woman."

I didn't know what to say. Was that a caustic remark meant to make me angry, or a product of her disjointed thoughts? Her glance cut through me as she continued, her tone softened now. "How will you turn them around?"

I realized it wasn't a question addressed to me. She was either a madwoman or a seer punished by the bittersweet gift of prophecy. I staggered away, shaken.

Even though I never saw the stranger at the library again during my stay, it was still my best visit ever. I went to the library a few more times before I left for Karachi, but he never came again. I read *The Chili Queen* from cover to cover and longed to discuss it with him. It turned out that I had a few opportunities in the future. I didn't make use of any of them.

SEVEN

August 1998
Karachi

The sights and smells of a Pakistani wedding are what lend permanence to it. There is a huge investment and involvement of all senses. Even years later, I can evoke the dainty sweet fragrance of the jasmine and the pungent scent of henna, and it reminds me of the day of our union—the day of my mehndi, the celebration of dance and festivities that precede the actual wedding day in a Muslim society. I smiled inwardly as I snuck a look at Faizan at the other end of the room, where he sat surrounded by friends. At twenty-three, I had lived up to the expectations of the society; I was getting married.

A group of friends had escorted me inside the hall. They held a large tie-and-dye print dupatta over my head, shielding me. The shapes of the print—dots, squares, waves, and stripes—established the light and shade around me. The playful shadow patterns walked beside me and some-times climbed over me like excited children clamoring to be a part of the festivities. Inside, I was a rare exotic bird that needed to be kept safe in a dual-purpose effort—safe from harm and safe from fleeing. I was bound, unable to escape, led by rituals, my future stamped. The *baraat,* or the groom's entourage, arrived later, led by singing and dancing friends. The hall sprang to life as they gyrated to a *bhangra* dance in the middle of the room in a quick flashing swirl of colors. The crowd cheered on the dancing, sweaty bodies on the throbbing, pulsating floor. That lasted a half hour, and then the *dhum-dhum* of the *dholki* heralded in the wedding songs that the two sides were attempting to sing in unison, often straying off key.

Amid singing and dancing guests, Faizan and I sat on separate stages called *seg*, one at each end of the room. They were decked with red and orange batik covers and a flowery curtain of *moghra* (jasmine) and *genda* (marigold) flowers, a mingling of the milk and saffron of our lives, the joining of the ordinary with the extraordinary, a tantalizing fusion of mind and senses. A heady fragrance rose from where the basket full of moghra bracelets laid near my feet for eager female guests to pick out and wear.

The intricately patterned mehndi on my hand had started to harden and was flaking off, but the scent was still intoxicating. When no one was looking, I chipped off a few pieces with my nail to see the color inside. I had spent six hours that morning with the henna artist from Meena Bazar, who was fashionably late and applied mehndi the old-fashioned way, with a stick dipped in an open jar of henna, instead of using the modern method of filling a plastic cone with it and squeezing it out like icing onto a cake. She covered my hands up to my elbows in meticulously designed patterns: circles after semi-circles, flowers, buds, and geometric shapes that all came together in an exciting display of exotic design. Green, tingling, cold foliage shot up my palm to my fingers and at once caked over, itchy and brown.

"This is *fe*, and this is *alif*," she had whispered as if passing along an ancient secret to me, pointing to the lower right side of my palm. Those were the first words she had uttered since she started her assignment. "*Fe* for Faizan and *alif* for Arissa."

Together, the entwined Urdu alphabets looked like a figure gyrating on top of a bed (ﺍﻓ). I blushed like a little schoolgirl. Traditionally, the groom had to find the first letters of his and his bride's name within the henna design on the bride's hand before consummating the marriage. I wasn't certain, though, that it was a deal-breaker.

She started painting my feet next. It took forever, since I am a size 10, but gathering from the oohs and aahs around me, I was satisfied that she had done a terrific job. I wasn't a big fan of henna—it required me to sit too still for too long. The henna artist, apart from her few words to me that seemed to also be a part of her job, was quiet and worked efficiently. Her large fingers, yellowed from the herb of her livelihood, cradled the back of one hand while she diligently worked with the other. Occasionally I felt the jabs of her perfectly filed nails. I was grateful for her silence, because I had had an earful of what the ubtan massage lady had to say every day. A gaunt woman of diminutive stature with a permanently displeased mouth, the masseuse had been visiting for two weeks and always served up dreadful legends of brides who disappeared on mehndi eve because they were impure or of infidel grooms who were kidnapped an hour before *nikah*, the marriage ceremony. I tried to tune her out by attending to the pain her massage inflicted on my body.

As I sat on the seg, all I could think about was the excitement of my new life and the tingling at the base of my skull at the thought of the adventure I was about to embark on—it all held promise, in abundance. Occasionally a friend appeared magically with a small bowl of lemon juice and sugar and dabbed a dipped cotton ball all over my painted hands and feet, rendering them sticky and useless once again. At night, Zoha held my hands over an open flame in the kitchen and held a candle to my feet in the dark. Those were all ways to guarantee that the henna produced the coveted burnt orange hue or the color of the bleeding sky when the sun is about to set. If the resulting color is not dark enough, there are whispers among the elders that the union might not be that strong. Of course, if the bride couldn't even produce a darker color of henna, what is the guarantee of that union? Who can hope for the success of that relationship? What kind of offspring would such a marriage produce? I remember Azra Apa insisting when we'd met with the henna artist earlier in the month that she use the best mehndi in the market, the one that was guaranteed to produce good results so that fate could be relieved of delivering any unexpected messages through color.

The color of the henna when I washed it off the next day before getting ready for my nikah was the color of burnt sienna—one of the very best shades. There were nods all around. The union would be a blissful one, the elders predicted, raising their hands in prayer.

The first time I saw you, Faizan had said, I knew I would marry you one day. How can men be so certain? My analytical mind would dissect each event, gesture, connotation, and conversation and put it all back together before announcing my say. Although in Faizan's case, even I had acted contrary to my nature by basing my life's decision on a chance meeting. It just felt right. It was perhaps the first and only time I had acted on an impulse. I wasn't as certain of the outcome of my decision as Faizan was, but I had taken a chance, one of the very few in my life thus far.

How did we get there? Two years after Zoha's wedding, Tehmina Bua, who I had sworn would not arrange my match, arranged our match. She flounced in after *chandraat*, the day of the full moon, like a charley horse doubling you over in pain. After the obligatory *dua salaam*, she pulled out an envelope full of prospective suitors' pictures from her overstuffed purse.

"I know, Tehsin Bhai, you said that Arissa would decide on her own when she is ready," she had said, mouth blood-red from her paan. "But Saheb, these days what do young girls know? They want more and more education, and soon they have more silver strands in their hair and their youth has fled."

Abu shook his legs impatiently, waiting for her to get to the point, a trait I had inherited.

"What I am trying to say is it is your duty to help her understand that she can get a decent house now to go in. Later on the choices will be very limited. Divorced or widowed, *bas*."

"I am well aware of my duties as a parent, Bua," Abu said a trifle harshly. I rolled my eyes at Tehmina Bua and got up to leave the room.

"In that case, you must look at these young men," Tehmina said, opening the envelope stuffed with photos. "You should consider yourself lucky that so many nice families are interested in your Arissa."

Tehmina Bua started listing the credentials of each one as I placed teacups on a tray inside the kitchen.

"This one is Kamran. He has a number of travel agencies in Texas. Very nice family, small. Two sisters who are married and no parents. No meddling in-laws." She nodded at Abu suggestively and continued, pulling another photo out of the envelope. "And this one lives in New York but is only here for a short while. He is an only child."

Abu was looking at his photo as I came in with the tray.

"Has a big degree in *Angrezi*. What do you call it?" Tehmina Bua fumbled for the right word.

"Master's in English literature?" I offered, sulking at her as I handed the first cup of tea to Abu. Protocol stated that the first cup was always given to the guest. Bua adjusted her glasses and glowered at me. We had many glaring matches, she and I, whenever she visited.

"*Han. Wohi.*"

I briefly glanced at the photo Abu was holding and nearly dropped the other teacup. Flustered, I handed it hurriedly to Bua and fled to the kitchen.

"What is wrong with that girl today?" Bua commented in annoyance.

"Nothing," Abu said, setting the photo back on the table. "She's been working very hard. Zoha had her baby last weekend, and Arissa spent all last week helping her."

"She's taken the place of Saira Bibi very well," Bua commented. "She will make a very good wife."

Abu cut her short. "I will inform you of our decision. I will have to consult with Arissa, of course, but I see a few good options here that I can convince her to review."

"Take your time, Tehsin Bhai, but not too long." She wagged a finger at him. "Good proposals are like birds. They fly away quickly."

After Bua was gone, I came back in the room and sat next to Abu. I picked up the photo on the table and looked at it. My stranger in the library was back. There was no mistaking his identity: he had the same conjoined eyebrows, the square jaw, the grinning face set against the backdrop of a Christmas window at Nordstrom with Santa smiling behind him. I didn't know him, but it felt right. I handed the photo to Abu and nodded wordlessly.

We were both clueless as to what strange game life had designed for me.

Mai Jan liked to say that the crows always show up at your doorstep when a visitor is about to come. It was unconditionally accepted as a rational expression for that infuriating cawing near your home.

But despite the noisiness of the crows on the rooftop that day, I was totally tuned in to just one person—the one in front of me. The magic of Faizan's presence again in my life rendered me stupidly speechless. His interview with Abu had ended a few minutes ago and there we were sitting across from each other in the large living room. In the ways of the tradition, we were expected to have a final conversation before our match was finalized. It surprised me how much of it felt like a game of chess, the way all parties treaded carefully, working within the realm of tradition, making sure nothing was done thoughtlessly or in error.

Faizan glanced at me like a lab technician would look at a specimen, wondering what he would find when he finally ran some tests. The extrawide coffee table that separated my seat from Faizan's made me feel too distant. I longed to sit next to him, inhale his aftershave, perhaps stroke his cheeks. I felt my face turn red.

"Isn't it amazing how these things fall in place?" Faizan said finally. "Who would have thought we'd meet again."

I looked at him but my mind was vacant, I had not a single intelligent thing to contribute and I was deathly afraid of sounding stupid. I felt like a schoolgirl—awkward, clumsy, prone to folly. He stood up, crossed over to my side and sat down next to me. I looked at him gratefully. "You have a great smile," I finally said and then blushed.

"Oh, you pay compliments too," he smiled. "I thought you were always honest."

"I am being honest," I said irritably.

"Aha, that's what I was looking for. I like sweetness with a dash of spice."

I couldn't believe I had played right into his hands. I also realized that my anxiety had melted away. "You're impossible."

"Are the crows always this loud at your house?" He walked over to the window and opened it up. A few women down the street were engaged in an animated conversation, suggestively looking at the house every now and then. "And are your neighbors always this nosy?"

"No," I laughed and extended a jab of my own. "Only when they think there is someone at the house who needs to be chased away."

He turned around and the ends of his lips curled upward into a grin. Check mate!

After he left, I went out onto the verandah. Early evening's amber sky was punctuated by a few lazy gray clouds. Crows by the dozens were perched on the palm trees across the tall gate, perhaps tired by the day's racket. They were quiet now, enjoying the peace, adding to the serenity of the rushing night. A clap of thunder disturbed their respite and they flew off in a noisy panic, their black flapping wings filling the sky, bringing an earlier than usual darkness. I remembered what I had read once that contradicted the South Asian myth. In Greek mythology, the cawing of the crows is regarded as a bad omen, signifying loss.

"Shooo," I whispered to the terrified crows. "Go away and bring me good fortune."

A life-altering occurrence usually brings with it a series of premonitions leading up to the actual disaster. You can ignore it, or you can take caution. We did neither.

In the noisy pandemonium of Karachi's busy street of Saddar, Faizan was weaving his car in and out of traffic, face puckered in concentration. For once, he wasn't smiling. It made me uneasy to see him that serious. We had been engaged ten days. He avoided colliding with a red Suzuki and almost had to slam on his brakes to avoid hitting a truck that overtook him from the side, making no allowance for his space. He cursed under his breath and then smiled at me. We had stopped at an intersection. A man came by with moghra and rose garland bracelets on a pole. Faizan rolled down the window and beckoned him over to ask about price. The scent from his merchandise permeated the inside of the SUV.

"*Kitne ka diya, bhai?*"

"*Das rupiya, Saheb.*"

Faizan reached into his pocket and held out a ten rupee note. He bought two bracelets for me. He knew my weakness for those. A beggar woman in tattered clothes limped in from the side, as soon as he paid the man and started to roll up the window. She looked inside the car and pushed down firmly on the window with two grimy fingers, stopping its upward progress. Her expression was macabre, face caked with grime. I panicked.

"Firedancer! There's misfortune in your fate," she said, looking directly at Faizan. Her voice was eerily unreal, her gray eyes blazing with angry passion. She glanced over at me. "Giant flames will be his blanket one day. Tantalizing, scorching flames will chase him." She raised her index fingers in the air and twisted them around in a strange and maddening dance. "Like this, he will dance with fire one day, but he will not win."

The light turned green, and Faizan pushed the accelerator hard on the floor as the car shot forward, tearing the woman's hand away from the window. I didn't dare look back, and I couldn't look at him either. I had plucked every petal off my bracelets by the time he dropped me home and discarded them in the trash can almost as if they were somehow tainted.

She didn't ask for money, I remember thinking. I refused to let my mind go further than that. The event found its way into one of my compositions much later. By then, the firedance was long over.

EIGHT

September 2001
New York

When I felt the slight brush of a kiss on my forehead, I didn't want to open my eyes. My dreams always threatened to flee if I opened my eyes too quickly. I wanted to remain in this one for as long as possible. I was inside a beautiful rainforest with butterflies flitting around, busy and focused in their quest for nectar. There were some horses grazing in the distance. A koyal chirped in the trees, giving out the mango call. Occasionally squirrels dashed near my feet. Suddenly, I spotted a snow-white lamb escaping through an open gate, and I rushed to close the gate. Pregnancy dreams were great—vivid, colorful, and totally out of control. Most of the time I was able to recall them completely upon waking up. I had even started to maintain a diary for the ones I could pen down. There were others too erotic for me to even share with Faizan. They embarrassed me, even in sleep.

"Goodbye, *Jaan!*" Faizan was saying, and I mumbled a response although I am not sure what I said. Faizan left early most weekdays for his job at Windows on the World. I loved it when he called me *jaan*, the traditional name for a sweetheart. I turned and went right back to sleep, trying to find the place where I left off, but the dream was gone. There was no sense chasing after the lamb. I slept fitfully the rest of the morning.

Somewhere from deep inside the building, I heard a little scream but attributed it to my cloudy state of mind. The paper-thin walls in the apartment complex in Jefferson Heights hid nothing. Couples fighting at night usually wore sheepish expressions the next morning in the elevator, certain that their voices the night before had carried through the walls. Lives weren't private; marital problems were out in the open, bare before the public.

I tried to snuggle with the body pillow on my side. The early fall New York mornings were so harsh. All I wanted to do was lie in bed until the sun came up. After the fifth month of my pregnancy, I could no longer sleep on my back and had started using a giant pillow for comfort. This meant that Faizan got cheated out of his half of the bed, but he seemed not to mind. Some mornings, I woke up to discover guiltily that I had hogged the entire bed as well as the covers and Faizan had slept on the floor at the foot of the bed with only a thin blanket.

I decided to ignore the urgent knock at the door. It's probably a salesman, I thought. They snuck up easily when the gate downstairs opened as people left for work in the morning. The knocking grew more insistent, and I got up and looked around groggily for a gown. My feet landed on some papers that I'd worked on the night before, freelance work for a beauty salon's newsletter. I slept in the nude most days. I found the heated apartment too hot and sweated profusely during the night. Faizan liked to snuggle up to me when I slept in that state. That was the extent of how close he could get to me these days.

I made my way slowly toward the door in my nightgown and opened it. Juhi stood there. Her eyes were glazed over and swollen. Juhi and I had been close friends ever since I knocked her down the first week I moved in the building as I was coming down the hall with my big laundry hamper. We struck up a conversation and found out that we had many common interests. I liked the frizzy-haired, dimple-cheeked, easygoing woman with a penchant for dry humor. She was an art instructor by day at Queensborough Community College and an Iyengar yoga instructor by night.

"What is it?" I grabbed her hand to escort her inside. Was she in trouble? "Is Surinder back?" Surinder was the abusive man she had been dating awhile back. It had been a disastrous relationship that she had ended weeks ago.

She shook her head and went to turn on the TV. Yoga instructor Maria Jimenez was leading her group through some breathing exercises. Frantically, Juhi grabbed the remote and changed the channel to CNN. "Breaking News" was written across the top of the screen, and the image below showed thick bellowing fire coming out of a building.

"What...what's going on?" I tried to squint at the screen and reached for my glasses on the coffee table. It was the North Tower of the Trade Center. The world as we knew it was crumbling down in front of us, glass chunk by glass chunk, metal piece by metal piece, floor by floor. It was 8:55 a.m. I had slept through the moment that would forever alter my life.

Faizan, my silent mind screamed. Juhi came around and grabbed hold of my shoulders and sat me down on the couch. My body was shaking uncontrollably, and her hands kept slipping off. I blinked back tears and watched with blurry eyes as people, dazed and bloodied, passed by the camera: a man's arm at a crooked angle, a woman's terrified face covered in blood and grime, panicked firemen looking for comrades, saving lives, losing their own, running toward the smoke-filled hallways to save one more life, never to return. And as we watched transfixed, another plane crashed into the South Tower.

Together, we screamed. Abramovitz's Satan had delivered its blow.

"He doesn't have a cell phone! I need to reach him!" I screamed into the faces of the friends surrounding me as I started to get up. I remember seeing Joe, the building manager's face in front of me. He gently pressed down on my shoulder and pushed me back on the bed. Juhi sat next to me, spent from crying. They had all trickled in like ghosts in a matter of minutes after the news broke, the people in my life, blending together into a sea of faces that I can hardly recall now, some taking charge, some treading past me carefully and taking over my other needs, heading to the kitchen, keeping the steady supply of tea and coffee going, moving life along.

"You need to stay here, Arissa," Juhi said, holding my hand in hers.

I looked at her but I didn't see her.

"I have to get to him. You don't understand."

I got up and this time shoved the persistent hands aside and rushed to the phone. "I can call the restaurant," I said to those gathered around me, their eyes full of sadness and pity. I laughed hysterically. "Don't look so stricken. He's probably okay. My Faizan, he's a fighter."

My trembling hands misdialed the restaurant a few times before getting it right. The phone kept ringing; there was no answer. I slammed down the phone and raced to the closet. In front of dear friends who had never seen me out of my hijab, I peeled off my nightgown and put on a pair of jeans and a red shirt, my modesty of little importance to me. I saw some avert their gaze and some look on as if spellbound. As an afterthought, I picked up the neatly folded veil from the top shelf.

"I need to find him," I pleaded to Juhi, and she nodded.

"Then I'll come with you," she said.

The scream that reached my ears stopped me dead in my tracks and sucked the air right out of my body. But only for a minute.

Even as far as Hudson Street, the smoke and the smell of burning metal and sulfur were suffocating. I tried to block my mind and concentrate on my steps. *One. Two. Three. Faizan, I am coming.* The closer I got, the faster my feet moved. I didn't know if Juhi was still behind me, and I didn't care. As I made my way down the street, the temperature rose and the air thickened with smoke and dust. The dust clouded my vision, blocked my breathing, but I kept going. As I neared Liberty Street, I caught the first glimpse of the six-floor-high flaming pile of debris: glass, steel, concrete and metal that were once the towers that defined the New York skyline blown away by raging swords of fire.

Wretched terror spoke of death in my ears and sickened my soul. The ground slipped from underneath me, and I went down on the slick street. This was too big for us, too big for me. *This cannot be a part of our lives. We live a sheltered existence.* I said that a couple of times under my breath as it gradually became my mantra. *We live a sheltered existence.*

The panting next to me alerted me to Juhi's presence as she scrambled to hoist me up. I pushed her helping hand away and stood up resolutely, edging my way past dazed and wounded men and women frantically rushing away from the mass of debris. A man with half of his tie blown away walked past me stunned, and I realized that he was missing an arm. He had in his other hand what appeared to be the remains of a file folder. *We live a sheltered existence.*

The debris and smoke were getting heavier by the minute. I was running the wrong way, a few people stopped to explain. Safety lies the other way. *Not for me.* I came across human barriers, blocking my path. I struggled to push past, my paralyzed mind unable to process the directions that were being thrown my way. *I can't stop. Not now,* my mind pleaded to them. My voice refused to comply.

I started moving sideways, away from protesting hands stopping me from getting closer. I passed by some documents murky from the water on the street, a shocked man in a suit sitting on the curb with a bandaged head, an abandoned cell phone that was still ringing, a briefcase with combination locks. I picked up a black jacket with burn marks around the collar. It wasn't Faizan's. I let it go. He was probably wearing his brown corduroy jacket since his black one was at the cleaners. When was I supposed to pick his clothes up?

It was then that I saw her, the woman on all fours, looking at a bloodied limb, with a wild expression on her face. She turned the leg around and around, searching for a familiar sign. Then she dropped it and stood up, almost colliding with me. Our eyes locked, her panic settled in my soul, my fear crept inside her eyes, and our hearts fused in our collective pain and loss, knowing without expressing that our loved ones were gone.

I felt nauseous and sank down again. Nearby a child screamed, and an angry outburst ensued. Ambulances and fire trucks screeched, and police sirens sounded. I closed my eyes and tried to regulate my breathing, my lungs taxed from the heavy smoke. My baby did a somersault inside me, awake by now, its slumber disturbed from all the emotions inside me, from the smoke, the stench, from the sounds. The dust colored my hair and settled over my soul like a dense miasma that kept on building. I had aged gracelessly over a matter of hours.

My stomach plunged as the magnitude of the situation sank in. It was over. He was gone. What chance did he have when 10,000 gallons of fuel moving at 470 miles per hour slammed into his space? He was a human, not God.

Never again will I live the same way. We are sheltered no more.

Years later, a little boy would ask where his father was. I would tell him that he sleeps with the angels.

"Good," he would respond by signing. "I bet he dreams about me."

I came home with something clutched in my hand that I wouldn't let go. Juhi pried it open from my fist. It was a piece of charred document from the ground of disaster that I had picked up somewhere along the way—a signed lease for an office on the 75th floor of the North Tower. Over the course of a few hours it had been converted into a death certificate. I walked over to the bureau and picked up the beveled glass clock. I studied it for a minute and then laid two fingers flat against the hands of the clock, hiding them from view. I willed time to stop its clockwise journey, but when the errant hands moved in disobedience, I quickly turned the clock around and emptied it of its battery. Then I set the clock back on the bureau, now hollow and soulless, stripped of its functionality. I had stopped time. Now if only I could turn back time.

I paced the apartment, restless and jittery, meandering in and out of hope and desolation. It seemed that my mind had accepted his loss, but my heart was in denial. I refused to sleep or lie down. I felt that if I did, I'd lose him forever.

Every now and then, someone flipped open the phonebook. Every hospital, every morgue in the metropolitan area had been called. Friend after friend called long-distance, my quivering voice faltering with every repetition. Surely if a thing is repeated enough, it does not happen. That's what the older generation said in Pakistan, but wasn't it for good news?

At some point around midnight, someone popped a Valium in my mouth and I swallowed hard, my throat feeling like there were a handful of pushpins in my throat. In a short while, my feet gave away from under me and gravity sucked me downward. Unblinking, I curled up in bed and closed my eyes. In my pill-induced haze, I felt that I was spiraling to the bottom of the stairs. I saw Faizan at Windows on the World in his burgundy and gray steward uniform with the epaulets and gold-striped sleeves. A maroon napkin rested on his right shoulder as he looked at a giant plane flying toward him through the glassy barrier of the restaurant. He turned around as I screamed his name, warning him of the danger. With a wave, he smiled and raced toward the open embrace of the giant wings. The flames caught him mid-air. *Firedancer.* A sound from the past reverberated inside me. I lost my voice as the whiplash hit, radiating from his point of departure, a coil of flame and fury. It slammed me into one corner of the room as the ceiling started to crumble and the floors buckled underneath. The building rocked like a ship in crisis, flailing and powerless. I felt the baby inside me cry out, a high-pitched screaming that went on and on. *Why doesn't Faizan listen?*

I woke up to Juhi restraining me on the bed as I thrashed my arms around. The scream had been mine.

"I have to see him, to say my goodbye," I wailed. "I have to find him."

Friends held me and grieved with me.

There are moments during that agonizing time that I remember with amazing clarity, but some days I have lost in their entirety. Valium helped me for days afterward when I couldn't stop watching the news. My throng of friends dwindled down as my family formed a protective and loving shield around me. As soon as air travel resumed, Abu flew in, and Ma and Baba came a few days later. Sian and Zoha arrived soon afterward, along with some other distant relatives. There was one I knew who wasn't there and should have been—the woman who'd given birth to me.

Waking was a nightmare, a realization of a life stretching before me without a partner, holding a baby made by two but who will be brought up by one. I was grateful for the senseless bouncing of my mind that ensued from taking the pill, the haze desensitizing my ability to think. Adrift, afloat, I was the only one with wings. I lived for those anxiety-free moments.

When a friend asked for a distinguishing mark to put on the missing person's poster for Faizan, I rambled on and on about the birthmark on his jaw as if it was the most important thing. I knew in my heart it was a futile effort. The poster would only serve as an obituary. I went along with it so they wouldn't think I wanted him dead. A grieving widow is closely watched. *She didn't grieve enough.* I was wary of those hushed judgmental whispers in shadowy corners. I gave power to those voices in my mind, and when I got it all together, I hushed them all up, one by one. The voices in my mind often asked me to do things I didn't want to do. *Kill yourself,* they would say, and I stared them down through the mirror. *Scream and don't stop.* I obeyed and screamed inside. Most days, I ignored the voices, refusing to empower them until they all quieted down, muffled at first and then gone.

When I close my eyes and think back I still see and feel the smoke and ashes falling over my head in giant loads, trapping me below, and I open my eyes just to block those images out. But even then, I can't stop seeing the image of the woman who'd paused near me and nodded a silent admission of our loss.

NINE

I got off the northbound No. 2 IRT and found out almost immediately that I was not alone. The late October evening inside the station felt unusually weighty on my senses.

The tired commuters had long reached home, back to the busy scuffle of an ordinary life—home-cooked meals, irritable kids, TV time, nagging spouses, and overdue bills. For me most things had a dismal film attached. My rose-colored lenses had been stolen. Time was the thief. It wasn't an ideal time to travel, Faizan always admonished. But he wasn't there anymore to have his say unless he woke up from the grave to give me a lecture on safety.

I heard heavy breathing behind me. Angry, smoky, scared. I could tell there were several of them, probably four. Not pros, perhaps in their teens. They walked closer sometimes, and other times the heavy thud of spiked boots on concrete and clanking chains receded into the distance. They walked like boys wanting to be men. They fell short. Why was there no fear in my heart? Probably because there was no more room in my heart for terror. When horror comes face-to-face with you and causes a loved one's death, fear leaves your heart. In its place, merciful God places pain. Throbbing, pulsating, oozing pus, a wound that stays fresh and raw no matter how carefully you treat it. How can you be afraid when you have no one to be fearful for? The safety of your loved ones is what breeds fear in your heart. They are the weak links in your life. Unraveled from them, you are fearless. You can dangle by a thread, hang from the rooftop, bungee jump, skydive, walk a pole, hold your hand over the flame of a candle. Burnt, scalded, crashed, lost, dead, the only loss would be to your own self. Certain things you are not allowed to say or do. Defiant as I am, I say and do them anyway.

And so I traveled with a purse that I held protectively on one side. My hijab covered my head and body as the cool breeze threatened to unveil me. I laughed inwardly as I realized I was more afraid of losing the veil than of being mugged. The funny part of it is, I desperately wanted to lose my hijab when I came to America, but Faizan had stood in my way. For generations, women in his household had worn the veil, although none of them seemed particularly devout. It's just something that was done, no questions asked, no explanations needed. My argument was that we should try to assimilate into the new culture as much as possible, not stand out. Now that he was gone, losing the hijab meant losing a portion of our time together.

It had been just 41 days. My *iddat*, bereavement period, was over. Technically I was a free woman, not tied to anyone, but what could I do about the skeletons in my closet that wouldn't leave me alone? The ones who placed their scrawny hands of blame around my throat and threatened to choke me?

Without looking back, I knew who the young men were. They'd been sitting right across from me earlier on the subway. No older than twenty. One had a half-shaven head with a swastika tattoo on it and was wearing an inside out pair of jeans. The second one had long hair and brown penetrating eyes that chilled my soul. He wore a nose ring and large combat boots. The third, slightly thinner one, sported a tanned leather dog collar and wore black, loose trousers that could fall to the floor with the slightest movement, chains around the hip. I felt sorry for their desperate attempts to make a declaration. A statement of uniqueness, the silent cry that we all carry in our hearts: I am important, look at me, a wailing that ultimately gets lost in the deafening roar of everyday life.

The fourth one intrigued me the most. He seemed to belong the least to the clan he was traveling with—a rebel among rebels. He seemed dejected and morose, with his fingerless gloves and trench coat that hung loosely on him. His statement ended with his big spiky boots. His immaculately parted blond hair clashed oddly with the rest of his ensemble and entourage. It seemed that he was uncertain of which path to take, the path of least resistance or the path of sure destruction.

Like it or not, you do stereotype. We all do. Together they were the sort you see on the street and you are certain they mean harm. But I felt no apprehension at their sight. Sitting across from them on the subway, I'd glanced at them listlessly from behind the death certificate I was examining. The document I had obtained that afternoon, the unnerving piece of paper that validated what I already knew in my heart, released to me without a body. It seemed like I was in the subway only a week earlier clutching a few Ziploc bags containing DNA—some hair samples from Faizan's hairbrush, his spare toothbrush, a cup he used for gargling—hoping they would find at least a body. That hope was long gone from my heart.

I had seen a list of what was required to wrap a Muslim corpse. Absently, I ran it like a laundry list through my mind. The items would never touch Faizan's body.

Kafan: 4 x 12 feet
Head Wrap: 4 x 4 feet
Body Wrap: 4 x 6 feet
Chest Wrap: 4 x 4 feet
Body Sheet: 4 x 8 feet

The teens kept looking at me, elbowing each other and laughing. The blond teen sent a spiteful glance my way and turned around to look out the window. Perhaps he did not find poking fun at a veiled, pregnant woman particularly amusing.

There were other looks I had been noticing, or perhaps that dreadful day had given me a heightened awareness of any kind of glance. After the first list of the hijackers' names and nationalities was published, many Arab and Asian immigrants put up American flags on cars and shops, signs of solidarity laced with the hope of evading discrimination. It was a desperate attempt to show loyalty to a nation under attack. Immigrant cab drivers were spat on and ridiculed, and ethnic restaurants put up "God Bless America" signs after some were vandalized. With every horn or commotion on the street, they jumped, then withdrew a little more within themselves, guilt-ridden with sins they did not commit. They walked faster when alone. Some women took down their hijabs, afraid of being targeted, and adopted a conservative but Western style of dressing. Men cut their beards. Many postponed plans to visit the country of their origin any time soon. Those who did travel preferred to remain quiet during their journey and chose not to converse in their native language even among family members. A few close friends changed their names—*Salim* became *Sam, Ali* converted to *Alan*—in an attempt to hide identities. When asked their nationality, they offered evasive answers. We were homesick individuals in an adopted homeland. We couldn't break free from our origin, and yet we wanted to soar. The tension in our hearts left us suspended in mid-air.

I, too, had witnessed all sorts of looks in the past few days, the gazes from familiar friends who had turned unfamiliar, the silent blank stares of strangers, the angry, wounded looks wanting to hurt, the accusatory sidelong glances screaming silently, *You did it, your people brought the towers down.* My people? They were not my people, those few whose beliefs don't even reflect the religion they rely so heavily on to justify their cause. They wrecked people like me more than anyone, who come to this country to lead a freer, safer life, to live among a civilization unaware of the struggles of those who live in restrictive societies.

Is it money they are after? I wondered. A priest had been robbed at knifepoint in the same vicinity a few weeks back by two teenage boys. Mentally, I took stock of what I had in my bag: a chewed-up ballpoint pen, a notepad with "Arissa and Faizan Illahi" printed in cursive, a death certificate, a MetroCard, a $20 bill, my ring that didn't fit me any longer due to pregnancy edema. My wedding ring! My heart pounded like a trapped animal's. I can't lose that! That's what I held close to my heart when ominous night shadows fell down around me in the dark and I looked hungrily at each new one, hoping that one of them was Faizan's, that in death, he would visit me, if nothing else to say goodbye and to hold me close one last time. But how can one see an absence? Touch a void? Look for a form where there is none?

They were moving closer. I could feel it, and I tried to rush my pace. The muscles in my back tightened as I sensed their gained momentum, the footsteps matching mine. As I broke into a trot, a thin hand grasped my wrist. I spun around and faced the four teens. They looked at me with feigned crazed expressions. Now that they were face-to-face with me, they were unsure of their next move. I jerked my hand loose and turned around slowly to resume walking.

"Hey," the taller one with the dog collar called out to me, his voice laced with venom. "Stop or I'll slice you." I turned around slowly and subjected him to a steely gaze. To an onlooker, I am obdurate, an old structure under new management. The station was deserted. It was late. I realized the delicate situation I was in, but I was amazed by my own composure.

"What is it that you want?" I asked in a stable tone. "Cash, credit card, food?"

They formed a formidable circle around me. The teenager in combat boots frowned at me and ran his sleeve across his face to wipe away saliva in a futile effort to intimidate me. I could smell their breath on my face. They had been smoking. I tried not to breathe it in. Secondhand smoking is harmful to a baby. Does it matter if the smoke isn't being blown in your face?

"Where is the good in you?" The blond guy suddenly moved in and grabbed my chin, cupping it in his palm roughly. "You race of murderers.

How can you live with yourself?" He jerked his hand from my chin. I felt the rising ridge where his nail had scratched me.

"Me?" I looked at him in amazement and then laughed. It was more a product of hysteria. "You have no idea. I am as much a victim as you are."

"Bullshit." The blond guy spat in my face. I didn't brush the wetness away and looked him directly in the eye. I saw something shine in the hand he held behind his back.

"The veil that you wear," he continued, pulling out his knife and aiming the point at my hijab. "It's all a façade. You try to look pure, but you are evil inside. You are the nonbelievers, not us."

I felt the thin veil rip as it came away from my shoulder. I stood waiting for the adrenalin to kick in, for panic to arrive. There was silence inside me. Knock, knock. No one was home. The pain in the young man's voice, though, was unsettling. It had the echo of a loss. I let him go on.

Next he moved the knife down to my long black jacket.

"Where is your God now? Do you think He is watching?"

"You're a moron," I taunted, my heart void of fear. "My religion does not preach terror. They are using it as a crutch to fulfill their own objectives. But you will never see that."

The blond teen scowled but grew quiet as the knife in his hand moved down, forming a single long slit in the coat from my chest to stomach, hardly touching the surface. I saw the look of surprise on his face as he went over the big bulge on my stomach and stepped back as if he had touched a live wire. I realized with a start that he had not been aware I was pregnant.

"Jesus," he recoiled. "There's a fuckin' baby in there."

The tall teen with the tattoo shifted his legs uncomfortably.

"Go on. Slice me," I dared, my voice angry, now. "This baby's father died that day, too. I suffered as well."

"Shut up, bitch." The blond teen moved in again, a sheen of sweat on his forehead, the knife close to my throat this time, so close it itched where it rested. If I leaned toward it, I might bleed to death.

I was tempted.

"You lie—" He teared up, stopped, and with renewed resolution looked at the knife in his hand.

"Man, Jimmy, I can't do this," the tall teen said, moving back.

Jimmy seemed to ponder his options for a split second before the sound of footsteps coming down the subway stairs caught him off-guard. Panicked, he dropped the knife. It clanged twice on the hard concrete before coming to rest. He followed his friends, who were halfway up the subway stairs by then. I heard a voice yell, "Hey!" followed by the sound of someone being punched and falling to the ground.

I collapsed onto my knees and closed my eyes from sheer exhaustion. A shock of pain uncoiled from my stomach and shot up my spine. I felt the restless flutter of my distressed baby and placed my hand on my cramping belly. It felt hard. There was a smell of dirty metal around me, rubber burning somewhere. My senses were suddenly heightened— or were they just now dying down? Bending forward in blinding pain, I watched my torn black hijab. *My baby,* I suddenly realized with a rising sense of panic, heart drumming against my chest.

"Are you alright?" The man kneeling down next to me had chestnut hair and was holding his midriff with one hand and a briefcase in the other. I realized that in their hurry to get away, the young men had delivered some blows to this innocent bystander. My eyes had a hard time focusing.

"Shit," he cursed, glancing at his watch. A flicker passed across his face as he weighed his options. How important was I to him? A battle within his heart, his conscience his only witness. I kept drifting in and out of reality as I rolled over on one side.

"I have to go," he muttered apologetically and got up on his feet. "I am so sorry," he said before turning around. "I'll call for help." But would he, really?

I mumbled incoherently. His footsteps receded in the distance, and a few minutes later I heard other footsteps rushing in my direction just as a train pulled up in the station and bright, blinding lights illuminated my surroundings. *Oh no, they are back!*

I mustered all the strength I had and screamed at the top of my lungs as my unused adrenalin finally kicked in. The two powerful hands that had suddenly scooped me nearly dropped me as I twisted and spasmed with all four limbs.

I can't lose this baby.

I have to get to a hospital.

A thought loomed large in my head suddenly as the fight went out of my body and my scream tapered off: *How loudly did Faizan scream when death came for him?* When the flames reached up to engulf him, what were his last thoughts? Were they about me, his unborn baby, or the life he'd never have?

For the past hour or so my baby had not moved, I realized with a growing sense of panic. In the seventh month of pregnancy, that's never a good sign. I closed my eyes and tried to anesthetize my brain with the sounds surrounding me—the thump-thump of the fetal heart rate monitor, the drone of the machine monitoring my contractions, the occasional sound of hospital personnel being paged.

The heartbeat is still strong, they assured me, trying to ease my concerns. I had been brought in by a stranger, I was told after I collapsed at the subway station. In my Vicodin-induced haze, I felt strong hands move me to a stretcher, and a young nurse who introduced herself as Jennifer brushed my hair away from my sweaty face and said gently, "We are taking you for an ultrasound to see how the baby's doing."

I nodded. Behind her compassion, I also sensed an exigency. There was a deep, disturbing silence within me that had created a chaos in my mind. The baby was totally still inside. I worried my belly, willing it to move.

How did I survive all this? I was unsure. I was certain the baby wouldn't.

I was in my second trimester and had missed my Level 2 ultrasound that was scheduled in September—an event Faizan and I were looking forward to with much anticipation. We had picked up a blank videotape from Wal-Mart to record our baby's first moment in front of the camera. I never thought I would be by myself for that first look.

The screen flickered on as the technician adjusted the wand on my abdomen, and after a few sweeps of images that looked like creased hunks of flesh, she hit the spot. The first image of the baby took my breath away. It was alive and kicking—a completely formed tiny human being that had beaten all odds. Right on cue, the baby took its thumb to its mouth and started sucking as I watched in awe. Despite the fact that the technician was a stern, harried woman with pulled-back stiff shoulders and a long face, I tried to rejoice in the moment. When I repositioned myself to get comfortable, her wand lost its place, and I was subjected to a cold stare. I was stunned by her total lack of empathy.

"I can't get a good picture," she declared in impatience after a few minutes of futile fumbling. The baby had decided to hide from the wicked technician, and I smiled inwardly; it had its father's sense of humor. "I'll get someone else."

When she left, I peered around the small, oppressive room. The air conditioning was on too high, and I felt tiny goose bumps on my arms. I was surprised by my child's silence. It was prancing around quite a bit on the screen, but I couldn't feel any of its movements. On average, the baby only wriggled once or twice for me during the day, at least the times when I really felt the tiny jabs.

Jennifer bustled in, accompanied by another, much gentler and jovial technician. The images were better than before. As the two chatted, I tried to concentrate on the baby. I spotted the telltale appendage between his legs even before the technician pointed it out. *It's a boy,* I thought to myself, *just as Faizan had predicted.* I had searched enough ultrasound pictures online to distinguish between the sonograms of a boy and a girl. The technician was silent afterward, taking measurements, recording, taking snapshots, and Jennifer fell quiet, too. At some point the technician nodded to her, and she left the room briefly. I didn't think anything of it until she walked back in with a doctor in tow—a black woman in her fifties, her dark weaved hair pulled back in a clip. I started to panic at that point. *What are they seeing?* All I saw was a perfectly formed baby boy. The doctor laid a gentle and reassuring hand on my shoulder as she peered in closely to examine the baby on the machine. The technician passed the coiled sheet of sonogram pictures to her and then shut the machine off and turned on the blinding fluorescent lights. I flinched and looked at the group in front of me in dread.

"Mrs. Illahi, I am Dr. Mitchell. We would like to do a Level 2 ultrasound on you to rule out certain things," the doctor declared in a critical yet measured tone. "Would you like to call your husband?"

Jennifer gently rapped the doctor on the shoulder and whispered something in her ear as I looked on, stunned. *What are they saying?* My mind screamed. In my sheer state of agitation, questions hung like overcast clouds in my mind but could not make their way out of my mouth.

"I am sorry, Mrs. Illahi. I did not know." Dr. Mitchell placed a gentle hand on my shoulder. Jennifer came around and propped me in a sitting position, pulling the sheet on my chest all the way down to cover me.

"I suspect fetal growth retardation," the doctor continued, "which may or may not be serious, but we need to do a Level 2 ultrasound to be certain. Possibly even amniocentesis, which is a painless procedure but carries a minor risk of fetal loss."

"*Allah!*" A cry came from me and the room spun. I had a gut-wrenching need to strike someone. Instead I clenched my fists to both sides of my torso and sank down on the hospital bed, a protective hand on my belly.

The doctor and nurse exchanged uneasy glances.

The fear that I had held at bay for weeks was back in my heart, weakening my soul. I thought of Ma, Faizan's mother, waiting at home for me and felt another wave of dread. I closed my eyes tightly. I didn't want to call her, but it seemed like that wasn't a choice anymore.

"Can I use a phone?" I finally asked in a voice that did not feel mine. "I need to tell my family where I am."

"You should ask them to come here," Jennifer suggested. "You'll be here for awhile."

Oh, no!

"Let me use a phone," I requested again. "I want to break it gently to my mother-in-law. I want to make this as painless as possible for her."

Ma's voice at the other end sounded panicked. "Arissa *bayta*, where are you? I have been so worried. I called every person in your phone book." I pictured her in my mind, the undercarriage of her eyes dark from worry.

"I came to the hospital to get myself checked out," I said, trying to sound calm. "They are telling me I might be here for awhile."

"What is it? What's going on?" She cut me off, alarmed. "Here, I will pass the phone to Baba. Give him directions. We'll meet you wherever you are."

I passed the phone to Jennifer. Heck, even I didn't know where I was. I turned around on the pillow and heard the nurse struggling to assure my father-in-law that I was not dying, and tender love washed over me for that couple who in a few days of being with me had put their grief aside and helped fill the shoes of a lost husband, a loving companion, a father, and a soul mate.

And all I could ever give them was one piece of bad news after another.

The results were in.

Dr. Mitchell ran a laundry list of things they had seen during the advanced ultrasound—heart defect, urinary tract malformations, kidney abnormalities, cleft lip. My heart sank as the list kept growing. I gripped the edges of the bed as Ma held my hand tight, squeezing it every few minutes, passing on some of her strength to me. She and Baba had arrived at the hospital a few hours earlier.

"What does all this mean?" I broke in, too frightened to hear any more.

The doctor shook her head and closed the file. "The condition still is compatible with life," she admitted, although she didn't phrase it as a good thing either. "We don't have the results from the amnio yet, but even then there is no way of knowing the full extent of the challenges until the baby is born. We will do weekly ultrasounds and monitor you closely. That is—"

We all looked at Dr. Mitchell questioningly.

"That is what?" Baba and I asked in unison.

"That is if you are willing to carry the baby to term."

The room lost all of its oxygen. I felt something akin to physical agony and saw my loved ones' faces turn ashen. Ma put her arms around me, cradling me like a child. I snatched my hand away from her and closed my eyes. I struggled to breathe, taking desperate gulps of air. I felt the baby kick and inhaled deeply to regulate my breathing.

"I will carry the baby to term."

My voice was croaky, broken. Like china on concrete.

Ma and Baba looked at me and nodded vehemently.

"Arissa!" Baba came to stand beside me, his voice shaky. "We will help you through this."

How could anyone help me? I was having an abnormal baby, all on my own, with no partner to share the burden with. This was too big. Mountainous. How did my life end up this way? They were so meticulously planned, the events of my life. We were supposed to have a wonderful life, a healthy, beautiful child. Not apart like this. Not by myself.

"We are here, Arissa," Ma said softly beside me.

Yes, but for how long?

I thought of the empty videocassette in our bedroom at home. What a start to my little boy's life: a lost first photo opportunity. Even nature determined that the moment was not important enough to be recorded. How did I get here, from blissful married life to stark bleak widowhood and now this?

A journey that took just 41 days.

I shut my eyes, wanting to hide from the world behind the blessing of sightlessness. When the nurse came in with my medication, I pretended to be asleep. It was only when I heard Ma's soft snoring that I opened my eyes and saw that she, too, had dozed off. It had been a long night. I sat up and willed my brain to think.

Yeh na thee hamari qismat. An old Urdu poet's verse rattled in my brain. *It wasn't in my fate.* I let it soak in and overpower my thought process. I tried to shut my brain down to avoid thinking the inevitable. Unsuccessful, I focused instead on recalling the rest of the lines by that controversial poet, Ghalib:

> I would not have resented death had it come only once
> Shamed, as I was after my death, why didn't I drown in a
> river or sea
> There would have been neither a funeral nor a tomb erected
> in my memory.

Through the window, I heard the slow crescendo of city traffic usher in the morning, but the room retained its silence. It was ironic to me that the world went on as if nothing was amiss when in just a few weeks, I had lost so much. The world did not care about one person's misery; it did not care about thousands of people's losses either. I wondered if the ghosts of the nearly 3,000 people who perished still visited their old dwellings. Perhaps they lingered in doorways, stood near their old beds, baffled at their sudden exit from the world, unable to accept that their place at the dinner table was gone. Did they cling to their loved ones, hover near their children, or try to touch them to tell them that really they had just shifted dimensions? That they still existed? Did they come back one final time to say goodbye? Did *he* come? Ill-fated as I am, did I sleep through Faizan's visit when his disembodied lips touched mine in a final farewell?

After Faizan, the child within me had provided me the will to go on. Not anymore. I wasn't even certain that I was doing the right thing in wanting to give birth to this baby who would have lifelong struggles. What would Faizan have said? Would he have agreed with me? Clueless, I rotated the hospital bracelet around my wrist and waited for an answer. There was none. I was alone in my struggle.

For the first time in many days, I took the rosary from the bedside table and started praying. Verses from the *Qur'an* on my breath flowed into my soul. Eyes shut, I found all the events of my life bouncing around my brain, the good and the bad, the moments when joy discovered wings and soared high, taking me along for the ride, and the moments when bleak shadow entered my life and threw the cloak of darkness over me and tried to suffocate me.

I saw it all, the benefactor's name on my lips, as the chronicle of my life opened up in my mind and spread its pages before me—recording every fleeting moment, every erroneous turn, every disturbing second and not allowing me the chance to go back and recreate the past. The deaf ears of history paid no heed to my entreaty. Instead, like wings they soared forward, adding new pages, carving out plans that didn't exist in my mind, marking directions I had not anticipated. It didn't matter that I was a reluctant traveler.

The cruel thoughts came to me when I had almost dozed off, like an unleashed sob at the back of my throat, cutting in its truthfulness and finality.

If I had woken up and given my husband his goodbye kiss before he undertook his last journey on his final day on earth, could I have stopped him?

If I had just snuggled against his chest and convinced him to get inside the covers with me that morning, would it have preserved his existence on earth?

And then, finally, the one that haunted me many nights: if I had listened when Faizan had tried to talk to me about his premonition of disaster, could we have averted it?

TEN

Evenings continued to create a looming apprehension in my heart as my life stretched before me, endless like the night, barren and unfulfilled. My child was no help either. Just when I'd doze off, he'd wake me up, lying low on my bladder, forcing me to get up to go to the bathroom. One night, lying half asleep, I felt the feathery touch of something outlining the contours of my belly. I shot up, heart thudding, raining blows on my belly only to realize that it was just the baby moving inside me, not an intruder. He stayed silent for the next few hours, too scared to move. I nudged him lovingly, seeking forgiveness. He refused. The baby, too, was mad at me. I stayed awake that night. Again.

Most days, I felt like I was spinning inside like a top, unable to stop. The world around me had a crazy quality to it. I looked at my surroundings with the eyes of a stranger, wondering why I had never noticed the shocking pink in the checkered print on my bed sheet. I hated that color and yet I had bought the sheets. Why? The fan on the ceiling had a black spot on one of its blades. Nights when I was unable to sleep, it seemed to grow until it took over the ceiling and inched closer to my face, almost touching my nose until I felt claustrophobic. I don't think I was going crazy. I didn't want to, I knew that much.

The empty space next to me in the bed seemed to grow bigger each time I looked, and the darkness magnified my loss to an incomprehensible degree. Throughout the night, I kept throwing Faizan's pillow on the floor and picking it back up, hugging it close for his warmth and scent. It still carried a faint whiff of his aftershave, which was diminishing by the day. I refused to launder the cover. Many nights, I just clutched his pillow and sat at the foot of the bed, one leg dangling down, the other curved at the knee, and stared out the window where moonlight streamed in and weakly illuminated the empty side of the bed, trying to make up for the person I'd lost. What can a few shimmering rays of the moon do?

There were nights when Sian and Zoha crept in and sat next to me, reminding me of when as children we huddled together after watching a scary movie. We left a light on in my room and slept on my bed, hugging each other's bodies, twisting and turning to find snug spots. Once settled, we were too frightened to move, too uncomfortable to sleep, afraid of closing our eyes lest the monster in the movie descend into our bedroom. One by one we finally closed our eyes, the many names of Allah on our lips. Even then we slept facing the fluorescent light on the ceiling. What harm can come to you if you face the light? Don't shadows fall behind? Or below?

Sian and I shared a special bond in our early years, because we were closer in age. Growing up, we skipped many afternoon naps to send Azad Baba to get us *phalsas* from the street vendor in the corner—the red sour berries that with their juice turned our tongues crimson. Afterward, we often indulged in a fierce competition to see who could spit the seeds out the farthest. Once we even aimed for Azad Baba. When Sian's seed struck his dark balding head, he turned around, scratching his head in confusion. We pretended to be busy with our marbles, trying not to laugh.

Other days, we chased the white puffballs—the flowerlets of the *shimul* tree, fleeing from their split pod—all across the yard until Ami rounded us up and took us indoors for our nap. We paused only to trace their wayward path as the gleeful seeds raced past the rose bushes and the bougainvilleas along the fence, bouncing off the windows, escaping from nature and manmade snares in their path. That memory always conjured up an image of me running in my snow-white shalwar with a red kameez and a trailing long batik scarf that seemed to stretch and grow as I ran and then took off into the air. I would later hunt it down but not before I was exhausted by the other chase. We never caught a single puffball, ever. They always traveled a little too high, a few fingers beyond our reach, like unattainable dreams.

The nights Sian and Zoha came to my room after Faizan was gone, I didn't know what brought them there, and I didn't ask. Could my screams have woken them up, I wondered? They never said anything, just sat with their arms draped around me. We watched the sky through the bare window, sometimes moonlit but most often stark naked, stripped of its jewels. We didn't need words and they could not talk about the man I wanted to converse about. Instead with their presence they acknowledged that the monster had been in the house and snatched away one of the inhabitants. Maybe it was time for silence, for mending the broken and for piecing together a life disintegrated by hatred. Long after they were gone, I still felt their arms around me the nights I stayed awake. Love has a curious way of finding its way through oceans and skies; distance is never a barrier. Those nights, I waited until it was too dark to see, and just as darkness lost its hold on me, I turned over and went to sleep.

My thoughts often went back to the week before the disaster. We had gone to bed late after catching the last show of Anthony Anderson's *Two Can Play That Game* at the Triplex. I woke up to screams. Faizan was convulsing on the bed, eyes closed. I tried to wake him up but couldn't. In desperation I slapped him across the face, and his eyes flew open, wild and bloodshot.

"Are you okay?"

He sat up, feet dangling off the bed, looking around with feral eyes. "I had the strangest dream."

"What about?" I leaned in closer and hugged him. I felt his heart beating like a frightened rabbit's in his chest cavity.

He didn't answer and pulled away, reaching for the glass of water on the nightstand. With his other hand, he unbuttoned the top two buttons of his plaid nightshirt. He had a panicked look on his face as he drank in big impatient gulps.

"Why can't I breathe?"

I could have bottled the anxiety that exuded from him. I took the glass from his hand and put it away. I leaned my head against his shoulder and rubbed his back. He pulled away and his shuddering body curved away from me on the bed.

"What did you dream about?" I asked again, feeling his temple with my hand. It was throbbing.

There was a long unsettling silence before he began.

"I...uh, I saw that Baba, Ma, and you were gathered around a bed. There was a person lying face down on the bed. It appeared he was dead, and you were all talking about him."

He paused and looked directly at me. "In the past tense," he added. It was as if he was telling me the plot of a movie he had seen. It seemed unreal, but then dreams rarely ever make sense.

"The man was dressed in a black suit, and his hair was oiled back with some rich black cream or oil," Faizan continued, staring off in the distance. "Possibly Brylcreem. No, it can't be that," he quickly corrected. "That is white. Anyway, it seemed from the conversation you were having that the man had been a victim of some form of a racial attack. While you were talking, he began reciting some unknown Arabic verses. He was chanting several, but the only one I recall was *Al Mani*."

Faizan shivered and fell silent. *Al Mani*. It sounded familiar but I couldn't recall where I had heard the word before.

"Then what happened?"

"The man started shifting his body clockwise on the bed. Slowly. So that his head came very close to you." Faizan looked at me as if he were seeing me for the first time. "You were startled but only slightly. It was a general understanding around the room that it was still a matter of time for him. You seemed undisturbed by his movement and simply put your purse on the floor to make room for him to rest his head. As soon as his head touched your lap, he flipped around and I…I saw his face."

I held my breath. "Who was it?"

"Me."

I inhaled sharply. He looked haggard. I snuggled against him.

"It's just a dream," I whispered, not sure what else to say.

"Right."

"Try to get some sleep."

He nodded and closed his eyes.

I stayed awake, unable to fall back asleep. I studied the maroon curtains on the window, eerily dark in the night.

"Jaan?" My voice didn't feel mine when I finally spoke.

There was silence. Faizan's steady breathing meant that he had probably gone back to sleep. I meant to ask him to recite *Al Mani* for protection. I had remembered what it meant. It was one of Allah's names, the one that meant "the preventer of harm." I tried to say it several times before sleep took hold of me and I gave in, my fear melting away. The verses cleansed my insides; I felt light-headed, safe. Dawn erased the events of that night from my mind, and possibly from his.

Ma came in each morning with a cup of steaming tea and helped me sit up, forcing me to face the new day. She smelled of soap and water, fresh like spring. She would draw the curtain and sit next to me and encourage me to talk. I studied her dark oval face while we conversed, the sun highlighting the lines on it, etched more by the events and people in her life than years: the father she had lost as a young child; an early marriage; some miscarriages; a mother-in-law who was hell-bent on destroying her marriage until her own untimely death created some much-needed peace; the tragic death of her only surviving son. In many ways I saw similarities in the structure of Ma's face and Baba's face, perhaps a product of going through similar life events that left wrinkles and lines at the exact same times on their beings, some at the exact same places. Ma's eyes were most astonishing, gray and ever hopeful, belying her age and circumstances. She pulled her salt and pepper hair back with a long broad clip, the only accessory I ever saw her wear. She was built lean and had a slightly extended abdomen from childbearing. It was ironic that she had no children left to show for it. Instead, she carved her space in the lives of others, giving more than she ever received.

In time, it seemed like Ma and I had a history, like old friends who had shared much. She started to talk about Faizan more openly once she realized that was what I wanted. Unlike most people, who dodged the subject, she talked to heal. I talked to hurt. I loved to suffer, to feel the sweet sickening slow twist of a knife at the pit of my stomach at the mention of his name. I didn't want to stop, didn't want any of the moments we spent together not spoken of, lest time would make me forget them.

And Baba reminded me so much of the old driver Azad Baba back home, with his rock solid strength and silent love.

As children, Zoha, Sian, and I loved running to Azad Baba's shed behind our house in the early morning hours, with its scanty furniture, just the bare minimum: a stool, a rickety chair, a *charpoy* with a few-decades-old blanket, a flat pillow with frayed edges. We usually walked in to find him prostrate on the floor, his two hands outstretched and clasped together in front of his bowed head as if reaching out to someone other than whom he was praying to. Perhaps he tried to touch something more alive, more tangible than the unseen God who exists only in the mind. Money, perhaps, which is more real and should be worshipped, or some unrequited love. Azad Baba had neither. He was alone, poor and aging. It was hard to imagine him being someone's father, brother, husband, or son.

Azad Baba was a sincere advisor in our lives. In our hearts, he was more than a driver; he held the place of an affectionate grandfather and even a mother at times. To us, he was a person born old who had at some point stopped aging any more. Even when I saw him twenty years later, he looked exactly the same: glasses almost falling off his nose that he slid back up every 10 seconds, scarce gray hair on the sides of a balding head that he covered with a turban each morning. He had the kind of smile that lingered in his features long after it had faded from his lips—the smile of contentment, of unadulterated love for us, the only family he had. We reciprocated, although not in kind. Class barriers prevented us from showing our affection for him. On days Ami was gone, he assumed many of her responsibilities, making sure we were well-fed and well-attended, ordering our favorite dishes, barking orders to Mai Jan as she scurried around completing her tasks under his watchful eye. He made certain that when the cat was away, the mice didn't play.

Azad Baba left when Sian left for college, long after Zoha and I were already married. By then Abu had a new life and family, a new set of problems to deal with, and not many remembered the graying old man who made our lives livable, more bearable. For the three of us, he existed in our hearts, a rock-steady memory that we invoked for strength in times of need.

In a way, I felt that Azad Baba had come back to my life in the form of Baba.

There was never a discussion about how long Ma and Baba would stay. The unspoken understanding was that they would stay as long as it took for me to heal and move on—the unconfirmed but stable promise of selfless parents, a product of a culture a continent away. They would leave once I healed and created a new life for myself that didn't have their son in it.

There were times when I did nothing all day but sit in front of the computer and pore over the stories of 9/11 victims, crying, re-reading and crying some more. I was fascinated by the story of losses, especially of the widow who'd committed suicide a month after she lost her husband. In a letter she left for her devastated brother, she explained that she could no longer go on living without the man she loved.

And I remember thinking to myself, *what kind of a wretched wife am I? I continue to live when he is gone. Am I made of stone?*

I realized in time that the source of my strength was the little tenant inside me, the symbol of someone's deep and unfaltering love, and the woman in front of me. I looked at Ma and felt the purest kind of love. How do you love a mother? It had been a challenging question for me. How do you love someone who was always a hazy presence in your life despite the connection of blood? In contrast to my own mother, the woman before me was the epitome of sacrifice and now a vital support for her daughter-in-law and would-be grandson—so awaited, so cherished, already an orphan.

Had my own mother ever called? I vaguely recalled receiving a phone call. Ami was by far the closest, living in Boston, where she ran a salon. She had not come. What was it she said on the phone? *It would be too awkward what with Abu being there.* I had felt the bubbling of a hysterical laugh within me; only Ami could think of her discomfort at a time when her daughter was facing the biggest catastrophe of her life. I felt pity for her, the woman for whom the petty things in life were larger than her family's needs. Perhaps for her we were always a distraction from what she wanted to do for herself in life. The marriage she destroyed, not having ever accepted it in her heart as a union of minds and souls, and the man she always blamed for not loving her enough, for the children who were always a threat to her independence. Her words were etched on my soul in dark, long, toxic letters: "I wish I never had you!"

Even years later, the words still had the power to sink my heart, if only for an instant, the words that took me back to a life that was structured painstakingly by Abu to be filled with love but was tainted often by Ami's lack of care.

In contrast, I loved hearing the voices of Ma and Baba in the predawn hours, soothing like the whirring of a ceiling fan with its familiar fall and rise of pitch. Baba always brewed three cups of tea before breakfast for Ma, himself, and me when I woke up. That was their quiet time, and even in the first days they were with me, I understood the importance of those revered moments and never interrupted them. It amazed me—they had been companions for 40 years, and they still enjoyed each other's company. Throughout their son's death and afterward, they held each other through the waves of sadness and the ripples of lost hope that crashed against the giant rocks of desperation and made it ashore—always together, generously passing on that gift to me. My own life as a child had been so different; I was convinced marriages could only bring pain. Mine had, too, but the circumstances were very different.

It made me question my own looming motherhood. What kind of a mother will I be? A loving, doting one or resigned, inattentive? What I felt sure about was that I would try really hard to be good but tip the scale over on one side by my obsessive and constant self-analysis.

On panicked, sweaty, insomniac nights, Valium was my solace. I refused to think of the habit as an addiction, only as a means of coping.

"You have to stop taking it," Abu chided me the night he caught me popping a pill at 1:00 a.m. "It's not healthy for the baby or for you."

I scowled like a teenager, a fist held to my throat to prevent myself from choking out the words in my mind. *Baby! What about me? How do you expect me to get past all this?*

I grabbed a jacket and headed out, ignoring his calls. I didn't know where I was going, only that I needed to get away from this house of people who cared, sometimes a little too much. I needed to grieve, to go somewhere where I could think privately with spirits and shadows as my companions, not mortal beings.

Faizan's death had opened up some possibilities for me but none that I was excited about. For instance, I could go out anywhere late at night and didn't have to think about making him crazy with worry. I could go to a bar and drink, maybe even get picked up.

But did I really want all that?

Of course not. All I wanted was him. Back. Worrying about me, loving me enough to stop me from ruining my health, my life.

I headed up the street, watching the streetlights cast shadows that loomed in front of me like ghosts looking for trouble.

The moon hung low, laden with sorrow, and insisted on traveling with me, a forced companion. When I turned a corner, it, too, left my side. I walked four blocks, not knowing when I would turn or if I would ever return. What was it that I wanted out of life? How much did I care about the well-being of my unborn child?

Faizan had asked me once if it bothered me, being a woman. I wondered if he meant being bounced off the walls between acceptance and new roles with very little wiggle room. I said no. I lied.

The truth is I am a planner, and new situations and new roles take that away from me. I hate having to start afresh, plan anew, plot out probable challenges along the way. Until I have it all together in my hand, I remain agitated, anxious. The new twist in my life had caught me unaware, and I had not found my balance yet. I was living day-to-day, one breath at a time. Slow in, slow out. Groping in the dark for some form of equilibrium and always coming up empty-handed.

I saw a homeless man sprawled in a corner sleeping with his mouth open, snoring, a crushed Budweiser can near him, a reminder of the night's events. I passed by an old sneaker, a forgotten Frisbee, a torn blanket. Past that, there were a few teenagers huddled in a corner passing cigarettes to each other. They turned around when they saw me and for awhile, it brought to my mind the incident at the subway. I lowered my head and kept walking. They lost interest and resumed their smoking. I looked back and saw one of them cough in quick succession. A companion thumped him on the back and they all laughed. It somehow created a rip in the serene fabric of the night. In front of me stretched a night of shops, lampposts and apartment complexes, occasionally startled by houses that talked in their sleep. They yawned and creaked and sometimes groaned. I passed by one and heard angry exchanges from within and then the sound of glass shattering. I moved quickly, hugging my shawl jacket to me. When I turned a corner, I almost tripped over a young couple embracing. They seemed to be high schoolers meeting secretively; their guilty expressions were a dead giveaway. I watched them with something akin to maternal anxiety. The girl clumsily tried to button up her open shirt, a nipple still peeking out. They must know. Surely they must know about monsters that strike in the shadows, the ones Ami told me about long ago. What made these teenagers so fearless? So gullible? Don't they know that even towers who flirt with the sky can come down? That steel and concrete can become the rubble of the future and dreams can be destroyed in a heart-stopping second? That knife-wielding strangers wait around corners eager to strike? I wanted to say something. I even opened my mouth to speak. I did! But then I didn't. Some rights I had; others were not mine. I turned around. I needed to face this brutal life, not for me but for the little person inside me who would feed off my courage.

I entered the apartment and saw Abu sprawled on the couch in the living room. His eyes were closed. I studied his face, the wrinkles that had appeared in just a few days, and guilt overpowered me. How dear he was to me. I went to the medicine cabinet and took out the bottle of Valium and emptied its contents into the trash can. As an afterthought, I chucked the bottle in as well. The sound of the bottle touching the bottom of the trash can jolted Abu awake, and he sat up.

"You're home," he said.

"Yes." I walked over to him.

He got up with a sigh. I offered a hand to him and then a hug.

"Sometimes I am not the easiest daughter to be around, right?"

"You do make life interesting," he laughed. "I wouldn't want it any other way." He grew quiet and then said, "Will you be okay, Arissa?"

I knew he was thinking of the time when he would leave.

I nodded. "I'll be fine. How can I not? My life isn't mine anymore." I patted my stomach. Abu looked down and touched my belly gently. He was silent for awhile, and when I looked at his face, his lips were moving in a silent prayer.

ELEVEN

In the last week of November, we finally received word to proceed with the absentee funeral. A funeral without a body, we learned, wasn't a common concept.

The casket we saw was for a *janazah* service for another fallen victim of the attack, a Muslim. It was not an option for us, we were told later. It was a simple casket made of wood with wooden fasteners hugging it together, the only one allowed since wood, like flesh, disintegrates in soil. I looked at the green satin sheet inside the coffin with the flowing Arabic script in gold thread that read, "We belong to Allah and to Allah we return." Sunnah was to spread dust in the casket. From dust we come, and to dust we return. Why did He need the dust back? Did He not have enough?

There was a red satin pillow on one end of it. *Here is where Faizan's head would have been,* I thought to myself, trying to block the pain and let objective thinking take over, *and here the toes.* The entire 6 foot 3 inches of his body would fit inside, albeit a little tightly. How ironic that, being a Muslim, Faizan was cremated without his loved ones' choice. There was no body, no three pieces of cotton kafan that his body would be shrouded in. I often wondered how many people he saw to safety before he succumbed. He would not have thought of himself. Or of us. He tangoed with fire, just as he had flirted with life. He never believed in following a conventional way of operating in life, and in death he mocked us, too. Lit in flames, lost like a firecracker. Not a cry. Not a sign. Vanished, like he never existed. Snatched away like he was never mine. Buried, cremated, lost at sea or in the air, no one leaves this world without a trace. They leave behind a memoir of moments, cherished or despised.

It was like pulling teeth to have the imam of our mosque agree to *ghaibana namaz-e-janaza,* an absentee funeral. Abu presented case study after case study extracted from hours of research on having a funeral less a body, citing even an example of a cleric assassinated recently with no remains found, who had a casket at his funeral that contained only his wristwatch, a ring, and a turban—some possessions from his life on earth. He reminded the imam that even Prophet Muhammad had offered an absentee funeral prayer for an Ethiopian man named Negus. The imam finally agreed reluctantly, though he did not want a casket present. There will be protest against this practice, the imam warned. Abu reassured him by saying he would take his chances. Baba hung around, a dazed and distraught father, letting Abu take over a situation too grim for him to fully comprehend.

The ride to the funeral home was surreal. The morning sun was up, merciless and harsh, blinding Uncle Rizvi as he drove. As the car ascended a hill, it caused the spiteful sun to set, and I was grateful for the shade. There were many roadblocks along the way. Security was beefed up. Our vehicle was inspected four times before we reached Brooklyn.

There were a few things required to get a death certificate. We had no flesh, no identity. They needed Faizan's birth certificate, marriage certificate, proof of employment, and a completed presumption of death form. Prove to us that he existed, they tried to explain to us tastefully, so they could sign off on his obliteration. Mayor Giuliani had promised that one day all the families of the victims will have a memento by which to remember their loved ones. "We will give every family something from the World Trade Center, from the soil and from the ground, so that they can take it with them," he had said.

What can the soil from the ground give me? Just the validation that the body comes from dust and to dust it returns. Except that some exalted ones never touch the earth. They merely fly away.

"Whatever the religion, having the body gives people some real sense of consolation," a minister of a local church had said on CNN. "I would want it myself."

I felt angry at that declaration. *Would you? Do you consider having a body a consolation? Is* that *closure?* Or would finding Faizan's body be another thing that would scratch at the scab that had formed on my bleeding heart? I felt for the families who got called as piece by piece their loved one's body was recovered, then a toe, now a bone, the blueprint of DNA linking them together in a chain that could not be challenged.

I looked at the two things in my hand: a 3 x 5 photo of a smiling Faizan taken in Karachi during a vacation, and his white shirt that he'd loved so much. The shirt read, "Today, I will do something different!" and bore a ketchup stain that no amount of washing could remove—a permanent mark, a difference that couldn't be shaken. I would have dropped those inside the casket were we allowed one.

The towers had obliterated flesh and identity, the news media said. The closure wasn't for me. It was for everyone else. I will hold on to my grief, my Faizan.

I won't let go.

I clasped my hands tightly together as *thana,* the funeral prayer, began, and bowed my head. I was impervious to the sideways glances of pity around me, the clasped hands, the solemn faces. I had started to ignore them. I was tired of hearing the litany of all the proper things to say at such a time. None of them sounded right to my ears or comforted my heart. Loved ones hurt me the most. They wanted to talk about everything but him.

"If you stop talking about him, it will be easier to let go," said Azra Apa, my cousin, who had flown in from Miami for the funeral.

"Healing will begin when you accept that he is gone," Uncle Rizvi observed, laying an arm across my shoulder.

Accept that he is gone? Never! Abu held my hand but didn't talk; Sian and Zoha looked at me in dread, teeth clenched, waiting for me to snap. It seemed like only a matter of time. Ma and Baba waited for me to mention Faizan. The tension became palpable as the circle dwindled down to immediate family members. Their sidestepping hurt the most.

I recalled running into a middle-aged woman with fiery red hair who had always made a point to avoid Faizan and me. She lived across from us on the second floor, and her home always smelled of French onion soup. She never smiled when we greeted her and never acknowledged our existence. A few days earlier, however, she came up to me as soon as I got off the elevator.

"I am so sorry for your loss," she blurted out. "He was a fine man."

Somehow that didn't comfort me.

"Oh, did you know him?" I snapped. "Or are you sorry that you never bothered to get acquainted with him?" My questions threw her off completely.

She winced and walked away in a hurry. As long as I lived in the building, she never spoke to me again.

Subhaanaka allaahumma wa bihamdika wa tabaaraka ismuka wa ta'aala jadduka wa jalla thannaa-uka wa laal ilaaha ghayruka. Glory be to you, Oh Allah, and praise be to You, and blessed is Your name, and exalted is Your Majesty, and there is none to be served besides.

Exalted You are, but You couldn't prevent this from happening either. What kind of a god does that make You?

After the prayer, Baba gathered me in his arms, and I let him weep. He cried noiselessly, without exhibition or audience. When he pulled away, my shoulder was wet and his beard was soaked in his own tears.

Sons are not supposed to die before their fathers, and fathers should never have to attend their son's *janazah*. The world had just flipped on its side in our household and in many others across the country.

Beneath the drone of the F-16s flying low over the city, New Yorkers were slowly resuming their normal lives. But what was considered normal anymore? In the aftermath of 9/11, that definition had significantly altered. New York, a melting pot bubbled over, was now a boiling pot of lost innocence. Makeshift memorials went up daily. Wherever you turned, there were photos of lost loved ones of all ethnicities plastered on walls, bus stops, even shops. Some of the fliers were dog-eared and yellow from being in one spot for too long. Occasionally rain washed them down, or a sunny day rendered them stiff and crisp. They died and were reborn daily. The laminated ones merely shed tears when it rained and quickly dried. The collective group of souls they portrayed were betrayed by humanity, united in their legendary departure, their faces next to each other as if they somehow belonged together. The truth was that perhaps they had never even met one another. For me, the sea of faces all fade away until one remains—the one who represents them all, a loving family member, an innocent civilian, a hard-working citizen, gone never to return. His struggle, his tenure in life cut short, his dreams unrealized. His *jihad* was so different from the misguided, misrepresented, and misunderstood interpretation of the word that existed in some circles.

I didn't realize I was being stared at until I stepped back and almost collided with the man behind me. A flyer on a pole had captivated me. It was of a young man with glasses. Something about him reminded me of Faizan. Perhaps it was the hopeful quality of his face or was it the boyish smile that left a permanent imprint on his face?

"Pardon me," I apologized, adjusting my veil.

The man frowned and looked away. There it was again, judgment by association. He seemed to be in his fifties but held a cane in his hand.

"This one's mine," I pointed to the flyer of the young man. I have no idea what made me say that. "Which one's yours?"

He stared at me in disbelief. "None," he said finally.

I turned to leave.

"I am sorry," I heard him say but I could not stop and answer. My scab had been scratched again and I was too busy bleeding.

TWELVE

There is something so ironic about death, I thought to myself as I ran my fingers over the picture frame on my nightstand. It makes your appreciate what you lost even more. The trouble is you can't take death away and restore life.

The photo in the frame was taken my first week in New York as a married woman. I was laughing alongside Faizan, awkwardly clenched in his embrace, still not used to the idea of being affectionate in public. He was smiling—an expression frozen in time, his body bathed in sun, almost fading away. Now a dimension away. Somewhere he existed although my mortal fingers couldn't reach him and my words couldn't recall him. I winced as my finger touched the lower left corner of the frame, where the glass had chipped. I looked on in a foolish fixation as a drop of blood stained my stomach in the picture. I was reluctant to rub it off. Over time, it would dry and become a permanent fixture on the frame. It also became a symbol of many things for me: the clot that forms a baby, Faizan's life lost for an unclear and deadly cause, my own bleeding heart at the knowledge that I had traveled through time to return to the state in which I had entered the world, wailing, alone, exposed, and covered in blood. Faizan's half of the picture, on the other hand, seemed to fade every time I looked at it. Was it my imagination, or could it be that my healing had finally begun?

It didn't seem like it from the shaving foam on the countertop that I refused to remove, his towel that still hung on the rod where he'd left it after his last shower, a faint waft of his aftershave preserved in its careless folds. I used his hairbrush to comb my hair daily and watched in a senseless absorption our entwined locks caught in its teeth; we would never be that close again. I recalled a date on the calendar stuck to the fridge. November 29. It was circled, and "Faizan's eye appointment" was scribbled underneath in a familiar handwriting, an event that would never happen. *Should I call the doctor?*

I looked down at the clothes on the bed—Faizan's and mine—and felt a deep sorrow uncoil like a serpent from within and twist around my innards. How do you weigh loss? Define a lost love? I grabbed Faizan's blue shirt that held many memories for me and clutched it close to my heart. I had taken it out of the hamper the morning he shifted worlds, and slept with it for many nights. How do you fill a void? Kill an emptiness? I moved it down between my legs, but I could not invoke the memory of his touch, not even hear a sigh caught between the walls, no whispered word from the past carried through the wind. I imagined Faizan's hands on me, making every cell come alive in my body, the way they did the very first time he ever touched me. Before we were even married. There was total silence within and around me. With my lover gone, it seemed like the one inside me too had passed.

❧———————❧

Faizan had picked me up one night to go visit his parents, days after our engagement. We drove to a Pizza Hut that had recently opened in Karachi, ordered a medium pizza, and brought it back to his parents' house. It was my first visit to their two-story Bath Island home, with its red brick exterior and walls all around that were twice my size, prison-like, punctuated at the top with strategically-placed triangular chunks of glass to keep intruders out. It seemed very quiet when Faizan parked his father's silver

Land Cruiser outside; even the lights inside were turned off. Surprised, I turned to Faizan.

"Do you think they have already gone to sleep?"

He smiled and shook his head. He used his keys to unlock the door.

"Should I go upstairs and see where they are?" I asked, a little worried, slipping my leather sandals off near the door as was customary. A daughter-in-law visiting her future family for the first time is considered a big event in many households. It troubled me that no one was around to welcome me. Was it an omen for the future?

I started to move toward the stairs, but Faizan pulled me back and enveloped me in an unyielding hug.

"They're not here," he whispered hoarsely against my cheek.

"What do you mean?"

"They've gone to Hyderabad to visit some relatives." He took my hand and put it on his chest as he pulled me around to face him. He was wearing his signature smile, a feature I had grown to love in just a few days. "Arissa Amaan, do you realize that you ask too many questions?"

I heard a ringing in my ears. His heart sounded like raindrops landing on a pond, rhythmic and hurried. My knees quivered, and he embraced me again, my palm still against his heart. He cupped my chin and raised my face. I was too shy to look directly at him. The world around us took on a new flavor. The hum of the refrigerator sounded like a serenade to my love-stricken ears. When his lips caressed mine, I leaned up on my tiptoes as my naked feet sank deep into the tribal rug on the floor. My very first kiss! It was a little brush at first, and then with his lip, he rimmed the edges of my untrained mouth open and started kissing me openly, passionately, finally free from all barriers that had kept us apart. My heart was like a hunted animal's, thumping and throbbing.

"Don't leave me ever, Arissa," he moaned against my lips, and I quieted him with another kiss, surprised by my own passion. The fluid sounds of our excitement for the most part were contained within our throats; we were still too frightened to voice them lest the walls had ears, lest they had voices to alert the world.

"I can't believe we are finally here," Faizan whispered. "I never thought I'd see you again."

"I came back and waited for you but you never came."

"I was afraid." He kissed the top of my head.

"Of what?"

"Of myself. Of you. That perhaps you wouldn't feel the same way."

"I think I did," I said, looking in his eyes. "Although I didn't admit it. Not even to myself."

We were silent for a minute, swaying against each other, reflecting on God's strange ways of bringing people together. The tradition of arranged marriage had done just that in our case.

His fingers were moving down my body, exploring slowly and then quickly. Every pore in my body hungered for his touch; his hand was a flaming torch that left my body ablaze, tingling. Like a drummer, his fingers invoked a stimulating rhythm without ever touching the surface. The melody that rose in my mind had a haunting tune; I closed my eyes and slipped into a different dimension, where barriers are dropped and shame has no place. We were in no hurry, and I wasn't about to end whatever it was that was happening to me. Not even when I felt his hands slide under my long shirt and unhook my bra. Not even when he pulled my *kurti* off by slowly raising my arms. Featherlike, his fingers walked over the tight muscles of my neck and then slipped to my breasts, as my nipples quivered and came alive, surprised by their own maturity and eagerness to bloom. I didn't stop him even when his hands slid down further toward my navel. The sensation felt both foreign and familiar to me as my protesting hand gripped his fingers and then let go as gently, but firmly, they traveled even further. I felt my trousers slip down my legs and bunch up around my ankles. I shivered as the cold air touched my naked body invasively. I realized with a start that throughout it all, his fingers had barely come in contact with my flesh.

I was quite taken aback when his hands stopped suddenly. My body rebelled at the abrupt end to its exploration, and my eyes flew open. I found myself standing disheveled and shocked in front of a wall-sized mirror in the hallway that was stained to look antique. I was completely naked save for a silver watch on my wrist in front of a person who was not even my husband. The watch was his gift to me.

He was right behind me, his expression a strange blend of yearning, surprise, and pride as he brought his lips against my ears and moved his mouth to the back of my head, leaving the wetness in my hair.

"I just wanted to look, Arissa." His breath was a caress and his next sentence almost a moan. "You're beautiful, and God, you will be mine one day."

His heart was thudding against my back, and I could tell that it took every ounce of his willpower to not cross the barrier that society had set between us. His body protested. I knew because I felt him come alive against me.

I took Faizan's shirt back to the closet to tuck it in amid my clothes on the shelf. Something on the top shelf of the closet caught my eye. It was a green manila folder jammed with papers. I opened it and felt the earth slowly shift underneath me. My knees felt weak and wobbly as I made my way back to the bed. It was Faizan's dream project. *Soul Searcher,* it said in big caps, by Faizan Illahi. *Countdown to completion: 143 days,* it stated in a small font at the top. He even had a completion date in mind! My hands grew clammy, and the folder fell from my hands, the papers landing in a pile on the floor. Brushing away tears, I sat back on my haunches and started sliding them back in the folder, putting the pages back in order.

Soul Searcher was Faizan's novel in the works, the one he had mentioned to me the first time we'd met. He had shown it to me only once, when we were engaged and he was two chapters into it. You're the author's soul, he had told me then, insisting that I inspired him to take the novel to a whole new level. I thought his writing was beautiful. I had so many questions, but he was evasive about answering them.

"You will get to read it all once it is finished," he had said simply. "You have to be patient. Good authors take time."

There again was that self-assurance that had attracted me to him in the first place. "Perhaps we should just dedicate one weekend where we can sit down and discuss your greatness."

But the truth was that the work was good, flawless from the beginning. The characters were perfectly composed, the scenery was balanced— it had just the right texture and flavor to render it unforgettable.

I opened the manuscript to page one and traced the words that had been etched in my mind ever since I read them a few years ago.

> I am their conscience; I am their eyes. I am the one who puts the fear of God in their hearts. They think to themselves, *the tiffin wallah knows. We cannot hide from him.* You see, it's because I am an arm's length away, lurking just around the corner. My senses are eager to grab hold of any tidbit for my memory book, which I neatly file away in the three compartments of my mind. The biggest one is the section of sins, *gunah*, the chamber of the landlord where all things evil exist. Then there is the pure, milky-white chamber of love I call Barsa. The third is a place for repentance that is home to Baba. They are the chambers of secrets, of untold stories that have not been checked out yet.

From the very start, Faizan presented the protagonist as a person you felt empathy for without making him too black and white. There were enough gray areas in the character to make him a living, breathing person, prone to confusion, prone to mistakes. Faizan never showed me any future drafts. Perhaps he felt that I didn't ask the right questions. He always reiterated that he would feel comfortable sharing when he was close to finishing. He never reached that point. Or was it I who failed to reach that point in his eyes?

I was picking up the folder from the floor with the reverence of a holy book when Ma entered. I quickly shoved it under the pile of clothes on the bed.

"Arissa bayta, lunch is ready." She sounded hoarse; the voice of a woman who had cried many nights by herself but always woke up with a vow in her heart to be a healing balm to others around her. She held my hand through my rough time, her grief secondary to mine, as she took over the housework and the apartment, leaving me free to figure out my life, my future, and that of my unborn child. But the leisure time let me grieve more and heal less, and in her kindness, my mother-in-law had given me the freedom of coming close to lunacy.

The days after Faizan's death were a blur to me. Relatives and friends from all over had gathered to help and support me, overwhelming at times and much needed at others. Then, like fall, they started to disappear leaf by leaf, going on with their own lives and work, until only two remained: Ma and Baba. I felt I could snap like a twig most mornings, just as Zoha and Sian suspected before I chased them away, Zoha back to Karachi and her children, Sian to Ohio where he was studying public administration at Ohio University. Abu left before any of them to go back to his new family, people who were real to me only in pictures, the few I received of a wife, who often looked bored, and her son, who was seven and whose smiles always revealed a few missing teeth. He was adorable, though, plump-cheeked like his mother. My stepmother.

Ma was silent as she looked around my room, nervously eyeing Faizan's clothes on the bed.

"Are you cleaning up?" she asked, voicing a bereaved mother's silent fear that perhaps her daughter-in-law was getting rid of all signs of her son and yet knowing in her heart that the world does move on. It had just been sixty days. Sixty days without the love of my life. I was not a widow in iddat anymore, but I couldn't let him go. Not yet.

"Yes, just organizing a little bit," I replied, frazzled. I decided to change the subject. "What's for lunch?"

I chided myself as I ushered her out of the room even though she was not done answering. Why did I not try to assuage her fear, the woman who lived completely for me and put her life on hold to piece mine back together? Why did I have this constant need to hurt people? Was it because I myself hurt in so many different ways? What was that thing Ami had said to me once when I hurt my knee as a child, "I'll feel sorry for you if you want me to"?

That need had not gone away.

I was an ungrateful brat.

And an inconsolable widow.

That night, I opened the manila folder again after I did the dishes and escaped from the kitchen. The apartment was silent. Ma and Baba had retired to bed. I traced the text without reading the content. I imagined the pages in Faizan's long hands as he turned each page lovingly, cradling them as only a mother would.

I read all night and did not know when dawn broke the night's back and pushed forward into a brilliant sky. Faizan's work was his passion in life—beautifully crafted, words like gems beaded together into a sturdy necklace.

Under the sweltering sun of the Karachi summer, a panting rider on a bicycle was making his way up the road, meandering through autos with blaring horns and red-tongued rickshaw drivers chewing tobacco and shouting obscenities at the same time. Nothing fazed the young rider. His shirt was drenched at the armpits with sweat that had seeped down both sides of his body. The city was a splattered mess of life. The buses that zoomed past him and at times forced him off the road were muddy and unabashedly adorned—the groomless brides.

I did not realize that I was crying until the pages in my hands curled from wetness. I *was* the groomless bride, a *baywah*. I cried for Faizan's unfinished work. I cried for the child he would never see, for the wife he'd never hold. It seemed debilitating to sense the loss from his perspective.

Ma walked in with a cup of tea. I did not sense her presence until I felt the bed slump on one side from her weight. The rustling of pages informed me that she had discovered my treasure.

"This is—?" she asked, her eyes hopeful and sad at the same time.

I nodded. "His work."

She breathed in and picked up some more pages. Her hands trembled.

"Did he—?"

"No, it's not complete," I answered before she finished her thought. She looked at me and then turned toward the window at the sound of a common grackle that had just landed on the ledge, its purple velvety surface shiny with the promise of a new day. Ma stood up to turn the light on in the room. I blinked several times and still my eyes hurt.

"He invested a good number of his days in this project, didn't he?" Ma turned her attention back to the pages in her hand. She lifted a handful close to her face and inhaled deeply. "It still has his scent."

I sniffed at some pages, too, and we both laughed. We hadn't laughed in days.

"I used to hold his shirt when I slept on days he was working late," I admitted, curling my fingers around Ma's, stroking the calluses that strayed down her palm. "He never understood why."

"When he started sleeping in his own room at age two, I used to take the shirt he wore during the day and sleep with it," Ma replied, patting my hand and kissing the tips of my fingers, her eyes brimming with unshed tears. "He was such a good baby. Slept all night from the start. I had to wake him up to feed him." She paused and looked up at the ceiling, lost in memories.

"We have to keep him alive in our minds—in this baby's life!" My statement came out like a plea.

"We will, *Insha Allah*." Ma nodded, and she seemed grateful. I was surprised how little we mentioned God lately. It was as if we felt that He had wronged us. I was thankful that Ma didn't ask me to let go and live my life as other people had done. But maybe it was important for her to keep the memory of her only son alive. Through me, through my unborn child.

"But to fulfill his dream, his work has to be finished. It was such an integral part of his life." She looked at me and then her eyes brightened with a secret knowledge. "Who better to do it than his own companion?"

I looked at her questioningly and then realized that she meant me. I shook my head, trembling at the credence of such a project. "I don't feel adequate to handle—"

"But you must!" Ma pleaded, holding both of my hands in hers, squeezing them together. My ring grazed the fingers next to it, and I tried not to wince. I shook my head. The papers were once again strewn all around us.

"You have to piece it all together," Ma said, looking at them. "You have to give it life so he can live in these pages."

I was surprised by the passion in her voice. It was as if for days she had been losing herself piece by piece and had just realized how to put herself back together again.

"Promise me!" Ma yearned, her eyes wild as she shook me by my shoulders. "Promise me, Arissa!"

And wretched woman that I am, I could not even give her that. I could not even lie.

She matched my stubbornness.

And so began our days and nights with just one debate.

You can do it.

I can't.

Yes, you can.

No, I can't. I won't.

You will. Just watch and see.

How do you end a story that's not yours? Add another sentence where there is a pause? Infiltrate the story with a comma when really there should have been a period? Punctuate with an exclamation point where a period would have sufficed? What if you kill something breathing and breathe life into something the author wanted to eliminate? How do you get inside the mind of a person who isn't there? Fill the shoes of someone who will never again fill his own?

It's ridiculous, I told myself, *I cannot finish his work.* His words had an ethereal quality, placed on a pedestal very far from my reach. How could I even think I could do this? The work was not mine to finish. My words wouldn't compare to his. They would lack the perfect lilt, the flawless pitch, the faultless tone, the right humor, the creative flair for changing scenes. How could I match his skill?

"You're right. You can't," said Ma, always the wise one. "But think of it this way, what is the worth of his work if it is not finished? It will never bring any good to anyone. And who better to finish it than another writer? Faizan would have said that, too."

"I am a business writer," I reminded Ma. "I write boring corporate stuff!"

Would Faizan consider me a good enough writer to finish what he was certain would be his masterpiece? Wasn't he the one who had tons of things to say about my work whenever he reviewed something for me? Not enough zing, too many adjectives, mixed metaphors, wrong use of commas, verbs not at par with their subjects, shifting tenses, unparallel sentences—the list was endless.

All the same, he was the one who once said, "Next to me, I would say you are a darn good writer."

Modesty was never his virtue. Neither was clarity.

I was snuggled on the couch, in the middle of my fourth reading of *Soul Searcher*. It stopped at page 110, leaving many questions unanswered. I sighed and leaned back against the silken dupioni pillows that I had planned to crotchet and bead one day. The little packet of yarn and hooks sat forgotten in the kitchen drawer and in time had slid under the many books of recipes I owned. It seemed like such a bad idea now. The pillows seemed grotesque and misplaced against the wide back of the oversized couch, too big now for just one person. What were Faizan and I thinking when we bought it from Pier One?

I suddenly had a fresh view of the accent wall where the fireplace was situated. In the excitement of moving in, I had painted it a screaming burgundy and then sponge-painted it with splotches of blue and yellow. That was another bad decision. I remember Faizan being pleased with the wall, but I hated it as soon as it was done, even before I'd put all my supplies away. A framed painting of mine with two sunflowers and a rose on a stark white background served as a focal point. The painting was one of my favorites.

Ma came into the living room and dropped something in my lap.

"Look what I found."

They were two identical ocean-blue booties, perfect with little zig-zaggy crochet trims and bobbing snow-white balls hanging from a white thread.

"These belonged to Faizan when he was a baby." She came around to settle down beside me and fingered the socks lovingly. Her breathing was uneven. In time I learned that she got that way when she was particularly zealous about something.

I cupped the booties in my palms and buried my face in their soft wooliness. They lacked the fragrance of a young baby but had eons of history within the fibers.

"I started knitting these seven months into my pregnancy, and in the last two months, my fingers were swollen twice their size and I couldn't knit anymore. At that point, I had just finished one."

I looked at her, long and hard, tearing my eyes away from the little socks. What was she getting at?

"Your Baba finished the other one. He had never knitted before, but he learned for my sake and for the sake of our unborn child."

I saw Baba enter the room and tower above us before moving away to the kitchen with heavy feet. He opened the refrigerator door, and the light from within illuminated the tears on his face before he slapped it shut.

Ma lifted my hand and placed her palm against mine. I turned my attention back to her.

"This is how couples who are in love fit, like two identical socks, like a pair." Her voice was breaking but avid. "Where one leaves off, the other picks up and finishes the task. For love, for the sake of the other. That's how God made us. In pairs, so that we complete each other."

And then he snatches one away, I thought, *and makes us realize that we're dispensable mortals.* Alone we come, and solo our return.

Without voicing it, we both knew Ma had won that round. We embraced and held each other. We had no more tears left. There was nothing left to discuss. This was our closure as well as our new beginning. Together, we would create a lasting legacy for Faizan. She with her selfless support, me with my pen.

I waited for the computer to purr to life and hungrily scanned the documents folder for the manuscript. I saw a folder titled "SoulSearcher-drafts" and my clammy fingers almost slipped off the keyboard. The most recent file in there was dated 09-07-2001, four days before Faizan was snatched from me. I opened the file to the title page. It stated simply, "Countdown to completion: 70 days."

That manuscript had 65,000 words. I quickly calculated that the hard copy I had discovered in our closet days after Faizan's demise wasn't the most updated version. I devoured the pages for the additional words. That was it. It was almost finished but not quite. How did he want it to end? I pondered over that unanswered question. How had the author imagined it? I wished for the hundredth time that Faizan had talked more about his project or that I had been a bit more relentless in my queries.

The novel was about a Pakistani *tiffin wallah*, a lunch carrier named Yavar. Following a hundred-year-old tradition in South Asia, the lunch carriers delivered hot prepared lunches from people's homes to offices. Wives of working men diligently prepared elaborate meals and stacked them in cylindrical aluminum containers for delivery. In the novel, Yavar goes through a rough childhood after he loses some family members in a mysterious fire. His father, who survives the disaster, is devastated and becomes a beggar, leaving Yavar to fend for himself. Yavar ends up becoming a street child of Karachi, making a day's living by polishing boots and carrying loads, trying to keep away from the many vices prevalent on streets like drugs and the sex trade. In time, a cleric and his wife take him in and raise him as their own. Yavar grows up to become a *tiffin wallah*, also becoming a friend and confidant to many clients. In time, too, the truth about his past surfaces, and he is able to piece together the events of the unfortunate night when he lost his family. The truth he uncovers, however, is worse than not knowing, and he struggles with how best to direct the course of his future.

The room was extremely quiet; I could hear the drone of the fridge in the background, the ticking of the clock in the hallway. Ma and Baba had gone for a walk to a nearby park and were going to take the bus and buy some groceries on the way back. We were running low on *dal*. Faizan had never been a big fan of that dish and I had been slow to replenish our supply of lentils.

And then it came to me, an idea so brilliant that I almost fell off my chair in elation. I steadied myself and looked at the papers on the desk and then at the words on the screen. It was perfect. It meant rewriting the whole manuscript, yes, but in the voice of another—the disembodied voice of the protagonist's dead mother. The narrator would be the person like my Faizan who had passed on. It would take longer, of course, but it would be worth it.

I lit some floating candles in a pan, which I carried to my bed. I gazed at the surreal, distorted forms the objects took on behind the flames until my eyes grew blurry from not blinking. I watched the candles burn out one by one throughout the night until there were none left. Then I turned around and went to sleep. I had paid my respect to the lifework of a man.

It was the seventieth day since September 7, the day Faizan had intended to finish his work. I had been unsuccessful in getting it done in time, but I renewed a promise to complete it. When, how, I didn't know. I didn't want to set a time to it, only a goal. I wanted inspiration and his spirit to guide me, to fill my thoughts with what he had envisioned. I wasn't certain he would comply. He had not been good at making contact since crossing over to the other side.

THIRTEEN

I made certain promises, and I assigned them numbers. If it isn't drawn or written in ink, I can't focus, and the nagging worry in my heart keeps me anxious until I cave in and devise a plan.

The first task was the toughest, and carried many consequences, but I wasn't sure for whom. Losing Faizan, the attack at the subway station, the ultrasound afterward—they all were collectively responsible for that decision. My world was not mine anymore and was soon to be inhabited by another human being, helpless, disabled, and totally dependent. His comfort came first of all. My decision to let go of an integral part of my life would only offer him one less chance of being singled out. That resolution would also offer him an opportunity to mingle and fit in better. I was certain there would be plenty of times when he would be regarded differently, and the least I could offer him was one less deviation from the norm. Assimilate and accept it all, I decided. Only this society can give my unborn child what my own can't—a chance for a better life and abundant opportunities that he could seize and avail.

"You can do anything you set your mind to," Faizan had said once, "with or without me."

I had swatted him with a paintbrush, leaving a fiery red mark across his cheek, and he had laughed and taken the brush from my hand and marked an "A" across my chest. Ironically, after losing him, the veil that I had worn since the day we got married had performed the role of that scarlet letter he'd marked on my chest. The one that shouted, "Look at me; I follow the same religion as the one who harmed you." I would have liked to add, "Please don't rush to condemn me," but a veil is only supposed to convey so much. Lately it had transcended into another role: the wearer was associated with supporting the acts of the attackers.

Was the decision easy for me to take? Of course not. It was my dead husband's wish that I was negating, but it was time to let go of that desire and nurture others. But how do you let a tradition go or justify it to people? Some choices are never yours; your life's events choose them for you, and you merely obey, whether you agree or not.

There was someone who needed to know my plan of action.

I suggested to Ma that we take an excursion to the 500-acre urban park in Brooklyn, the one famous for its scenic lake, its landscaping, and its forest. She raised an eyebrow, unsure of why the invitation was not extended to Baba.

"Go ahead," Baba said before she could respond. "I have some paperwork to handle this morning." He looked at me. "Make sure you bundle up well."

I nodded at his concern. He was very perceptive and perhaps sensed that this excursion was something other than just a random outing.

We took the B train to Prospect Park station and followed the mix of locals and tourists with their many cameras, backpacks, strollers, and babbling children headed to the park, meandering down the path through the Cleft Ridge Span Bridge. We held our jackets close to us like our two worlds, walking like only veiled women do, protectively shielding our bodies from being touched—an instinctive quality we had developed by living in a society at war with itself. Mostly we looked at our feet and occasionally at the sights around us, avoiding the gaze of the men nearby. I did this more so than her, since I was in the presence of a watchful adult.

I discovered that when I was with her, I was reduced to a childlike state, forever faltering, full of simplistic follies, unable to make correct judgments.

People nodded at us, and some stepped aside to let us pass. Many passed us by because we walked too slowly. The world around us couldn't match our pace. Ma's arthritis had been bothering her lately. I often heard her knees crack when she got up from a sitting position. A few days ago, she'd fallen in the bathroom and couldn't get up. Baba and I aided her and brought her to bed. By evening, she was back in the kitchen despite our protests, still wanting to cook the lentil and spinach dish called *dal bhaaji* and a fresh batch of chappatis.

"Don't stop me, please," she pleaded. "I am fine, everything is okay."

Nothing and no one was, but we left her statement unchallenged and backed off reluctantly. We all had strange ways of keeping our sanity. Ma found hers in the kitchen.

The view of the Prospect Park Audubon Center was breathtaking in its midmorning magnificence. It was a focal point for one of the most dramatic landscapes in the park with its slowly descending waterfall enclosed by a natural canopy, the serpentine paths, the carved bridges, and a beautiful view of the wide lake with its open mother-like embrace. We walked along the park's watercourse, watching the boaters traverse the water. The excited shrieks of children and the wails of the very young symbolized that there was still hope in the world. How I wished Faizan was there to see this. We had always wanted to take this excursion. Around us, the sunlight beamed with a magical quality, wanting to envelope us in its shiny embrace. Instead, we looked for shade and put on our shades.

I handed half a sandwich to Ma from inside my bag. She took a bite and looked at it. It was a simple sandwich that echoed our lives: green chili paste on rye with cucumber, tomato, and a single slice of cheese. With regret, I saw the crisp fallen leaves on the ground. *They will never find his body now,* I thought randomly. *Too much time has passed.* I shooed the thought away.

"Ma, I have decided to let go of my hijab."

I sensed her shoulders stiffen, but she didn't look my way. A sigh escaped her parted lips.

"I have given it much thought," I continued, studying her profile. "It isn't easy for me either."

Ma turned around slowly and then sat down on the blanket I had laid out earlier. I couldn't read her expression, but tiredness oozed from her. I kept standing, unsure of what to do with the rest of my sandwich.

"I started wearing my scarf when I was ten," Ma finally said, looking at me. "My grandfather, he was a strict man. When my sister and I were little and complained that after washing our hair our veils wouldn't stay put, he shouted, 'Drill it down with a nail. That's no excuse for going around with naked heads.' Our mother took pains tying our scarves down with bobby pins on both sides of our heads. After awhile, they did feel like nails burrowed into our skulls."

I tried to search her face once again for emotion but found none.

"Times have changed," she continued finally with a soft smile. "We have all changed. I am no one's judge. There are things I am not proud of. There are things I am sure you regret as well."

If only she knew.

"What I am saying is that, Arissa, it's your life. I know why you're making this decision, and I am not the one to stand in your way. It's always been a tradition in the family, but the tradition also was to live back home. We have modified our lives, and we do what we can do for those to come."

"He wanted to move back," I blurted out, unable to control myself.

Ma stopped and looked at me. She opened her mouth to speak and closed it again.

"He told me a month before…before—" I was unable to continue.

"You didn't know," Ma said simply. Her face was full of sorrow as she continued. "You couldn't have known that—"

"But as a mother, doesn't that make you—?"

We were unable to let each other finish our painful thoughts.

"Angry?" Ma concluded for me. "Who am I going to be upset at? You? The attackers who took my only child away from me? God? Where does it stop? The list will be endless if I let myself go."

I looked at the woman before me in wonder. Why didn't I have her ability to absolve others, her conviction, her clarity of vision? Does that only come with age?

"The truth is that there is a time reserved for each one of us. When it comes, we have no say, no power to stop it. No loved one's pleas work. Prayers," her voice broke, "fall on deaf ears, and the one who is to be snatched away will be plucked from this earth." Overcome, Ma buried her face in her hands. "Allah knows I prayed for the safety of my child every day! I—"

A sigh caught in my throat. There was nothing more Ma could say. We clung together, heartbroken and lost for words. How do you bring back a promise that you thought had the span of a lifetime, but was looted by blazing wings of flying machines? Besides us a hawk swooped down, so close we gasped and pulled away. It flew off in a diagonal quickly and we caught a glimpse of what it had stolen from the earth—a tiny baby bird who was probably out for the first time, learning to fly. Nearby, its mother chirped in terror. For awhile, the feathered world around us went berserk, protesting at the injustice, angry at the perpetrator. They failed to realize that the hawk merely followed its nature—preying for food. It had no other means of sustenance, or the realization of another's loss.

I pulled away from Ma and looked at the sun directly. Sun spots clouded my vision, and when I looked back at Ma, she was dotted from head to foot.

"Leave the guilt behind." Ma finally raised her head and looked in my eyes. "It has no place in your life. Yours or mine."

Sudden fog startled the sunlight and quietness fell around us. We finished the rest of our sandwiches in silence. I looked across at two toddlers at play, passing ball to each other, unsuccessfully most of the time. One of them kicked the ball high, and it missed me by inches.

A woman came hurrying over, perhaps their mother, panting and breathless from climbing uphill, and did a double-take when she saw two veiled women sitting cross-legged on the grass.

"I'm sorry," she began, her expression sullen like a lit flame.

We hurried to set her mind at ease, assuring her that the ball had not hit us.

"No." She waved away our concerns and glared at us. "I am just sorry they missed you."

With that she picked up the ball and walked away.

We stood up and quietly picked up our belongings in our in-between world. The line between a resident and an outcast had grown very thin. I threw the bags and used napkins in the trashcan. We each took a lesson back with us from the encounter that day: my decision was now strengthened, new plans germinating in my head, while Ma's stoic hold on tradition grew a few degrees brighter.

I decided to add one more item to my list of things to do: *Let the guilt go.*

Faizan and I had been lying in bed after our intimate encounter, our limbs entwined, looking at the moon from our window. I studied his profile briefly and planted a kiss on his nose.

"You're amazing, Faizan Illahi."

"You're not so bad yourself." Faizan laughed, tickling my toes with his. "I guess practice makes perfect."

"Oh, so you think you've perfected the art in two years of marriage?"

"Of course. I never do anything halfway."

We held hands, enjoying the silence and the stillness of the night. Outside, a baby house finch cried out, its slumber disturbed, breaking the sanctity of the night air. Faizan turned to look at the time and in his hurry, knocked over the bedside clock.

"Darn," he muttered as he picked the clock up. It had a crack on its face. He had had it since his graduation. The planner in me made a mental note to buy him a new one for his birthday. Maybe it was time for a change.

"Oh well," he laughed and turned over to hold my hand. "You know, Arissa, I have been thinking."

Oh, oh, I knew that tone well. That could not be good.

"We should have lunch together at Kudrows."

I laughed. It fascinated me, his ability to bring tension to a conversation and in a trice, ebb it away. He turned to sit up and faced me.

"No seriously, Arissa, I have been thinking and I have arrived at a decision."

I massaged his fingers. "What about?"

He held my wrist and placed my fingers against his cheek. "That we should move back."

It didn't register at first. The tone or the content.

"Where to?"

"Pakistan."

"What?" I jerked my hand away and snatched the blanket away to cover my chest, leaving his body bare.

"I think it's the right thing to do," he said, smoothing a crease on the bed. "Ma and Baba are getting old and they're at the stage in life where they really need me."

His words hinted at something unsaid that I could not grasp. The orange hue from the lamp added a few years to his face.

"Why? And most importantly how?" I flung my legs off the bed and paced the room, the juice of our intimacy spilling down my thigh. "Did it occur to you that you ought to consult me before arriving at a decision on a matter of this scale?"

"Our lives would be much more comfortable," Faizan persisted. "It's the right choice. Let's be rational about it."

"Rational, hah!" I wanted to physically injure the person in front of me. I knew the restaurant job must make him feel less adequate, but I didn't tell him that. I held on to some notions, antiquated or otherwise, without letting on. "Why can't they move here?"

Faizan shook his head. "They'd be miserable. I can't uproot them."

No, uprooting me is easier, I fumed inside. *Not once but twice.*

"What about me and our plans for the future?" My voice trembled from rage and started to rise as I continued. "Do I not have a say in the matter? Or do you think you can fit your wife in any corner and in any space to your liking?"

"You know that's not fair, Arissa. Consider this, it will finally free up my time to work on the book—"

"The book," I said with sarcasm-laden voice. "Is that all you care about? *You* and *your* dreams? *You* and *your* book?"

The last word came out accompanied by a spit and he turned away, hurt. I plopped down on the chair across from the bed, tired of pacing and looked up at the ceiling fan in irritation. The damned blob infuriated me and suddenly my anger shifted to the owners of the apartment. How tough was it to switch out a blade?

I looked over at Faizan who seemed lost in the sea of lavender foliage of the bed sheet and was struck by a strange realization: It was all wrong— the choice of the sheet, this moment, his choice. How well did I really know him, my own husband?

I took a deep breath to calm my nerves and tried again.

"Why is this not a topic up for discussion, Faizan?" I asked in a softer voice. "Why does it have a tone of such finality to it?"

He didn't answer right away.

"I just think it's best for us as a family. I just feel it," he said. "When we have a child—"

I turned away. It had become a sore topic. We had been trying for the past year or so to get pregnant and had been unsuccessful. I cringed every month when my suspicion was confirmed that I had yet again failed to conceive.

"Jaan, it will happen, and if we are in Pakistan, Ma will help us in raising our child."

I refused to look in his eyes, and being on the defensive, took his comments personally. "You don't think I am qualified to raise a child on my own?"

"Of course you are. I am sure you will be a great mother, and the support system that we have in Karachi will enable you to have a career later on."

He stood up to go to the bathroom, an expression of hurt on his face, reminding me yet again of how trapped he seemed in our low-ceilinged apartment. When we moved in, we laughed at how Faizan could touch the ceiling when he was standing.

In that moment, I was incapable of consoling him or myself. I never thought Faizan would want to leave the United States. That wasn't in the plans, at least not in the ones he had laid out for me earlier. I had outlined a whole series of events. He was presenting a new set of blueprints altogether.

"I don't think it's a good idea," I shouted to him from across the room. "I think our children can have a better future in this country, especially if the child turns out to be a girl."

I heard a flush and then the sound of faucet drowned his next few words. He came out and stood across from me, arms crossed. "Arissa, I don't want to argue with you, but my mind is made up." For once his voice was harsh and unrelenting.

"In that case, *I'll* give you a choice," I said with fury. "You can decide whether you want to leave me and go back to Pakistan or stay here and be with me."

I didn't wait for an answer and grabbed my pillow to spend the night in the den.

He never mentioned the move again.

FOURTEEN

November 2001

After my visit to the pier, I took a subway to Wall Street and wandered around aimlessly. In the glass pane of a Starbucks, I stared at the new me—bold, unabashed, sans the veil that I had retired within.

I slipped in and ordered a grande coffee of the day. It was too strong, and I drank it too quickly, burning my lips. I never liked putting the lid on the cup and sipping from the tiny opening. When I left, I carried the coffee with me even though it was tepid by now, an oily film on its surface that trembled as I walked. My baby stretched within me as the caffeine jolted him awake. I patted my stomach lightly.

"Good morning, little king," I whispered. "It's a bright, new day."

I sat on the steps of the Federal Hall National Memorial, right next to a large statue of George Washington, and watched a steady stream of people go in and out. News reported that the hall had sheltered 300 people on September 11. I was amazed by the sulfuric smell that still lingered in the air. For a long time, there had been the stench that reeked of lives burned. Dust even now settled on buses when they were in the environs, slowly moving through downtown as if life had been sucked out of them. New Yorkers walked differently now, always watchful, looking over their shoulders in fear, eyeing each other guardedly, unable to relax or let go.

I stood up to leave and without realizing it left the empty cup behind. For a brief minute, I stood under a pole cluttered with signs outside the museum. Two of them said "One Way" but pointed in two opposite directions. I didn't know where I was going or what I was doing. "Checkpoint Ahead," the yellow diamond shaped one at the very bottom stated simply. I started walking down the street, feeling like a couplet with a lost stanza, a jingle that had lost its beat. Walking was therapeutic for me. It gave me a chance to order my thoughts, to assign them slots in my mind or to jerk them loose. The wind at the nape of my neck pierced the cold through my skin like a shot. It jolted me, the breeze ruffling my hair in its silent invasion, the air whispering a song in my ears that was not familiar to me. I felt naked, like a prostitute, my wares exposed for all to see. In reality, the busy world around me scarcely noticed my loss or collective losses. I longed for the veil I had let go.

I didn't realize I was part of a procession until I was flanked by men and women on all sides holding up candles, signs, and banners, some with children piggybacked on their shoulders. The peaceful march had started down lower Broadway from Union Square. I tried to read the signs and move out at the same time, almost stumbling over a placard. "We Want Our Sanity Back," it said. I smiled to myself. *Who doesn't?* A man in a red sports jacket reached over, picked it up, and handed it to me, laughing broadly as if he had done me a favor. I hugged it to me, the wrong side out, not knowing what else to do. I realized that it was an antiwar march. I moved along the sea of bodies reluctantly, keeping my face low. It was useless. I didn't feel anything one way or the other. The war on terror wasn't mine to win or lose. I had lesser goals, my own mini-wars to contend with. A woman moved up the line holding a sign so big she was having trouble working its width and marching at the same time. "Compassion Rather Than Belligerence," her sign said. If only a dictionary came with that.

I was in the front flank, but I don't know what or whom I represented. A deceased husband? A wanted pregnancy now challenged? Or a child doomed in-utero with a damaged existence? I heard the tut-tut of sympathetic relatives in my mind.

"*Bechari*," they whispered to one another. It was a title that I hated. It rendered me a pitiful subject for everyone's scrutiny and constant analysis. "Can you imagine being a *baywah* and pregnant at the same time?"

And that title again. Baywah, the Urdu word for a widow. It hit me like the cold slap of the snowy winter whenever I heard it. Widow. An echoing sound that loops around me forever. Even when I hold my hands to my ears to block it out, it somehow still manages to reach my brain. Cursed. Broken by loss. Baywah! I had read in the news that the Indian-administered Jammu and Kashmir government had prohibited the use of the term after rights groups deemed it derogatory and aggravating to the bereaved. Call them "wife of deceased," the directive said; if they are Muslim, refer to them as "*zouja marhoom*," or "respected wife of the deceased." However you phrased or dignified it, it was still a stamp of loss permanently affixed on our hearts. Would calling us this or that change that reality?

Some days ago I read about the lives of widows in Nigeria and the age-old traditions of discrimination and isolation that leave them destitute. Hair scraped off their heads with a sharp razor blade to make them easier to spot in public and subsequently shun. A bizarre ritual offered them some redemption, one that required the widow to sleep with a member of her deceased husband's family to banish the spirit of the departed.

How will I ever redeem myself from my widowhood?

I silently inched away from the crowd without being noticed, and then stopped to watch the procession pass. Losses mean different things in different parts of the world. Where I come from, healing begins with forgetting; in other societies, healing is achieved by dedicating yourself to certain causes. The concrete walls of women's hearts in the peninsular landmass of the Indian subcontinent seal off emotions, thereby achieving absolute sterility that can only lead to isolation. The dreaded word *death* scares my people; losses make them uncomfortable, nervous. They do the only thing they know to do: shy away and distance themselves. As I do now.

At home I checked the item "Lose veil" off my list and studied the next two entries. "Move," the second one stated simply. Scrawled beneath it in just the last few weeks was the last entry.

"Complete *Soul Searcher.*"

I was ready to face the weekly ultrasound that the doctor had ordered for me.

I put on Faizan's turtleneck sweater—the green one he'd worn the day we met. It was twice my size but hid the contours of my body well. Next, I slipped on a pair of loose khakis. In the mirror, I studied my almond-shaped eyes that angled up toward the far corners of my head and scrunched up my nose. I hated that feature of my face, and yet I had been told by many that that was my best attribute. I maintained that my hair was probably a better selection. It was long and thick, although knotting easily after a bath.

Losing the veil had given birth to a new worry in my mind: what should I do about my hair? At home, I was used to just coiling it up on top of my head with a clip. I ran my finger through my hair. I had always worn the same hairstyle, parted down the middle, one long plait tumbling down my back tied with a black or blue band. It hadn't mattered anyway; it never showed through the long scarf I wore. I had once used a piece of cable wire to tie the ends when I couldn't find a band.

I untied the plait and shook the strands loose, looking at my hair as if noticing it through the eyes of someone else. I started to part it in the center but midway decided against it and swept it back in a skull-tightening ponytail.

I stood back and felt a kick in my belly. I smiled. *The baby approves. That's all that matters.* It was all about looking at life through a one-inch square and allowing myself to study just one moment at a time.

The apartment complex where Faizan and I lived was only five stories high and was built in the 1920s. It was one of the few garden complexes in Jackson Heights with its shuttered porches and Spanish-style ironwork separated by wide green pathways that offered views of the courtyard to the street. The apartment itself was quite minimal, a one-bedroom home with a small den and hardwood floors. It was always dank in there, kind of a decaying smell that never went away no matter how much incense we burned. There were three windows side by side in the kitchen that I particularly liked although they didn't have much of a view, not unless you enjoyed watching a starving artist in his underpants across the street, dozing off on his balcony after a night of drinking.

Faizan liked the apartment because of its easy access to the subway and various bus routes. The great district of Queens known for its multilingual ethnic neighborhoods is a broth of many tastes: Colombians, Mexicans, Indians, Bangladeshis, Pakistanis. Although ours was considered a safe neighborhood, one had to be more careful on the subway under Roosevelt Avenue or busy Northern Boulevard.

Often on weekends, Faizan and I visited 74th Street between Roosevelt Avenue and 37th Avenue. Trolling down Jackson Heights, our arms linked together, *kulfi* cups in the other hand, full of spindly noodles and pistachio ice cream topped with oodles of rose syrup—such were our simple joys. That's what I missed most, the times when we bonded wordlessly, almost magically.

Walking among folks from the continent we came from lifted our spirits, although we rarely stopped to converse with anyone. They were a calming presence in our midst, moving around urgently as if living in the present would somehow devour them. I always slowed down my pace when I saw them. I envied the little children in such groups. Their perpetual joy was spellbinding, their carefree rejoicing of the instant refreshing. They were always a few steps behind, enamored by a bug, then a bike. Innocent souls touched, moments etched onto one's heart.

Occasionally, Faizan pulled me to him and planted a full kiss on my lips in a grand display of affection when we passed a seemingly conservative group. He almost always got the reaction he wanted. He thrived on seeing their absolute shock and surprise at the brazenness of a South Asian man and the veiled woman by his side.

I rode the elevator down to the apartment lobby and saw Melvin, a neighbor who always had a ready smile for me but lately looked away when he saw me coming. That day he stared, and his eyes widened in disbelief at the absence of my veil.

"What's new and different, Mel?" I teased as I walked by without stopping.

He grunted in response. *Oh yes, nothing is the same.*

Is the veil really a barrier, as Jack Straw indicated, or is it a symbol of modesty? It is different for different women. It irritated me that it was a political game for some high-ranking individuals, a tug-of-war of sorts, a way of attaining the limelight albeit negatively. The debate provoked the community and suddenly united us while we had a hard time agreeing on just what exactly our faith was about. Or did the love for our own religion really mean that we should hate other faiths? It made me reflect on what being a Muslim meant to me. Wasn't the whole concept of Islam based on tolerance, peace and bridge-building, or was it just a very well-kept secret that only a handful knew?

Outside, I ran into a boy I had seen around the apartment complex. He seemed to be about seven and had long chestnut hair that kept getting in his eyes.

"Hey," he said. "You're the lady who…who—" For lack of the right word, he gestured wildly over his head, forming a halo with his arms. *Yes, that's me, the angel,* I thought wryly, smiling at him, waiting for him to complete his thought before realizing he probably never would.

"A scarf?" I offered.

He snapped his fingers. "That's it, a scarf."

He looked at me curiously.

"Your hair?"

"Yes."

"It's very—" He was again at a loss for words and scratched his head, his baseball bat and cap tucked between his legs. "Shiny…and…and long!" This time his eyes brightened up as the words came through for him at the last minute.

"Thank you." I ruffled his hair just as I heard his mother call out to him from the second-floor window.

FIFTEEN

The ringing of the phone broke through the silence at the dinner table.

I had had enough of answering pestering reporters and funneling my way in and out of the building through them. They were all looking for one story because they had beaten the rest to a pulp. *Muslim harmed by Muslim, how do you react?*

How do you?

I hadn't even decided in my mind how to answer that. Our common-ness didn't make a good enough story. Like a sack of potatoes, we are all lumped together. Incessantly. Insistently. Now that makes a good story.

What was it the reporter from the *Observer* had said over the phone? He seemed nice at first, and I was amicable, offering all the answers he needed. About our lives, Faizan, his work at the restaurant, the enormity of my loss. And then the inevitable question came.

"Mrs. Illahi, being a Muslim, how does it feel to be attacked by your own people?"

If he were there in person, I probably would've clubbed him with the phone. Instead I inhaled deeply and formed a thought: *I don't know, Mr. Cloomin. Have you ever been in a similar situation?*

My voice had a sullen, monotone quality when I finally responded. "They are not my people."

"They have the same religion as you."

No, they don't. They don't have a religion.

"Did you lose anyone in the events of 9/11, Mr. Cloomin?" I finally asked. My voice was trembling but icy.

"No, ma'am," he answered. "I'm from New Jersey. Most of my family lives and works there. I was most fortunate."

"So in the aftermath, you have not been on all fours at Ground Zero, looking through debris for a sign of your loved one." I held on to my tears. I did not want to let on how fragile my world really was. "Examining fingers? Toes? Recalling from memory what your loved one's limbs looked like?"

Ma gasped across the room, and I looked at her sharply. *Don't cry now. Not now,* my stern eyes told her. I turned back to the phone. When I continued, my voice shook from rage.

"When you put all your potatoes in a sack, you should know they all have unique flavors. Some are rotten, some fresh. Just because they are clumped together doesn't make them all the same."

There was a shocked silence at the other end of the phone. The bitter pill of reality seemed hard for him to swallow.

"They are not my people, but I don't think you are smart enough to figure that out."

With that I slammed down the receiver.

So we let the phone ring.

And it stopped.

And then it started ringing again.

Ma started to get up, and I stood up as well.

"I'll get it. Why don't you finish eating?" I suggested.

I picked up the phone, armed with a furious retort if it was a reporter. When will peace return to my household?

"Hello, is this Arissa? Oh, um, I mean, Mrs. Illahi?"

The nervous voice at the other end was a woman's, the kind that you never can take seriously because it has such a chirpy birdlike quality to it.

"It is."

"May I call you Arissa?"

I was getting irritated. "What is this about?"

"Mrs. Illahi…Arissa…my name is Ann Marie Beaumont. I think I might have met your husband before…before, you know—"

My heart stopped.

"Are you there?" The woman was nervous.

"Yes, I am here. You were saying?"

"Faizan. Your husband served me on the morning of the 11th. I saw him right before—"

I didn't realize I was kneeling until I felt the harsh floor underneath. I cradled the phone with both hands as if dropping it would make me lose something precious.

"Are you sure?" My voice was scarcely above a whisper.

"Yes. I saw his name in the paper. It's an uncommon name and I remembered it from the name tag he wore. I can't say how sorry I am for your loss. I didn't want to be a bearer of bad news, but by now, I think you—"

Her voice trailed off meaningfully.

"I lost my husband in Vietnam," the woman continued. "I know how important it is for a spouse to know about the last moments of their companion's life. I never did."

There was a respectful silence as we both meditated over the memories of our fallen men.

"Your husband served me that morning. My daughter and I had a ritual of having breakfast there at least once a week. She used to work at Fiduciary Trust in the south tower."

"Oh!"

"She made it, Arissa. She's fine." The woman laughed, a little uncomfortably. "I couldn't believe we both cheated death in one single day."

"And there were those who didn't."

Not even when they were forewarned by their dreams. Not even when they reminded their spouse to move away and the surviving one refused.

"Yes. Quite right," the woman said quietly. There were a thousand questions I wanted to ask her but none that I had the brain function to evoke. I needed to meet this woman. See the face Faizan had seen in the final hours of his life.

"I need to ask you for a favor," I said after a pause. "Can you meet me tomorrow morning for coffee?"

"I'd be happy to."

"I'll always be indebted to you."

"It's my pleasure."

What a wonderful woman, I thought, and as an afterthought I asked hesitantly, "What was the last thing Faizan said to you?" My hands were shaking as I twisted the phone cord around my ring finger and waited for her to respond.

"More coffee?"

Of course.

And we both laughed.

Ann Marie was a woman well into her sixties, built like a farmwoman and sporting fleshy cheeks with numerous blackheads riddled on her nose, huddling together as if for comfort. Outside the coffee shop, she enveloped me in a giant hug, squishing my pregnant belly.

"You are so tiny," she commented, blinking away tears. "I couldn't even tell from behind that you are carrying a baby."

I smiled. "I am glad you came."

"Would not have missed it."

For once the sun was shining. We wandered outside aimlessly after buying coffee. The park across the street looked inviting, and we headed there. I was surprised by how youthful Ann Marie seemed despite having a daughter close to my age. She'd lost her husband when her daughter was just one. I glanced over at her as we sat down together on a bench.

"I remember his smile," Ann Marie said after awhile. "It was kind and sunny. Put you right at ease."

I tried to see Faizan through her eyes, the eyes of a stranger. I pictured him in his uniform, pouring coffee, making small talk, laughing his easy disarming smile. He did everything with a quiet elegance, an even grace. He hated imperfections in his appearance. A hair out of place, an unpressed shirt, a missing button, even a hint of a hole in a sock irritated him. The scar he didn't seem to mind. In death, too, he chose to simply disappear rather than let his loved ones see him in a less-than-perfect state.

"Presentation, my dear wife, is the key," he used to say. "How else can you leave a lasting impression?"

And he didn't miss making that final impact on a total stranger either. The memory of another day at the park a lifetime ago flooded in, carrying with it an insurmountable amount of sorrow that washed over me.

"When does it get easier?"

She looked straight ahead.

"That takes me back in years, that question."

Then she looked in my eyes. "It takes a very long time. The hole in your heart never goes away, but after a while you fill it with what you have left in your life. Your life's events, transitions, everyday distractions. They gradually cast a blanket over the pain, but underneath it all, the emptiness exists and continues to exist." She nodded toward my belly. "A child helps."

A jogger passed by in a red tracksuit, a chocolate Lab beside her panting to keep pace. The sound of "Last Night on Earth" filled the air despite the headset on the woman's ears. I vaguely remembered hearing it somewhere in my past.

> You know she's going to pay it back somehow
> The future is here at last
> The past is too uncomfortable

For once I let the tears flow, and so did Ann Marie. I did not want to tell her about the challenges of my unborn child. We were joined together by a chance meeting, unified in our sorrow, years apart in our losses.

Widowed.

Wronged.

Yet free from the pull of vengeance.

The guilt was there for me, though.

SIXTEEN

I walked in to a blinking answering machine and looked at the caller ID. The familiar number on the screen made me sigh. I started to hit the delete button and stopped. I had been deleting Ami's messages without playing for awhile. She called at least once every two weeks. I had a feeling she spoke to Ma and Baba too when I was not around. It bothered me but I didn't want to bring it up.

Out of curiosity more than anything else, I decided to hit play and sat down on the couch to listen.

"Hello bayta, "Ami's voice sounded tired and sad. "Wish I could talk to you and see you. I might be coming to New York in a few weeks, I would love to—"

I stood up and hurriedly pressed delete just as Ma came into the room, a towel over one shoulder.

"Was that your Ami?" she asked, tying her wet hair back.

I nodded.

"Why don't you talk to her sometime?" Ma suggested cautiously. "She clearly misses you."

"You know how complicated it is." I put a pillow on my lap with a sigh. "It's just not worth it."

"What's so complicated about a mother–daughter relationship?" Ma asked.

I glanced at her with a sad smile. "She's not you."

"True." Ma touched my cheek lightly. "But my dear, you have to remember that you are not her either. To a mother, the most precious gift in life is that of a child. I lost mine. Don't deny her the chance to be with you."

She placed the cordless phone in my hand. "Call her."

I looked at the phone and felt a rising tension. "I don't feel ready just yet."

Ma nodded. "Just don't let a lifetime go."

Her words took me back to the fateful night of the Khans' party.

The night seemed dabbed in sticky dew, the kind that clings to your pores and sits on you like a spider's web, tight and unrelenting. From deep within the recesses of our home, an angry and shaken voice rose until its unwavering pitch finally woke me up. I sat on my bed, eyes wide open, heart thundering. Will this night never end? It seemed that it was just hours ago that Abu and I had driven back from the Khans' party.

The voice wasn't unfamiliar, but the urgency, the anger, seemed compounded. Final, almost as if a record was being generated. The wings of history swooped down to take their notes in painful slowness.

"You think I am a *veshya*. A whore. That's what you think, Tehsin." Ami's voice was a mixture of hysteria and panic.

I stared at the pitch-black darkness around me, my heart thudding against my thin nightshirt. The night shadows crept nearer, frightening as quicksand, drawing me in. The wind from the open window worried the curtain that rose up in protest and twisted itself once over. It was an exchange between my parents, but as usual, I could only hear one side of the story. My soft-spoken Abu never yelled or spoke above a certain volume.

He wasn't built to break. Only to join.

"I hate being your wife, a mother. You stifle me, you and your kids. Especially them!"

The shadows danced closer, now reaching up to caress my hair, my knees, my eyes. They entered my spirit. I felt their cold hands on my heart and the chill of being unwanted. Unloved. *What am I lamenting?* I thought. *The loss of a love that I never had?* No one in the house had it either. Does everyone know how to fulfill the role of loving? It's surely not built in the mainframe of a body's design.

"I can't be a prisoner here, now or ever." The voice grew to a higher pitch. It was almost a scream.

I slapped a mosquito on my wrist and felt my skin swell. Removing the covers, I stood up to close the window. Azad Baba had forgotten to burn the coil that evening. I decided to tiptoe across to Zoha's room, a swarm of mosquitoes over my head. Her door was ajar, and her face was facing the wall. I knew she pretended to be asleep for my sake, and I stepped out respectfully and closed her door. Sometimes silence is the best potion for families. When things don't make much sense, we could all rely on our own interpretation to maintain our individual sanity. Not everything has to be talked about.

The voice was slowing down now, broken by hysterical sobs. My heart felt for the woman who didn't understand her life. Walls apart, I cried with her in solidarity of blood and affection. Unfortunate as she was, she probably didn't even feel the love around her. At some point, I felt sleep enter my body and halt my thoughts.

I decided to meet Ami before I left New York. "I'll feel sorry for you if you want me to, Arissa," she had said to me the day I fell in the verandah when I was barely ten. Ami had propped me on the kitchen counter to examine my wound amid her cooking utensils and at least one pot of a terribly frothy *urad dal*. She was never a great cook. It was Mai Jan's day off. She had gone to visit her ailing father in Faisalabad. I had fallen off my bike and skinned both knees. Since I had no audience to witness my sad descent to the hard concrete, I'd rushed inside seeking sympathy and feigned a limp upon entering. For emphasis, I let out a yell of pain, and Ami peeked from behind the kitchen door, not in any undue haste.

As a child, I often searched for the rise and fall of her voice in my dreams. When awake, I hungered for her appreciation, her glances—mad, irritated, and even hurtful at times, I did not mind as long as they were directed my way. Oh, the things you long for.

Ami had not changed much since the last time I had seen her. Her face had an enduring quality that nature didn't mess with, although her complexion had acquired an almost *genda* pallor. Age had attacked other areas of her, though. Her body sagged now with age and the love pouches on the sides of her belly were now more noticeable. Her eyes were the same, wild and inquisitive—like a child's. Her high cheekbones were firm and held the skin taut on her face. I had not seen her at all in the distance I had traveled from being a blissfully married woman to a widow. She had visited me once when I'd first moved to New York, bearing the gift of a gold necklace. She had missed my wedding, as she had missed Zoha's.

Ma and Baba had excused themselves from the meeting, explaining their need to visit a relative in Manhattan for a few hours. Ami avoided my eye when she came in, and after a brief hug, she busied herself with propping and readjusting the dupioni pillows on my couch. I couldn't bear to look at her. After awhile, she stood up and looked over at my wedding photo on the wall with a wistful expression on her face. Sympathy was the last thing I wanted from her.

"Ami?" I said after what seemed like a lifetime.

She turned around, and I was surprised to see tears in her eyes. She tried to speak, but her lips only trembled. Her emotional state left me feeling uneasy. I felt wrath uncoiling inside me. How could she pretend to show sorrow when clearly she felt none? She had not come to see me when my whole world had fallen apart and I needed someone to pick me up, hold me close. Instead, I was comforted by another mother who'd been a stranger to me until three years ago.

I turned away and marched to the kitchen to do the dishes that were piled high in the sink. I didn't have the energy to deal with theatrics. I had seen enough of that growing up. I knew this visit was going to be tough. I didn't know just how much.

Ami followed me to the kitchen and leaned against the door. She had regained her composure. "You have a beautiful apartment. It has traces of your talents. The subtle details that make something yours and unique."

I looked at her in silent defiance and continued to rub a tray with the scour pad.

"I know that you are trying to finish Faizan's manuscript." Ami took a step toward me. I looked at her in surprise. "Your in-laws return my calls, unlike you," she explained with a smile. "I think it's admirable what you are doing."

I turned around without a word and continued my assault on the dishes, my elbows in soapy suds.

"I know, Arissa Jaan, that you think I have failed you as a mother." She sighed. "I don't know why I can't do all that life requires me to do."

"Like love your children?" *How many times do you forgive a person?* Even words grow rusty from being spoken so many times.

Ami looked flustered. "Don't say that. I always loved you," she pleaded, voice breaking. "It's very easy for you to judge me. I never claimed to be perfect. You have no idea how hard it has been for me. I...I—" Her voice, weary with whispered excuses, trailed away.

"Cared too much about your own self?" I finished for her.

Arissa, I chided myself, *you are not helping*. I had vowed I'd make the visit as pleasant as possible, and I wasn't living up to that promise.

Ami's lips were so tightly pressed that her cheeks were gaunt from the effort. "I didn't know how to love in the conventional way." She exhaled and walked over to a jar of cookies, unscrewing the top. She peeked inside and picked out my favorite: butter pecan. "Arissa, can we not start over?

I have many regrets, and I live with those thoughts every day. They haunt me, taunt me—"

"You didn't come," I cut her short, my anger now boiling over, "I needed you, damn it, and you didn't come."

"I am sorry, I am…I wanted to. You know that."

"No, I don't!"

Ami staggered away and collapsed on the couch.

I flung the washcloth on the counter and stormed after her. "What do you want now?"

"I want us to be friends." Ami looked up, trembling arms outstretched.

Friends? The word hit me with the force of a wet towel on my face.

"Okay," I agreed, turning away from her embrace. "Like Juhi."

Ami looked at me blankly.

"A friend who is there but doesn't have to be and has the choice to leave whenever he or she wants, right?" My voice was dripping with sarcasm. "With no tangible ties like blood to be a barrier? That is smart. Very smart. A good escape route."

"That's not what I—"

I turned away and walked toward my room. I locked it from the inside and slumped against the door. The visit was over as far as I was concerned.

The break in the light underneath the door revealed that Ami was standing on the other side. She didn't knock, but I felt her there. Breathing. Silent. I put a shaky hand on the door to feel her presence. How I wanted her to love me. Love us. Oh, the many doors that would have opened for her had she knocked, even once. But as always, she lost the opportunity. The light corrected itself as she moved away. Why did I always expect her to do something that was just not in her nature?

I heard her let herself out after fifteen minutes. I wondered what she was doing in the apartment for that long. I found my answer in the lingering stench of smoke and the stubbed-out cigarette in the sink.

SEVENTEEN

Juhi carried a box of books to the end of the hall and collapsed on a nearby stool. She was two months pregnant, and in between helping me pack and move boxes despite my protests, she managed to puke in the bathroom every two hours. She looked pale in the cropped gray sweater she wore over a pastel shirt and cargo drawstring pants.

"Stop lifting boxes," I scolded. "You are not doing anybody any favors."

She made a face at me and hurled a pillowcase at my belly. "Look who's talking," she jeered. "Miss Fat Princess herself."

I ignored her and taped up the box labeled "miscellaneous." Packing boxes in the eighth month of my pregnancy had not been easy. I was a trifle nervous that all the boxes I had labeled since this morning—a grand total of 10—were all tagged the same. The ones that Ma had packed were more carefully named: "clothes/Baba," "kitchen utensils/top shelf," "painting supplies/Arissa." What had happened to the planner in me?

I missed Ma already. She had gone to Atlanta to assist in the postpartum care of her niece, who had delivered twins a weekend ago. Ma's sister lived in Pakistan and had been denied a visa to come help her daughter. Ma had assured me she would be back in time for the move. I couldn't be selfish, although I was already missing my own cherished *aloo* paratha squares in the morning; the tea slowly steeped to murky perfection;

samosas, the meat-filled deep-fried wraps; *bhajiyas,* the mouth-watering fritters; and the never-ending list of magical items that appeared on my table at each meal time.

Ma had left me in the able hands of Juhi. A few hours after she left, Juhi turned to me and said, "Guess what?"

Her eyes had the glimmer I had learned to dread. It usually meant some new dead-end boyfriend's emergence in her life.

"I'm pregnant."

I nearly dropped the vase I was wrapping in a white sheet. I wasn't expecting that.

"What?"

"Yes. I found out yesterday."

That probably explained the dark circles under her eyes, the fatigued look. I looked at her in shock.

"Who, I mean—?"

"Raj. Rajesh. But it doesn't matter who, really." Juhi waved her arms.

"What do you mean it doesn't matter?" I looked at her in confusion.

"I think it's really exciting," Juhi continued, ignoring my question, putting a small box full of crystals in a slightly bigger carton to prevent breakage.

I turned her around by her shoulders to face me.

"What do you mean it doesn't matter?" I asked again, a little more slowly this time.

Juhi sighed in mock sadness and touched my cheek. She had a red bandana on her head that made her look unusually young. "Poor Arissa, always the worrier. Perhaps your aura needs adjusting?"

I shrugged her patronizing hands away. "Juhi, do you even realize how big this news is?"

"Of course I do," Juhi said in exasperation, walking over to the stove to check the pot. She lifted the lid and peered in. She sniffed at it and then clutched her abdomen and raced to the bathroom. I stood outside listening to her retch.

"Are you okay?" I called out.

"Oh, just heavenly." She emerged from the bathroom with an annoyed look on her pink face. "In case you didn't know, the only time a person is throwing up over a toilet bowl is when he or she is not feeling well."

I handed her a wet washcloth and studied her while she wiped her face.

"Have you told Rakesh?"

"Rajesh. And no."

"He has a right to know."

"No, he doesn't. He made it perfectly clear at the beginning of our relationship that having a family was not in his plan. Besides, we aren't seeing each other anymore. It's just as well."

"So what are you going to do?"

She looked at me as if I had just grown a second head.

"I'll do what you did," she said. "I'll build my life around my child."

I felt very tired and sat down on the couch.

"It will be hard without someone to share the burden." I studied my ring finger that still had a ghost-like band encircling it. Juhi laid her hands on my shoulders and started massaging them.

"You don't think I know that?" Juhi asked softly. "I *want* a baby. I'm 41 years old. Even I know that a special someone is hard to find." She came around to face me. "And equally hard to lose."

I looked away. Juhi had no idea what she had just done to her life. It could be the most perfect thing for her or just the opposite.

"It would've been nice if you were here," Juhi said, sitting beside me. "Our children could become friends. We could move in together. Maybe even become lesbians."

We giggled. Somehow I could not picture our children playing together. Whenever I thought of my son, I always thought of a severely challenged child, barely able to walk. I had the image of the worst possible scenario stuck in my mind. I figured if I allowed myself that, having a marginally disabled child would be a tremendous blessing and a boost at the same time. No, it was easier to remove myself and my child from the present. Being near Uncle Rizvi in Houston would be better.

"Why do you do that?" Juhi's voice broke into my thoughts.

"Huh!"

She had moved on from the subject and was now holding a painting in her hand that I had not finished packing. The painting was an awful one with a beggar woman engaged in a bloody fight with a little boy, fire dancing in her eyes. I had tried to tell Juhi about the woman who'd brought us the prophecy of firedancer, but I could never bring myself to relate that story to anyone. It seemed that if it was untold, I would allow it lesser power to affect me, although lately the woman had started appearing in my dreams. I put the painting face down on the floor and walked away from it.

I sometimes forgot that Juhi was an art instructor. We never conversed about art much. To her it was a career; to me it was not. It just wasn't a factor in our relationship. I had been to the Metropolitan Museum of Art with her once, a year ago. We never could see it all. The Islamic art section had enamored us the most, especially the Turkish *Tughra*, a handsign of Sulaiman the Magnificent with its bold calligraphy. We had laughed about how we wanted to have such elaborate signatures on our immigration papers.

"It would drive the officers insane," Juhi had said, laughing. "We would insist on signing with gold ink."

We had made plans to come back and finish seeing the museum. We never did.

"Your themes were subtle before," Juhi was saying. "Like that sunflowers painting you have in the den, and the girl reading a book that you gave me for my birthday, and the abstract that reminded me of a peaceful ocean with seagulls flying above that your Abu took with him last spring."

I didn't know how to answer that. My subject matters were never hidden, but since Faizan's departure they had become more intense, almost fiery, invoking disturbing feelings in the onlooker—red magnolias oozing blood instead of nectar, a man in his last dying moments with his killer, a mother holding a dead infant.

As I was quick to point out to folks, painting was not a career—if it were, I would be out of a job. I painted to liberate the thoughts and images within me. I merely provided them release.

As a young child I'd entered many art contests and never won anything. Impressionism with a unique blend of postmodernism, that is how an art teacher had once described my work, his glasses balancing on his long nose that looked like a cliff with a steep fall. I had quickly realized it was his way of being nice and to get me off his hands quickly. I barely passed his art class.

My work had few admirers. In time I realized it would never become a career, not a successful one anyway. Abu enrolled me in a painting class one summer when I was in my teens. The instructor was a cheery guy in his early forties with a goatee and sideburns, and that summer of Ramadan, I was his only student. Most of his paintings, being of intimate and nude subjects, were draped over in respect for that month. The instructor had a strange habit of sidling up to his students and making them jump. By the next summer he was all over the news. Jilted by his lover, he had gone on a shooting spree in a co-ed college and killed several students. The thought that I had been in such close proximity to a madman sent shudders through my body.

I wondered if all gifted folks are slightly mad. Would my challenged child be gifted in some way? I believed that in life, we all make an impact somehow. Some with brush strokes, some with keystrokes. Still others with their genuine hearts.

"I'll miss you." Juhi came around and stood in front of me, her eyes brimming with tears. "Who will I do laundry with now?"

I was speechless. I had no words to describe what she had been to me and what I would miss the most.

When I put my arms around her and hugged her, she smelled of cinnamon and warm summer.

After Juhi left, I picked up a book that had fallen to the floor from an overfilled box I had marked "miscellaneous." For awhile, I couldn't move. The book, titled *Surviving Susan*, a shoddy Victorian romance novel, had seen happier days and was responsible for some of the lighter moments in my life. Half of its cover was torn off, and the bosomy lady in the arms of a dark man had lost a breast. It seemed that the man was about to drop the woman on her head. It was pretty comical, but my heart did a flip when I reminisced about the novel's presence in my brief married life.

Faizan and I had found the book by accident. When we moved into our apartment, abandoning Faizan's bachelor pad, we had discovered a box of books left behind by the previous owners. The box contained romance novels, a genre Faizan and I didn't care much for, but this particular book was different. Something about the art of the cover was so side-splitting that when we gave the box away to a library, we kept that book. It offered us many laughs for its author's ludicrous way of writing love scenes. The writing wasn't that great, and every chapter had at least one sex scene. It became a bedroom study for us, and we frequently acted out scenes from the book. Somehow, despite the bad writing, it almost always got us in the mood. One particular day when we had just finished cleaning house and were lounging in the den, I saw Faizan pick up a seemingly tedious report by Amnesty International on Pakistan. At once, I pulled out the novel and flipped it open.

"'She looked at him with her forest green eyes,'" I read aloud. "'There was passion in them.'"

I saw Faizan put the report face-down on the chaise. *Mission accomplished*. I smiled inside.

"Brown," he corrected.

He moved down on the floor beside me.

"'She looked at him with her russet brown eyes, large as potatoes,'" I began again, improvising this time. "'There was *passion* in them.'"

I batted my eyes at him. He laughed and snuggled in closer. "Much better."

"'Her breath on his face was sweet like honey, and he wanted to drink from the source.'" I sniffed his face and then sneezed all over him before I could stop. He ducked and then came near again. I laid the book on one side, carefully dog-earing the page where we left off. Our noses and knees were touching. I kissed him.

The empowered female character in the novel fascinated us. She was the one who usually initiated the foreplay but disappointed us when she came to a certain point and then automatically slipped into the gender-dictated role of waiting for the man to make the final move, kind of like how we were.

"'He circled his arms around her waist and pulled her on top of him in a primitive, almost animal-like force,'" Faizan recited from memory. He rolled over on the floor like a dog, panting, limbs in the air, and then grabbed me and brought me down on top of him. I giggled. Just then the phone rang. I started to get up and he groaned.

"Her rejection was like a germ that spread in his innards."

He came after me on all fours as I dashed toward the phone, now taking artistic liberty with the author's voice.

I picked up the phone breathlessly as Faizan wrapped his arms around me. "He yearned for her sweetness."

It was Abu. I tried to pry Faizan's hands away from my waist. He wouldn't give.

"Her full breasts tormented him day and night, giving him not a moment's peace," Faizan whispered, trying to unbutton my shirt as I struggled to button it back. I mouthed at him to stop and twisted my body to get out of his embrace. Even when out of Abu's sight, I couldn't picture talking to him without a shirt on.

"How are you, Arissa?" Abu was asking. "What were you doing?"

That's never an easy answer. The voice carried over into the room, and Faizan smiled at how flustered I was.

"Tell him we are making love," he whispered in my other ear. "Ask him to leave us alone."

I answered in monosyllables, letting Abu do the talking, very conscious of my shirt wide open as Faizan proceeded to lick his way from my bellybutton to my left breast.

"He drank from her nipples as if they contained nectar," he breathed against my skin. "He wanted to squeeze and pinch them, to punish her for how she tormented him—"

I struggled to regulate my breathing.

"Is Faizan around?" Abu asked.

I thrust the receiver gratefully in Faizan's surprised hands. I stepped back, buttoning my shirt, trying to keep from laughing.

He struggled to talk, mildly irritated by my trickery. I ran my fingers down his waist where he was the most ticklish. He swatted at my hand, brushing it away. Undeterred, I let my fingers trail to the other side of his waist and traced the contours of his side. For added impact, I nibbled on his left ear.

"Um....er...there's someone waiting for me. Can I call you back?" Faizan finally said. I fled to the bedroom.

"You'll pay heavily for this," I heard him say. Then he paused before adding. "At last she would pay for the torture she inflicted on him day and night."

I held the book up to my ear. I willed for it to bring back the laughter it had once given us. I shook it, tugged at it, as if worrying it could give me back some past moments. I rubbed the soft cover, now aged and wrinkled, against my cheek, urging the lifeless piece to talk to me. It was just like praying to God. It probably answered in some way, but certainly not in a way that was to my liking.

What had attracted me to Faizan? It wasn't only the way he knew all the right things to say to make me cheer up after a bad haircut ("Don't worry. Your pretty locks are banned from public, and I don't think your veil knows what is and is not fashionable") or the way he taught me how to hold the spatula just right to flip the omelets ("Why do I have to do all the things around the house? Didn't Mai Jan ever take a day off when you were back home?"). Perhaps it was how he always had plans for us for the weekend, most of them surprises, annoying me at first and then pleasing me by how perfect they were, or the many visits to the museums, retreats, and movies. Maybe it was how he never let me carry groceries myself, not even when I was not pregnant, always hauling the heavier loads himself. The things only he could say after lovemaking ("That's amazing—remember that next time"). I forgave him even when he made absurd, unpardonable conversation about art; at least he tried to take an interest in what was a big part of my life. Perhaps it was the way his hand moved over my body and triggered just the right spots to make our union fit for historical records. He taught me to cross the bridge of bashfulness to love in easy strides. I shed the cloak of shyness and reveled in the glorious dangers of lovemaking. He taught me to burn and heal again. And then he burned me one last time and abandoned me forever.

"You can't force a cow to smile."

Faizan had the strangest phrases to offer in any situation. It seemed like he had his own dictionary of idioms. That or he enjoyed annoying me by distorting them. This was in response to a gripe about an old friend that I was reporting to Faizan. I had recently met a former classmate who had changed considerably to the degree of being standoffish. After having a short one-sided conversation with her, I realized she didn't share my excitement at the meeting, and I was quite taken aback and offended by her formality and lack of enthusiasm.

"The correct version is you can't force a horse to drink—"

"Cows, horses, sheep, domesticated animals…it could be anyone."

"Not all animals *that* can be domesticated *are*."

"No, some have to be trained to accept domestic responsibility and still fail at it miserably." He took a jab at my lack of culinary talents.

"You're impossible."

"And irresistible," he reminded me.

And that was how he cheered me up. He simply made me forget.

His laughter was what I missed the most. There was only one way to describe it, imprisoned laughter, the kind that bubbled from somewhere inside him. He held it captive until he couldn't anymore and then it burst from him, echoing and bouncing all around. Just when it was about to die down, though, it managed to find its way to another's lips and the cycle began again.

I woke up with a start in the middle of the night, feeling strangely disassociated from my limbs. My body was warm, but my hands and feet were tingly and cold, shocked pores raised in protest. I looked at the contours of my slumbering spouse, his chest rising and falling in peace. I found a comfortable spot and turned over but my agitated movements woke Faizan up and he glanced at me groggily.

"You okay?"

I nodded. "I can't sleep."

He sighed and got up, making his way to the bathroom like a drunkard. I rolled over onto his side of the bed, enjoying the warmth he had left behind. I woke up the next morning to find him asleep on my side, leaving me undisturbed, his warm breath on my face. In and out. In and out. I didn't realize that in just a year's time, I would have the whole bed to myself but no warm spots to find comfort in.

I sat up with a jolt, a stark realization in my heart. *I am pregnant.*

And I remembered the night I had conceived.

I was sitting on the bed lost in thought when Faizan emerged from the shower, a towel low around his waist, beads of water glistening on his chest. I was startled when I felt the spray of water and looked up to see him grinning. He was towel-drying his hair with one hand, the skin around his eyes creased from smiling. Crow's feet, they called it. He had developed those early in life.

He hovered over me and planted a kiss on my head, parting my thighs suggestively with his leg, leaving my nightgown open.

"That, my dear, right there is a true work of art," he declared, settling down beside me as he flung the towel across the room.

"Huh?" He had caught me off-guard. It amazed me at how comfortable he was in his own skin. He sank down on the bed on his back and pulled me on top of him, running his fingers up my leg.

"The question of the hour is," he said, "do you feel inspired to create a masterpiece?"

I comprehended at last, although his words were fading fast as my body came alive. He smiled and cradled my head on his wet chest, keeping me imprisoned in his embrace for awhile. Passion made me impatient; he breathed noiselessly, normally, prolonging my agony.

"Yes, I think we are both inspired," he concluded, nibbling at my ear.

I silenced him with a kiss on his mouth, stroking the birthmark on his jaw, shaped like a half-smile, as if his own needed to be underlined or somehow emphasized. It fascinated me, that blemish on his face. I caressed it tenderly. The mark of beauty, they called it, an imperfection left by nature so he could not claim divinity. In a way he still achieved it in my eyes by his early demise. He could not be held at fault for that or in God's eyes declared a sinner. I wasn't with him long enough to love him less.

He flicked off the lamp, and we lay there among sheet and shadows; black, gray, giant, small and in between. The eager moon watched in anticipation, peeking in from the window, a cosmological coincidence. It moved in our midst, waiting, illuminating the stage for our act. Impatient pleasure was trapped within me as I laid a sweaty hand against his damp chest. The heat that radiated from his body inflamed my soul, shocking me with its absolute familiarity. He removed the gown from me gently as if separating obsession from fulfillment. My pulse quickened as I heard a seam rip, betraying that somewhere within him there was an urgency he masked. He moved his hands over the familiar contours of my body, making every pore come alive, starting at the collarbone, lingering at sweet spots, unleashing the woman within me. There was a storm in our midst as his fingers traveled down my body, followed by his mouth. There was no quick way to get where we wanted to go. He knew my body well and like a matured lover took time to grasp the subtleties and refine his movements. And then he moved inside me like the unforgettable lines from a familiar book, easily, precisely, and with surety. Home was here, in senseless, mindless moments of pleasure. What more was there?

It wasn't until he moved away from me that I allowed myself to breathe.

Our very first fight was a nightmare. We were newlyweds, uncertain of how to assert our own sense of individuality in the relationship and how much we wanted to submit, each one wanting a larger share of power. We had not perfected the art of stepping carefully through the minefield of theoreticals in a relationship. It started over the first cup of tea in the morning. I had arrived in the United States a few days earlier and was still getting used to the pace of the electric stove in the apartment that didn't heat anything quickly enough. New York was too cold. It was the kind of cold that chilled you to the bone. It made me nostalgic for warm things back home—potato and onion fritters and hot flour chappatis.

I eyed my husband of twenty days over the steady steam of hot tea that separated us. He was engrossed in reading the *New York Times,* his glasses halfway down his nose. He was nearsighted but he still used his glasses to read. The rest of the time he preferred to stay away from them. He was right to do so—glasses made him look ridiculous in a geeky sort of way.

"Now that you are done with your master's," I began, taking a long sip of the hot tea and enjoying the warmth of it on my tongue, "what are your plans?"

Faizan looked at me over his newspaper and removed his comical glasses.

"Do you really want to know my plans?" he asked suggestively, nudging my toe.

"I'm serious, Faizan," I said, picking up a piece of toast and slathering butter on it. "Are you going to look for a job? Should I look for one?"

He grinned back at me. He knew me already. My mind had shifted into planning mode. Things that were up in the air irritated me, as did limited knowledge. We had decided after our engagement that I would spend the first year getting used to the new environment. I wanted to explore some freelance opportunities and work from home. We planned to start trying for a child in two years, and we agreed that I would start working after the child turned two. I felt better knowing how it would all pan out. In my naiveté, though, I had not factored in many things; for instance, conception takes awhile in some cases, loved ones can disappear, and children can deviate from textbook norms.

"I already have a job lined up," Faizan stated simply and took a sip of his tea, shaking the newspaper to smooth out the creases. Some crumbs flew across the table and landed on my lap, and I swatted them away. He turned his attention back to the paper.

"You found a job? Already?" I put the buttered toast back on my plate and looked at him in amazement. "When did that happen?"

I really meant, *when the hell were you planning to tell me?* We were too newly married for me to say that, though.

"Just as soon as I was certain I'd be adequately rewarded." Faizan was still in a joking mood, and seeing my dark expression, he concluded, "But it seems like I will be out of special favors. At least for awhile."

I continued to stare at him, willing him to answer my question. And then it came.

"I'll be waiting tables at Windows on the World."

There was an ear-piercing silence that knifed through the air around us. I looked at him in disbelief. He seemed not to notice my shock; his face had disappeared inside a book review column.

"At the World Trade Center? Faizan, are you serious?" I was getting a little testy now, switching to English, not wanting to address him any-more with the most familiar *you* word in Urdu that was reserved for either close loved ones or God. "With your master's in lit, you are going to wait tables. You have got to be joking."

Faizan looked at me patronizingly. "Arissa!" He clicked his tongue in sympathy. "Waiting tables isn't so bad in America. You make more money than you would teaching. I am sure you didn't know that."

I didn't. So I said nothing.

"You need to broaden your mind," he continued. "It's actually quite fun to wait tables. You meet many interesting people and make great friends. I did that for a long time when I first moved here."

"But—" I hated that my comments were so transparent.

"Besides it'll free up my two days in the week to devote to some serious writing and finish my novel."

He laid the paper down on the table and put his right hand on mine. For once Faizan was serious, realizing my anxiety.

"We'll be well provided for. I'll teach two classes at the university some evenings. I really have to do this. I can't finish my book with a full-time regular job. It won't be an affluent lifestyle, I understand, but you won't have to work, at least not for awhile."

"I don't mind working, but this sounds so...so—" I wanted to say *foolish* but couldn't. I eased my hand out from underneath his. "Have you given this enough thought?"

"Arissa, do you really think I would bring a wife here and not provide for her? You think I am that irresponsible?" His impish look was gone, replaced by annoyance.

"No, I didn't mean—"

"Then trust me, I can make it work." Our eyes locked. He saw the fear and uncertainty in mine and looked away, hurt large in his eyes. "It's no use. You don't believe in me or my work."

He got up to leave the table, upsetting the teacup that held only a sip. The spill on the table was hardly more than a drop, and I did nothing to wipe it away, too consumed with the discussion at hand.

"Please don't say that," I pleaded. "Your work is wonderful. I think you are really on to something."

"So what is it then, sweetheart?" He turned around, and his tone was cutting as he stood in front of me. Then a realization seemed to flash across his face. "Is it that you would be ashamed to introduce me to your friends and reveal my profession? Are you going to love me less if I wait tables? Or is it that you are so high-maintenance that you fear that my meager salary won't be able to sustain you in all that you are used to? It has to be something from that list."

I had never seen him so rattled, and I gasped and stood up, fuming with rage. He had hit the jugular with at least one of those comments and caught me totally off-guard. I fled to my room, grabbed my purse, and started to storm out the door.

"Don't forget your hijab!" he called after me.

I ignored him and slammed the door. The sound echoed down the hall, and I saw an old woman three doors down open her door and look at me questioningly, a chocolate-spotted Ocicat in her arms. I gave her a weak apologetic smile and got on my knees, rummaging in my purse for a scarf. I emptied the contents of my purse onto the floor, and my wallet, lipstick, and blush fell in a fanfold around me. No veil. The light thud across the hall signaled to me that the woman had closed her door. Tired, I slumped against the door and watched the morning tick away into the afternoon. *He didn't even stop me,* I thought angrily. I would learn in the next few months that that was how Faizan resolved conflicts, a quality I grew to appreciate. He gave me room to think over fights and disagreements and then always made amends first.

I allowed myself to think over the events of the morning without bias and with some level of clarity. Would it shame me if my husband waited tables? Does it bother me that Juhi's boyfriend works as a defense contractor and Zoha's husband is a successful businessman? When did I become that shallow? At noon, I stood up, dusted off my skirt, and went back inside the apartment. Time to expiate.

In time I also learned that Faizan, cheerful and boisterous in his boyishly cute way, almost always got what he wanted or what he set his mind to—except one time when I left him no choice but to see things my way.

The water felt good as it cascaded down my body, slapping the red tiles below; I enjoyed its liquid embrace, its unquestioning, predictable steady stream, continuous through the times. I tried to wash my feet that were virtually hidden from view due to my large abdomen. I cleaned via sensing, feeling the water pass between my toes and seep down the drain.

Drying quickly as I got out of the shower, I reached for the bathrobe and hesitated for a minute, looking over at the full-length mirror a few yards away. In two easy strides I reached the fogged-up mirror, my bathrobe discarded on the floor.

At first glance I almost keeled over in disbelief. I had never seen myself nude in my full-blown pregnant state. The giant swell of the baby was like a globe under my breasts—an entire world within me, with faultless temperature control, unending food supply, and the necessary tools for survival. Stretch marks crisscrossed along the entire circumference of it as if exuding ownership. My nipples were primed for suckling, waiting for the sweet sensation of a baby's lips on it.

Right on cue, the baby started to hiccup, and my belly reverberated from the act. I watched in awe as he stretched. A little hand shot up from deep within me and pushed against the walls of my abdomen—a palm print on my belly. Then the baby withdrew his hand, leaving me breathless. The seconds ticked away as did the hiccups. He had gone to sleep. I pictured him inside me, a perfectly formed human being, very different from the stark black-and-white ghost-like images I had seen on the scans. I imagined him in his sleep, his head bobbing on his chest, immersed in the essence of survival, unaware of his future and lifelong struggles.

I dreaded the moment of birth a few weeks later when he would be on his own, fighting for a chance at life. No longer dependent on my body for anything but milk. The pulsating lifeline, which provided him sustenance now, withered and torn. How would he fare? Would he make it then or not?

I refused to think further and reached for the bathrobe on the floor before stopping suddenly, flooded with memories of the past. I looked again at the mirror and reminisced on the journey I had taken from a shy untouched girl naked in front of a man for the first time to a pregnant widow. The nights in the early days of marriage when I refused to let Faizan touch me until the lights were turned out. "But I want to see," he would beg, and I would shake my head. "Feel me with your touch," I implored. "Sense me with your heart." Days later he told me that darkness added a mysterious quality to my beauty—it kept our union strong.

I stood with my back against the mirror as I tied the belt of my bathrobe around my waist. Then I left the bathroom quickly.

EIGHTEEN

December 2001
Houston

My heart thudded against my chest as I turned the steering wheel to the left. The car grazed the curb and steadied. I felt my breath quicken. This driving business was tough. In Houston, I was forced to learn how to drive. The public transportation system didn't take you everywhere, and with my many prenatal appointments, it was easier to get around in my own car. Uncle Rizvi offered me a few lessons, and after some fits, starts, and emotional moments, I was finally able to get behind the wheel on my own. He also helped me find a used Toyota Camry and concluded with pride that I was well on my way. Except, I had this fear of oncoming traffic since my days of living in Karachi, where I'd witnessed many accidents and near-misses and could not quite get comfortable with the idea of driving on my own. In Houston, I drove only in the right lanes as if venturing left would mean certain death. Buses and trucks running parallel to me still distracted and frightened me. I wrote down directions and then memorized them. I was the product of a country where I always expected to be driven to places. My brain just didn't process and resolve geographical challenges effectively. To get around, I plotted my destinations carefully, always starting at a familiar point to avoid getting lost. "It's all in your mind, Arissa Apa," Ruhi, Uncle Rizvi's eighteen-year-old daughter, told me. "With practice, the fear will disappear."

I was grateful for the counsel of my relatives, the family of three who had made our transition to Houston fairly easy. We were renting an apartment a few minutes away from where they lived, and they routinely called or checked up on us during the day. Jamila Aunty, Uncle Rizvi's wife, stayed home and worked as a Mary Kay sales representative in her spare time. She was a sweet woman who talked incessantly; you could not get a word in edgewise.

The two-bedroom apartment that I rented was minimal but functional for the four of us, still larger than the one we rented in New York. Although rents were higher near the Children's Hospital area, Uncle Rizvi had secured it for me at a great price. Money that my widowed state had provided would pay for that, and I had planned to look for a job in Houston. *Blood money,* some folks in the media had jeered. Yes, but we didn't want our loved ones killed for that money. Nothing could compensate for their loss. I admired the steadfast commitment of my in-laws toward us. Upon our arrival in Houston, they gave me a copy of their will that stated that upon their departure from the world, my unborn son and I would be the sole heirs of all their assets, not that we lacked for anything.

While we were settling in, the world was changing at breakneck speed, rapidly deteriorating. I lamented the world that callously abducted and killed with no conscience or respect for human lives. Unreined, unchecked, the radicals struck the four corners of the globe and left masses of innocent Muslims easy targets for others' hatred and venom. We were regarded as a race gone bad, mad. The people of our adopted land had lost faith in us, and we couldn't trust our own. The line between allies and enemies was growing thinner by the day. Watching our backs had become a habit, a necessity of the strange times we lived in. We struggled to know ourselves only to lose ourselves in the interpretation of others, in the hyphenation of our worlds.

There were times when I wanted to take the drenched fabric of elucidation in the media and wring it dry of the false analysis presented daily on channels across the country. It irritated me, the world with its unjust notions, its constant stereotyping. *Why did they attack us?* The question popped up everywhere. I heard it again when I was flipping stations in the car. A talk-show listener had called in to offer his take. "Let's go to the fundamentals of why they did this to us," the caller suggested. "Why do they want to harm us? Is it because of the teachings of their religion?"

"Precisely," answered the host, suddenly a subject-matter expert. "Their faith teaches that if they harm nonbelievers, they will go to heaven."

I winced. Don't they know that terror has no religion? That religions don't preach terror?

I looked on as day after day the media tried, sentenced, and hung my faith. Day after day analysts applied new interpretations to the religion, broke the backs of bridges, and erected barriers too sturdy to take down or overcome. Gaps widened, our hearts divided, we struggled privately, each one of us, to make sense of our shrinking world. I witnessed the lynching of a religion and race again and again. Apart from the religion that we strived to preserve came another necessity of the times: salvaging our reputation. What proof did I have of the innocence of the rest of us? Couldn't I be considered a living attestation like many others? Couldn't Faizan, with his intention of leading a common life by earning an honest living? The trouble is people like us stay too low and off the radar to ever be of any real use or value to the media. Our anonymity and obscurity rendered us useless. We created nothing newsworthy and powered no conflicts. What is a story if there isn't a divergence? Our ordinary lives were a bit too normal to be sensational.

The drive downtown was made trickier by the never-ending rain. All night it had rained, giving the soaked city not a moment's peace, and at the break of dawn, it paused for a bit and started afresh. I worked the wheel nervously, prayers whooshing out of my half-open mouth. Interesting how you reach out to Him only in times of want. In tranquil times,

He rarely gets the time of day. The city was a splattered mass and still held on to a wraithlike darkness. The taillights of cars in front of me bled an electrifying red on the slick road when they stopped. My leg ached from all the stop-and-go action. I adjusted the collar of my east-west fusion tunic with some degree of anxiety and wondered if I had made a wrong choice in clothes for that day. Did I look too casual, non-serious, inexperienced? I picked up the job clipping that had been my companion for the past half hour. The ad was short and direct. "Need an associate editor for a South Asian publication," it said, along with a phone number below. It was my very first real job interview. Permanent employment, it promised. Should I have worn a suit? The clipping fell from my hand to the floor of the car. I started to reach for it and jerked back up when the driver in the Chevy behind me honked in impatience.

I parked a few blocks away from my actual destination to avoid having to parallel park, realizing with annoyance that I had forgotten to bring my umbrella along. By the time I reached the building, I was completely wet, my hair clinging to the sides of my face like I had just come out of a bath.

Stepping off the elevator onto the third floor, I first saw the sign on the reception desk that read *Chamak* and then noticed the short, middle-aged woman in a blue scoop-neck sweater. She seemed a little out of breath as she worked the floor briskly, passing out some papers. She had wide hips that made her gait just a little awkward as she walked.

"Look at this memo, everyone," she barked. "Naomi, make sure you call Rahman's son and schedule that interview."

A small woman at the reception desk nodded in response.

"And someone call that artist in Atlanta. We need his headshot for the Chitral piece."

"I'll do it," a male voice called out from a distant cubicle.

"Where is Maria? I need some caffeine. She went to Starbucks a year ago—"

The woman started to walk toward an office and then saw me, dripping all over her burgundy carpet. She stopped in mid-sentence and beamed.

"You must be Arissa. Hi, my name is Cyma," she said, extending her hand. Her gaze fell on my swollen abdomen briefly before she lifted it back up to meet my eyes. The warmth had not waned from the revelation, and I breathed a little easier. I stood there nauseous from nervous tension, hands clenched on both sides, and then sprang into motion and shook her hand a little too vigorously. As soon as I let go, I felt embarrassed at how icy cold my palms were. She had a strong hold, nice and firm, and waved her hands around as soon as I let go.

"Do you see this? Madhouse, I tell you." She widened her eyes dramatically for added effect. "And I love every crazy minute of it." Laughing, she led me inside her office. She had a flawless complexion and a face that sported a permanent grin. Her sparse hair was tied untidily at the back with a flat clip.

I nodded in appreciation. I believed her. The office was buzzing with the vigor of real working people, the dull hum of meetings, the whirring of the copy machine, and the ringing of phones. Even the air had an official scent to it, one of cardboard boxes, fresh ink, and stimulating fresheners. As soon as we entered her office, Cyma picked up a piece of candy out of the bowl on her desk and unwrapped it. She bit off a square, looking at me thoughtfully. I tried to settle down. I had trouble fitting into one of the smaller chairs and moved to another wider one. I wondered if Cyma could ever fit in any of those. I found my answer in the wide leather swivel chair across from me and the matching ottoman across the room.

The office was nice, full of sparse but trendy furniture, with stacks of paper everywhere. The papers were neat even in the disarray and frequency with which they were scattered all across the room: on the floor, the desk, even the couch. In one corner of the room, above the decorative pot with the *naqqashi* pattern, was a carved silver frame with a portrait of a woman in *chador* shielding her eyes from the sun. I recalled the work to be similar to a Pakistani artist's whom I was fond of back home. Eqbal Mehdi was his name, and he had the mystifying ability to capture the most intimate moments and moods through his figurative work almost as if he had somehow touched the soul of his subjects. Although I wasn't a big fan of realistic work, the details Mehdi captured in his work—the lights and shades, the folds of garments and drapes—were somehow absolutely mesmerizing to me.

"It is his work, in case you are wondering," Cyma said, nodding toward the art, neither of us needing any further reference to the originator. "He is still on hiatus last I heard."

"I admire his work," I commented, "although some argue he paints pensive women in regal attires far removed from common people."

"There's a trace of royalty in all of us," Cyma said with a chuckle. "We are a kingdom unto ourselves; the world is our subject."

"He does paint women in commonplace settings, though," I stated, laughing along with her. "At least we can allow him that."

"Yes, but really, are humans *that* perfect?" We both glanced at the painting again. The mole above the woman's lip in the art failed to mar the perfection of the rest of her face. Most of her body was shielded by her long chador. She had a melancholy expression.

"The famous Bernini once said that art is overcoming every obstacle, making something sublime out of what you've been dealt."

Truer words were never spoken. I wondered what hand providence had dealt to the woman Mehdi had painted. Perhaps a jilted lover or a lost child? Maybe a dead lover?

Cyma beamed at me and sat down. "So you are interested in working for the magazine?" she asked. "I have your resume here somewhere."

"Yes," I answered shortly, turning my attention back to her as she rummaged around her desk briefly before producing my e-mailed resume.

"Do you know what we do?"

I wracked my brain to think of an appropriate answer. I had read a bit too much on the magazine. In fact, I had memorized the contents of its entire Web site. Googled it a couple of times and found more information. Some nice, some not so nice. It got bad press when a piece about a Pakistani model ran with a photo of her in a bikini but received kudos for reuniting a family of five separated for ten years. Two family members had been in India, three in Pakistan. I had seen the photos of the tearful meeting and actually felt quite overcome myself.

"Let me assist," Cyma suggested after she had waited awhile for my response. "We are—"

I cut her off. "A nonprofit magazine that received funding recently from the Cultural Arts Council of Houston to produce a magazine that projected a better image of South Asia, specifically the South Asian community. The magazine itself has been in existence for four years."

I paused as I remembered reading that it isn't advisable to cut off the interviewer. Cyma seemed impressed so I dared to continue. "You interview and highlight the accomplishments of that community in arts, science, literature, and drama and seek to highlight the culture of that race."

"Quite right," Cyma responded. "The grant will help us through another four years, and then we will have to look for additional funding."

Cyma handed me two issues of the magazine. A beaming Nepalese pilot was on the cover of one, a Pakistani fashion designer on the other. I flipped one open to check the layout and was quite impressed. They probably had a good designer on board.

"I like the samples you sent of your writing," Cyma said after I had leafed through a few pages. "If we hire you, you should know that I cannot guarantee you continued employment after the four years are up."

That's a long period, I thought to myself. I no longer planned for that long. Short, easy, accessible goals. One at a time.

"I can work with that understanding."

"Good," Cyma said. "I can only offer a small salary for now since you have no experience working full-time, but we can review it again in three months. Sound good?"

"I have a few thoughts to share."

"Yes."

I looked at my hands folded in my lap. "I am appreciative that you don't look at my advanced stage of pregnancy and discount me for that reason. I have to let you know that I will be the sole caretaker of my child when he is born. I have been made aware that it…he has some disabilities, the extent of which is rather gray at the moment. It's just to say that my work will have to revolve around such challenges. I don't want you to be in the dark."

Cyma seemed to chew on that for a minute.

"Nice of you to be upfront about that," she said, and then grinned broadly. "I like you already. Of course we will work around your schedule. After your child's birth, you can work with us as a contractor if you like. You set your own hours and work whenever, wherever. As long as the work gets done, we are all happy."

I smiled gratefully at her.

"Then we will see you on Monday for your first day of work." Cyma shook my hand, faintly dismissive.

"Of course." I suppressed the urge to hug her.

I got out and almost danced on the damp sidewalk. I had my first regular job ever. Things were moving along as I expected. The move had been great on so many levels.

Juhi had her very first ultrasound!

She wrote fast and furiously. Even in e-mail, her personality came through as she wrote in breathless sentences broken by ellipses, not three, not four, but six or eight. She never capitalized her "I"s either, and the editor in me cringed every time I came across one.

She wanted a boy, she admitted. All I could pray for was that the child was normal. The baby was due next August. "What have you been up to?" She asked. "Found a balding Pakistani guy yet?"

"No," I wrote back. "They seem to all have headed east or to the East coast."

"In that case, I'll go hunt for one," she wrote with a smiley face at the end of the sentence.

Getting used to the noisy pace of *Chamak* was easy. The crew was supportive, team-spirited, and made me feel right at home. Sidra, a content editor at *Chamak*, reminded me of Juhi with her quick wit and vibrant personality. We went out to lunch a few times and decided we meshed well together. The work helped alleviate some of my anxiety over the future. Ma and Baba were delighted to see a bit of spark back in my eyes. I actually had a focus when I got up in the morning. In just a week's time, I interviewed an Indian astronaut, a Pakistani chef who ran a successful restaurant on Hillcroft, and a five-year-old brainy daughter of Indian parents who solved math problems in her head. The most moving interview I did for the magazine and also the most difficult one was of a woman who had lost a son at the Pentagon on September 11. I found it a little hard to be objective in that piece. Human tragedies are such popular reads, Cyma reminded me. It seemed like we lived in such a sadistic society, constantly seeking out the unfortunates among us.

Not much travel was required. Most of the work could be done over the phone or by e-mail. The farthest I went to cover a feature was Dallas. Some interviewees even liked questions to be e-mailed to them and responded in the same manner, although that stripped out some of the human aspect. Emotions don't translate well in e-mails, and I found that sensory cues we receive from face-to-face encounters are lost in such exchanges.

I spent hours searching online for interesting people from the subcontinent. The immigrant stories inspired me the most with their level of sacrifice; so much had to be let go to get something in return. It made me even more nostalgic for the pieces in our lives that are lost once we move from one continent to another: the moghra and the mangoes that no longer give off their exhilarating aromas, the henna that loses its hue and scent, the relationships that suffer due to the dynamics of the new society, and the language we lose. It makes you miss loved ones more, the ones who are always present to solve any issue—personal or impersonal—with a joint resolution; and the neighbors who are always eager to bring over hot dishes for no other reason than to share and exchange gossip. What do we gain by moving to a new country, alienated at once from our own type and land? More freedom? Less anonymity? Distinction that we want to lose? And when we are finally ready to call the new society our homeland, does it accept us willingly?

Ma's glance lately held a silent question reminding me of our pact—completion of a son's dream. *I have not forgotten,* I tried to relay to her with my thoughts. I'd merely set it aside to give it the attention it deserved when I had the time. I saw it in the looks Ma directed toward the bureau in my room where she knew I had stashed Faizan's unfinished manuscript after the move, right underneath the painting of the roses. I had created that piece the year I got married: white roses against a fuchsia backdrop, the bashful curling petals encircling the virgin center. Faizan had been thrilled with that composition. He said it reminded him of me as a shy young bride.

With gentle fingers Ma traced the edges of the bureau when she talk-ed to me about life in general: my work, her day, the unborn child. I could see the reverence with which she cleaned that piece of furniture every week, always using a fresh unused cloth. She approached it almost as if she was tending to a grave or hailing a grave to the status of a shrine. Instead of flowers, she planted kisses. I had seen her once, head bent low on the bureau when I walked in, lips tenderly touching the surface, a tribute to her dead son. I retreated among the shadows, afraid to disturb the sanctity of the exchange—the silent conversation between a mother and the spirit of her son.

"You have to piece it all together." I recalled her words from the dis-tant past. "You have to give his novel life so Faizan can live forever in those pages."

I remembered my own uncertainty, my hesitation at the enormity of the task. I had caved in at Ma's persistence. It was all such a long time ago: the discovery of the manuscript and our struggles to decide its fate.

I had survived, I realized with a degree of pride. I had not succumbed to the pain of my loss.

NINETEEN

We were headed to the hospital. No waiting-for-the-labor-to-begin fun for me, the doctors had decided. The baby had to be delivered immediately. It was measuring three weeks behind at thirty-six weeks. My doctor could not wait anymore and did not want to take her chances if the birth happened during the holiday time when the hospital operated on a skeleton crew. In a way, I was thankful that closure was near.

Inside the cab, Ma arranged and rearranged the bags on the floor. An arc of gold dust shimmered in through the car window, tracking her every move. Every few minutes, she opened a bag in a panic, certain that she had forgotten something. Baba, who was seated next to the cabdriver, turned around after many such searches and gently commanded Ma with his eyes to calm down. She nodded and sat back, offering me a weak smile. I noted that in her hurry to get dressed that morning, she had only applied lipstick to her upper lip. I opened the large purse next to her and pulled her lipstick out from the zipper section. I quickly painted her bottom lip and slipped the lipstick back in. Baba looked back at us and smiled. So much of how we operated was based on predictability nowadays; I knew Ma's organizing skills, she knew by now how forgetful I was, and Baba, always a pillar of strength, could calm us down without uttering a single word.

I stretched my neck and looked outside. Above me, the clouds were rolls of cotton that had gathered around the sun, wanting to drown its glory or at least diminish it. Instead the rays bled onto the clouds, rendering them a shocking crimson, bloodlike in their intensity.

In the vastness of the world around me, I felt miniscule, like a bubble, a guest of the moment. Now here, then popped. Upsetting neither the world nor the composition of air. Even God must find it hard to keep track of us all, the way we scurry in and out of bodies. Prayers getting lost in the traffic. Children coming to homes already with many, while childless couples were overlooked. The wish to bring back a cheating husband granted to his mistress instead. Being an omniscient God could become challenging after a while. If only He ran it like a business and outsourced some activities: a contractor for prayers about careers; another for prioritizing requests to spare lives. Life could be simpler, for Him and possibly for us.

Perhaps?

The rays of the sun seemed softer now, the fight taken out of them. A yawn escaped from me, and I hurriedly clapped a hand to my mouth. How could I be sleepy at such a time? I fingered the little wooden sculpture in my pocket that Juhi had given me. *Zarek, give me strength,* I prayed. *God, divine powers, anyone who is listening, save the little king.*

Juhi had created the sculpture for me as a parting gift. It was of a tiny sleeping baby curled up in fetal position, an expression of immense peace on its face, fingers curled up on its sides.

"Call it Zarek," Juhi had said to me. "In Greek, it means, 'May God protect the king.' Keep it near when the time comes. I created it out of gentle and healing thoughts."

You have no choice but to take a yoga instructor very seriously when she says something like that, especially one who talks about balance in the body, quieting of the mind, and cleansing of the aura in the same breath that she talks about her failed relationships and her unplanned pregnancy.

Raian came into the world silently under the watchful gaze of many—Uncle Rizvi, the obstetrician, the pediatric surgeon, the geneticist, the anesthesiologist, and an army of nurses. I felt the pull and tug in my abdomen as Raian was brought out via c-section. He and I were separated by a thin curtain that was placed on my abdomen between us so women like me don't lose it from watching themselves bleed. When I didn't hear him cry, I thought the inevitable. Then I caught a glimpse of his raised blue hand in the air as he was whisked away and knew that he was going to make it. My heart overflowed with a disconnected and untitled love. Uncle Rizvi rushed out behind the entourage of the two specialists and nurses that accompanied the baby. Hormonally imbalanced, I immediately felt sorry for myself—upset at not being able to see my baby's face, tearful at doing the whole thing alone.

Raian. He's here. My little king, the voice inside consoled me.

"Possible bilateral choanal atresia," announced a nurse who came back while they were cleaning me up. They were all silent as they worked intently and briefly acknowledged what the nurse said with nods or raised eyebrows.

Sensing my concern, one of the nurses leaned in. "Blockage of nasal passage," she explained. It was Meredith, whom I had befriended earlier. "They will likely insert an oral airway to help him breathe."

I looked at her blankly.

"Maybe surgery," she continued and then nodded at me. "I'll get more information for you."

She assigned her task to another nurse and escaped from the operating room. I was again among strangers, tugging and pulling at my stomach, making me whole again until the next time my life took me apart.

"They need to get him to the Children's Hospital nearby," Meredith informed me when she came back, trying to sound optimistic but failing. "They might have to run some tests."

Pain washed over me, making me nauseated.

"I have to get to him," I pleaded, my throat dry. "Can I see him?"

Meredith laid a hand on my forehead, promising nothing.

"Soon," she said. "Very soon."

Raian, be strong.

"I think I have found the perfect name for our son," Faizan declared one day when he returned from work. "We should name him Raian."

"You're sure we are having a boy?" I asked, folding a tiny sweater that Azra Apa had sent from Canada. It was a gender-neutral yellow with ducks on one side and strings that tied in front. I was four months pregnant then.

"Of course," Faizan said, kissing my cheek and hanging his steward jacket on a hanger. His face was lit up with a serene smile. "Do you have doubts?"

"You definitely don't want a daughter?" I asked, trying to keep the anxiety out of my voice.

"That's not it." He shook his head, sitting down beside me. "I love little girls. A mini-version of you! Life couldn't get any be better." He rolled his eyes, and I swatted him with the sweater. "But we are *not* having a girl."

"You're certain of that."

"Positive."

"The ultrasound's in a few weeks," I challenged.

"I know, and we are prepared." He glanced over at the blank videotape on the mantel, still in its packing.

We settled down for dinner. I was famished. The chicken curry that I had attempted to make that day looked quite enticing.

"Faizan?"

"What?"

"What does Raian mean?" I liked the name; it had grown on me. Ra-ian. I liked the way my tongue rolled up and touched the roof of my mouth when I said it.

"'Little king.'"

It was perfect.

"If it's a daughter we will call her Reesa," I suggested.

"It doesn't matter," Faizan waved his hand, dipping a piece of bread in the curry.

"No, it doesn't because we are not having a girl," I offered helpfully. God, the curry tasted horrid. What had I put in it? I tried to take a mental stock.

Faizan nodded. "That's correct. We are having a boy."

And that was that.

Even then, I could not picture him with a child in his arms. Fate had already decided that he was a father who would never hold his own child.

Abu had flown in for the birth, and he and Baba stayed with Raian his first night at the Children's Hospital. Throughout the night, we kept getting calls from the specialist detailing the happenings and what their next steps would be. My stomach dipped each time a call came. I kept listening even as the list surpassed the one I'd heard when I first found out about Raian's health problems—heart defect, breathing abnormalities, some vision impairment. Was there anything normal with my child? Half of the issues made no sense to me even when the doctors tried their best to strip out the technical lingo from their explanation. My sense of comprehension was slipping from lack of sleep and exhaustion.

At some point in the middle of the night, the calls stopped coming. The pain from the sutures made me nauseous, but I refused to take any medication, not wanting to end my suffering or cloud my thinking capacity any more than it already was. Finally a night nurse cajoled me into taking some pills, and Ma slipped them down my throat, warding off my protesting hand as only a loving mother could do. I noisily gulped down the glass of water she handed me afterward and turned around, totally drained. I woke up the next morning to Ma's hushed conversation on the phone. She turned and looked at me and then moved a few feet away. It was Ami on the other end of the line, I was sure of it. I was torn by conflicting emotions; I needed her but I did not want to see her right then.

The next day I was wheeled in to see Raian. At first I couldn't see him. He was neatly hidden behind all the paraphernalia attached to the various parts of his body. And then I saw him—a tiny shriveled-up bundle with an umbilical catheter and a feeding tube down his nose. He had billy lights on for jaundice. I touched him lightly on the cheek and withdrew my hand instantly as I realized how translucent his skin looked. It seemed that you could see right through him without needing an X-ray. His tiny body shuddered in response, perhaps recognizing a mother's touch. I floated between joy and insanity from seeing my child for the first time and realizing how much he faced.

For an agonizing moment, I watched helplessly as he stopped breathing. An oxygen hood went over his head next. "He has floppy airways," the nurse told us. Abu stood by, his face guilt-ridden as if all this were somehow his fault. His jowl had sagged over the years, a little weightier than I remembered it to be. "I would've done anything to spare you this pain," he said to me later when we got back to my room.

How much can you save me from, Abu? After all, my life, my trials are my own. Loved ones soften the blows life deals you, but ultimately it's not their reality.

I was finally able to bring Raian home a month after his birth. He was released on a ventilator and a trach and I was instructed to feed him round-the-clock from a pump. A nurse was assigned to us for two weeks to help us learn the process of taking care of him. Inside the house, I gave Raian a grand tour of the apartment but he fell asleep in the middle of it.

"Not much of a tour guide, am I?" I laughed, stroking the area around his cleft lip and he turned his head toward the touched side, wanting to suck. I picked up a picture of Faizan from my nightstand and brought it close to Raian.

"Meet your father, Raian. He was the one who named you. He is very far away."

I felt overcome, stopped, and then laughed. "He doesn't even call."

Raian looked at the photo briefly and then turned his curious but imperfect eyes towards me—unfocused, yet attentive.

I sat down in the rocking chair, not being able to take my eyes off him. He still felt light in my arms at five pounds. *There it is, my reason for existing,* I thought. The minutes ticked away as we bonded in spirit.

A movement near my feet startled me. Did the shadows just tremble and dance? *Who else is in the room?* I wondered and excitement crept at the base of my neck, leaving me tingling all over. *Faizan,* I whispered. The shadows stopped moving. The light from the lamp and the shadows it created were playing tricks on my mind.

It is just us, I finally admitted to myself, but my hopeful heart expected to see more.

A week later we were back at the hospital for Raian's feeding intolerance. And so our journey continued in this vein—two weeks in the hospital, two weeks out, with periodic heart-stopping moments when he fought for his very survival.

At home, Ma tended to me like she did to Raian; we were injured and wounded birds under her care. Lately her bones sagged with the brittleness of age, of unrealized dreams; her eyes spoke of dreadful losses. The eyes are where the process of aging starts in the women of our world. I had seen it many times, and I started seeing it in Ma as well. The eyes go through so much—seen and unseen—that finally cataracts threaten their vision, clouding the lens of life for them. Then age attacks their hearts. Although women's hearts are sturdier than men's, they get weak from carrying unfulfilled or shattered dreams for too long and from nurturing lives that break them into pieces every few steps. Finally age catches up with their knees when they refuse to carry the burden of life anymore for their owners. Who said being God's helper was an easy task?

Ma rushed around, getting things done for us, often forgetting to eat her own meals, panicking at every call we received from the doctor, dreading every appointment we went to, fearing the worst. I had never seen her so apprehensive and confused. Even then, like a battery-operated toy, she ran around fixing all the postpartum essential food for me that helped in speedy recovery and lactation: the *gur* treats, the *ghee*-laden parathas, dried fish, all varieties of dal, liver *saag*, and *katla* that helps in lactating—a round flat whole-wheat bread cooked in butter with almonds, pistachios, and a powder made from different herbs, as well as easily digestible vegetables.

"Do not refuse," Baba cautioned. "Mothers know best, and I am a better man today because I listen to her."

Milk flowed from me in a steady stream, predictable and bountiful. I filled bottle after bottle of nature's gift and froze most of it. Raian continued to feed from the gastrostomy button and occasionally from the bottle.

A few weeks later, the verdict was in, and we finally had a name for all of Raian's trouble: CHARGE. Not as in "charge ahead and get through it" but a syndrome that was attached to him and would continue to pose challenges for my child at every stage of his life. CHARGE was an acronym for multiple birth defects. There was no single treatment for all that he faced. The conditions were still dealt with separately. The calendar on the fridge now had little room to pen in anything other than Raian's schedule. Our lives were dictated by specialist appointments, checkups, surgical consults, tests, early intervention sessions, punctuated by frequent feeding therapies as nearly every part of Raian was explored, probed, refined, fixed, and adjusted. I had to take a six-month break from *Chamak*. I wasn't certain I would ever go back.

The move from New York was the best decision I'd ever made. Under Uncle Rizvi's care and Ma and Baba's loving presence, Raian and I started putting the puzzle of his life together. I tried to see life through a one-inch square as Anne Lamott suggested in *Bird by Bird*. All I had to remember was to fill that space with new ventures. Seeing life in that manner made it less overwhelming.

On the six-month anniversary of the attack on the World Trade Center, I saw on TV the monumental lights that shone heavenward where the Twin Towers once stood, reaching out to those who were lost. I looked down at the slumbering child on my chest, his tiny fist clutching the front of my shirt. Why do we appreciate the full glory of light only in darkness? I wondered if we touched Faizan somehow. Did he feel us? Did he see the new person that we had created from our union?

Not even curtains rustled in response.

"There are many of you who ask, 'Why me?' And the answer is, 'Because you were chosen.'"

I was attending a Children's Hospital workshop for parents of children with special needs. The instructor looked around the class and fixed her gaze on me. She was a tall woman with a shock of red hair and a large Celtic cross pendant on a chain around her neck. "You were selected for your compassion, kindness, and above all patience."

She paused for impact.

"Have you ever met someone who was hurtful and had a disabled child?" She looked at the class. "I haven't."

I pondered her words after the class was over. I'd never thought of myself as special in any way. Raian and I were the most common-looking folks, but our skin and his disabilities set us apart from the rest. I didn't even think compassion was a virtue I possessed. I definitely lacked patience. I think we all have a tendency toward some form of meanness. I don't think we are born with malice. I think it is an acquired trait, and I do believe God grinds it in batches and deposits some in all of us, whether we like it or not. We grow up to resist it, our conscience our rescuer, and when we snap, it all comes spewing out. Unchecked, uninhibited, we are all sadists by default. Just notice how many cars stop to gawk at an accident and what percent of drivers actually get out of their vehicles to do something about it. I don't claim to be pure and divine. I am the first one to stop, steal a look, and move on. My world waits for no one, and I don't wait for anyone either.

Some hide their sadistic nature better than others, and God gifts them in unique ways. I really think he has a sense of humor; it probably comes from all the dust he ingests from the grinding.

I also learned the lesson of life from a little voice in my ear when I finally allowed it to speak: there's no real sense in stepping out of the cave of your past if you get trapped in yet again by your existing baggage.

Outside the hospital, I shook the umbrella in my hand and an unwilling wasp slid off it into the grim brown puddle. It landed without a splash and writhed awhile before it swallowed enough water to end its life. I bent down to witness its final seconds with fascination. For a minute there, I thought I saw a spark of courage in its eyes, the will to survive but just like that, it was gone. Dead to the world. Consumed by murkiness and senselessness. In the grand scheme of things, how important was this life if it was compared to some others?

I sighed and stood up. Yes, there really was no sense in getting out of the cave if you were unwilling to dust off the reminders of your past.

Soul Searcher stayed in my bureau following Raian's birth.

Month after month, year after year, as a struggling student of motherhood, I learned its nuances, its joys and sorrows. I suffered more than my fair share of heartbreaks. Month after month, babies around us celebrated milestones with textbook precision. The entire span of time from helplessness to crawling to walking is typically covered in a year and a half, separated by the mini-milestones of finding sound, voice, and vocabulary. Month after month, my son stayed on his back on the mat, his intelligent eyes looking around, his frail, underdeveloped body failing to comply with the commands of his brain. I listened for the voice he never found, syllables I never heard him utter. He said it with his eyes; the love was there. I saw it in his smile and the way his face lit up when I entered the room. The joy of hearing your child say your name for the first time was not to be mine. Together we struggled to master sign language. I made more headway; he was the one who needed it more.

And then came the defining point. The day when some of it finally clicked for him while he was propped up with a pillow in a sitting position in the middle of the living room. Baba was sailing a toy plane off Raian's head, making swooshing sounds for his enjoyment. Raian joined his fists and signed his first sign when Baba stopped.

"More," he commanded.

Time froze for all of us. Not wanting to startle him, Ma and I exchanged glances and inched in closer. Baba did not look away from Raian although he must have felt our presence. My son did. He turned around and gave me his brightest, most beautiful smile.

"Mama," he signed, resting his thumb on one side of his chin. I fell to my knees and through tears, hugged him close to my heart. He was two and a half.

The next year, he crawled toward the TV a week before his third birthday, and on his birthday, he surprised us all by taking his first steps. We were late, but we were there.

Hope sprang in our hearts. All was not lost. He still had a lot to contend with even as I finally went back to work part-time.

There was once a hero who wasn't your typical knight-type. Nor was he perfect.

He had many challenges. His vision was as if someone had pulled a baseball cap all the way over his eyes so that his only vision was peripheral. He heard the world at the level of a whisper and had to strain to hear voices and sounds around him. In his household, every morsel he ingested was celebrated because it required the concentration of his every brain cell.

So what made Raian a hero?

Plowing ahead and smiling through it all! Just like his father.

There is so much of Faizan I see in Raian, and I am grateful for that:

the eyebrows that run in a single line without a gap above his eyes, the curled lashes, the smile that never vanishes and puts strangers at once at ease. He senses my presence in a room just like his father did without even looking up. How will I explain to Raian the absence of a father when he finally asks me? How will I explain the viciousness of the world and define hatred to a person struggling with so many physical challenges? How do you convey horror, contradiction, and terror? Perhaps I will instead steer him toward tales of the land we left behind, the country that shaped us and made his father the great man that he was. I might also tell him that when you leave a land behind, you don't shift loyalties—you just expand your heart and fit two lands in. You love them equally.

Before I had Raian, I measured my life in two major chunks: before and after Faizan. All other in-between events were minor and inconsequential. Raian's birth changed that and brought me closer to letting go. It provided me a level of distraction from my grief that a normal child might not have been able to give me. My life fell into a single-minded routine, milestones measured by Raian's accomplishments. I created a chart of my own and put green dots on days he did something new, like walk, eat, or laugh—all the events delayed but occurring at their own pace if I just held on one more day.

Raian had nine surgeries in a span of five years, including an open heart surgery to repair a large ventricular defect when he was three weeks old, a gastrostomy to assist with feeding at one month, and removal of adenoids due to recurrent obstructive sleep apnea at age two. He emerged from each one better, healthier, and stronger. By then Ma, Baba, and I had perfected the medical jargon—the names of the surgeries, the prognosis, the diagnosis, and the remedies rolled off our tongues as if we had always been caregivers to a disabled child.

When he was a baby I rocked him for endless hours, perched on a rocking chair, bonded in love. It calmed him immensely. When he learned to sit up, he bounced on my lap for long stretches of time, especially when he was agitated or confused. When he started walking at age three, late by all standards, he bounced on my feet. He could do that all day long. It regulated the rhythm of his body.

For Raian, because of poor coordination, even the simple act of walking posed its own set of challenges. Watching him play with other children or acquire a new skill made my chest swell with pride. He was a trooper and a hard worker. If at first he failed, he kept on trying—through frustration, anger, struggle, and in the end, victory. He walked with a side-to-side gait and had acute vision sensitivity to the sun. He typically had to tilt his head back in order to see better, and I had to sign at eye level. I also couldn't sign to him from across the room. He needed to be fairly close. At age five, he was still tube-fed as a supplement, and that summer we went to the Children's Hospital once a week for swallowing therapy. He hated textured foods to be mixed, so yogurt could not have chunks in it. He would swallow all of it and spit out the bits of fruit.

It was interesting to watch him as he converted his limitations into milestones. Living with Raian had its moments of mirth and meltdowns. When I talk about his challenges, I refer to them as ours. Our task was to overcome them together. He, of course, had to work harder. He displayed extreme enthusiasm for the work he did and all that passion was actually quite daunting for me at times.

I often wondered if Raian's challenges were nature's way of filling my days so that I would not have time to grieve. In my mind, it makes it all worthwhile when he holds up his thumb, index, and pinky fingers and signs "I love you" to me from across the room.

TWENTY

June 2006

Summer in Houston tastes like dirt, thick bellowing mounds of dust piling on and on until you can't breathe anymore. Sometimes a squalling wind arrives, pressing its puckered lips to the window panes. *Whooooo,* it shrieks, *whooooosh,* and then it cavorts over the pile of dust, depositing it evenly in our miracle-less world. The rain that follows washes it all away, leaving behind an acerbic mustiness that lingers until September brings in the moldiness that I associate with loss, the dull snicker of an autumn past.

At 6:59 a.m. my alarm went off and I turned over to hide my face in the pillow. I had a curious habit of setting my alarm a minute before my actual waking time. It gave me a moment to enjoy the comfort of my bed before the day's activities consumed me.

I had stopped dreaming about Faizan at some point, I realized. Perhaps it was because he was still so much a part of me. I remembered little things, the not-so-important parts of our lives—the way Faizan stretched in the morning and tiptoed around me so that I could sleep in. I led him to believe I did, although the truth was that with the first rustle of life next to me, sleep left my side. I kept my eyes shut, though, and pretended I was asleep. I studied him with half-open eyes as he stripped in the middle of the room and folded his pajamas neatly before placing them on the bench at the foot of the bed. I liked watching his naked back disappear inside the bathroom. He didn't turn the light on until he closed the door lest the light fall on my face and stir me awake. I'd still be awake when he'd come out. He had the unusual habit of always wearing his socks before he wore anything else, and then padding over to the closet to get his clothes. He took longer there, and I usually fell asleep at that point. He always kissed me before he left, and without knowing it, he would wake me up once again.

I turned and looked at the baby video monitor at the foot of my bed. I still turned it on to keep an eye on Raian although he was now five. On the black and white screen, I saw his dark head against the white pillow. He snored in sleep, just like Faizan. My little angel!

Time to get ready for another day. I flung my legs off the bed and marched toward the bathroom, but not before the tinkering of teacups in the kitchen alerted me that Ma was up as well, preparing breakfast for me.

Evenings were our quiet time, mine and Raian's, and he looked forward to his bath. It was a relaxing time for us. I would sit him in his tub and surround him with his bath toys: the yellow duck now faded, the sticky colorful alphabet letters, and the squeaky bath books. I found the sound of water slapping against his soft skin incredibly soothing. I wasn't certain which one of us reveled in those moments more.

Once when he was enjoying the post-bath immersion time, he grinned and pointed to the ceiling, head tilted. I followed his gaze to see the light from the window reflecting water above, cascading waves over our heads, and we laughed together. Not an odd notion in our already topsy-turvy world—a world that made complete sense to us but was baffling to the rest.

His trusting eyes looked at me, shining, and I felt weak from the message they carried. *My mother is my guardian. I am safe when I am with her. She cocoons me in the palm of her hand.*

But there were times I was pouring water over his body when my thoughts would turn sadder: losing Faizan, getting uprooted, losing control of the life that in my mind had some form of stability. And always I thought of the little girl who I had seen in the news, the one who was thrown off the flyover by her mentally disturbed father to exact vengeance against his estranged wife. Then he himself plummeted to his death behind her. His daughter miraculously survived. God works in strange ways. I don't know why she comes to my mind when I bathe Raian. Maybe I look at both of them as survivors, different stories, lost fathers, lukewarm endings. Then there are some with unbearable endings, like Yavar, the character in Faizan's novel and even Faizan himself. On some level, I felt I had failed both of them.

Soul Searcher called out to me from the bureau each morning.

"I am here," it said. "Look at me. Remember your promise."

And each day, I tapped the bureau lightly in response as if appeasing a child. *I remember. I have not forgotten.*

Every morning, I got dressed for work and kissed the folded veil on the bureau before I left. I took Raian to his special school a few blocks from my work. He had a daily schedule of academics combined with speech, feeding, oral, and physical therapy. He spent his days with children like him, struggling, trapped in bodies that limited their potential and with the power of their gifts affirmed that they were different but chosen. It was here that Raian found his love for music. It was here that he tapped to the drumbeats in his heart, the rhythm that granted him hope.

I am closer, I told the waiting manuscript. *I have not abandoned you. In my mind, I have already composed you. You are a masterpiece. And although I did not create you, I will complete you.*

Writing from a different point of view perhaps had added years to completion, but I felt content in my heart. I would do it justice, as long as it took. *I will not rush through it,* I told myself.

When Raian started school, I took the manuscript out of hiding. Waiting for the muse to strike was a luxury I could ill afford, so I set a time to write. Every other weekend, when Ma and Baba took Raian out to the mall or park, I dedicated that time to writing. Ma smiled all day and looked forward to those times when she was certain that the bureau drawer would open and the manuscript would come out. The computer would crank to life, and the day would bring a mother's dream a little closer to fulfillment.

Ma left little snacks for me on the desk, only my favorite ones— *samosas, pakoras,* and the fried round balls of flour in sugar syrup called *gulab jamuns* that were so soothing to the palate, sensual even—her silent acknowledgement for my contribution.

The main character of *Soul Searcher* baffled me. I kept going to the early part of his life, his life on the streets. It fascinated me, the notion of a child living that way.

And I worked hard, all morning, all afternoon, until the rest of my clan dragged in. Even when I greeted them and made small talk, I carried the haze of unwritten words that blurred my thinking capacity. Some nights, I feverishly worked until dawn, until my fingers cracked and throbbed from the repeated motion of typing.

It was all worth it.

I was committed. I just wasn't fast.

Those mornings when I finally crashed and tried to steal a few hours of sleep, I was in and out of fragmented, phantasmagoric dreams that made little sense. I saw two red-tongued boys huddled together eating red *phalsa* berries from a newspaper cone, spitting out the seeds. They cheered the one who made it the farthest or struck an innocent passerby. The neck areas of their long shirts were splattered with wide strips of pink juice dotted with red. I knew them both, and they seemed to fit well together in spirit, not in appearance. One of them was a younger version of Faizan, his hair thicker than I remembered, and unruly. The other was Yavar—the character brought to life for me by Faizan. They both had marks on their faces at varying places, uneven in length.

One of them belonged to the street and the other was responsible for putting him there.

TWENTY-ONE

The man sitting across from me in the waiting area had his head bowed as he looked down at his Italian Edwin Cap shoes. I studied the stranger like you would a person on a subway, stealthily without letting on, not because the person seems interesting to you but only to kill time. He had a sports cap on his head, forehead creased in tension. Clearly his shoes were not on his mind, although at the price he probably paid for them, they should have been. I knew that brand well. I had once seen Faizan check a black pair out at a store and then walk away with the understanding that they were way out of his league.

I was more relaxed at present; this was just a routine ear checkup. Raian didn't mind going in with the nurses alone, because the place was almost like a second home to him. I was not expecting earth-shattering news that day, so for once I wasn't nervous, although I felt sympathy for the stranger. At Children's Hospital, it could only be a father waiting for some news about his child. How many days had I waited in that seat, my heart weak with fear at the certainty that any news they bring me about Raian would be bad? Lately, the challenges had been less. The focus now was more on progress than life; survival wasn't an everyday issue anymore.

The stranger looked up, probably realizing he was being scrutinized, and our eyes locked. He searched my face for the fear he felt in his heart—was my child in danger as well? I looked away, giving nothing away, and focused instead on a Van Gogh sunflower print on the wall. I saw him look at me as many people from the continent I come from do, in an attempt to place me. In a world of the ones who belonged, we looked for displaced souls like ourselves—the ones who didn't quite blend—exhibiting a fervent desire to learn their history. I did, too, and made my own assumptions. I believed he was from Pakistan. And when the nurse called out "Zaki," my suspicion was confirmed at the familiarity of the name. She conferred with him briefly in a low voice, and he returned to his seat with a sigh, pushing the newspaper he was reading a few feet away. Whatever news he had heard from the nurse had probably not been good.

He and I, I thought to myself, *we have no history, no fights, no reconciliations, no repartee over not enough sugar in the tea or forgotten keys in cabs. None, not unless you count sitting across from each other in the waiting room, agonizing over what terrible news the doctor would bring. But history can join us together if I give in a little and inch closer just once and ask him about his children, his life.*

He looked claustrophobic and undid the top button of his green shirt. He looked at me again briefly and stood up to walk over. I opened my purse and started fiddling with the contents inside.

"Hi." His voice was hoarse. I looked up at him. He was sweating and obviously needed to talk to calm his nerves. "This is a strange place, isn't it?" He cleared his throat and laughed nervously. "My son, he is in there." He gestured toward the closed door leading to the room where many of my nightmares had been realized.

"Is he okay?" I asked.

He shrugged and sat down next to me, picking up the *Glamour* magazine in the seat and placing it on his lap. "They're running some tests. He got hit by a baseball on the side of his head. They're checking to see if his hearing was affected."

"I am sorry." *If that's the only problem the kid has, he is one lucky kid,* I thought, but I kept it to myself.

"You?" he asked after a pause.

"My son's here for a routine ear checkup," I responded cheerfully. "He finished up and accompanied the nurse to collect his stickers and such. Should be along shortly. He's been in there awhile."

At that moment, a nurse appeared with Raian in tow. I pretended not to notice how my companion's jaw dropped when he saw my child limp his way toward me, making indistinguishable noises and babbling excitedly, his pirate eye patch drawing attention from all corners of the room.

"It was great," he signed even before he reached me and enveloped me in a clumsy hug.

"Fantastic." I smiled, pulling back and signing to him. I beamed all around at the many pairs of eyes that were fixed on us in the waiting room. Folks who were until that moment immersed in novel plots or reading about Operation Iraqi Freedom in *Time* magazine were now our attentive audience. I took Raian's hand in mine, and we marched out together. I didn't look back at the stranger. This land still has opportunities for my little trooper. It will assist him in reaching his full potential, his mother cheering all the way.

We stopped for some ice cream afterward. With the many feeding problems Raian had, this was one of the few treats he could enjoy. Cones were difficult for him. The different textures of the ice cream and the cone always made him gag. He liked plain, even-textured ice cream; strawberry was his favorite. I looked at his face, all pink and milky, and he was the most adorable person to me. Two Iranian women passed by us, scarves on their heads. People looked up from their conversations and stared at the pair. The women appeared unfazed, conversing breezily in Farsi. They paused near our table and smiled at Raian.

"What an adorable boy," the taller one commented in a heavily accented voice. "What is your name?" she addressed Raian.

"He can't hear you," I said in a hurry, wiping his face with a napkin.

They appeared shocked.

Raian signed his name as if on cue and uttered a guttural cry. To me, it was a happy sound. It was perhaps not delivered with an acceptable indoor voice.

"He says it's Raian," I offered.

"Little boy with a sunshine smile," one commented with a nod and resumed walking.

The eyes around the shop had shifted from them to us.

The summer flew away from me in a frenzy of activities. Abu came down for a week, and Zoha joined us a few days later with all three of her children: the very active eight-year-old boy and the two younger girls, spitting images of their mother. By the visit's end, I was exhausted from entertaining my visitors while working, keeping Raian safe, interpreting constantly for people around me, and fitting in all of Raian's necessary appointments.

The visit also left a huge mound of new toys in every corner of the tiny apartment.

"We have to find a bigger place just to fit all these things in," I told Ma. She smiled in understanding. The next day when I came back from work, the place was free from all toy piles. They had been neatly and carefully stored away for easy retrieval in various closets around the apartment.

What would we do without our loved ones? They drive us over the edge and yet bring sanity to our lives.

After awhile, I realized that despite the growing and sometimes receding circle of challenges he faced, Raian was the one who taught me to be a better parent.

Raian had a special ritualistic signing that began when he woke up in the morning and didn't end until he fell asleep at night. He had a set of signs he went through, wanting to know exactly where everyone was and what they were doing. He also loved certain shows on TV that he watched after school. He memorized their starting times and validated them continuously with me like Dustin Hoffman in *Rain Man*. Our endless barrage of signing often ended in a tantrum for him when I refused to sign anymore. I felt like a horrible mother when I did that, but we all needed to rest and refuel.

This is what our typical signing went like:

Raian: Mummy?

Me: At home.

Raian: Raian

Me: At home.

Raian: Dada *(Baba)*?

Me: At home.

Raian: Dadi *(Ma)*?

Me: At home.

Raian: Mummy shower?

Me: Yes.

Raian: Raian shower?

Me: Yes.

Raian: Mummy ready?

Me: Yes.

Raian: Raian ready?

Me: Yes.

Raian: Mummy shopping?

Me: Yes.

Raian: Raian shopping?

Me: Yes.

Raian: Mummy sleep?

Me: Yes.

Raian: Raian sleep?

Me: Yes.

That repeated on and on until something new happened. Uncle Rizvi said that Raian's ritualistic signing is the result of multiple sensory impairments, not mental retardation; it helped regulate himself and the world around him. Raian was missing so much of the sensory information that in our daily lives we took for granted because of his blurry and peripheral vision, hearing aids, people seeming to talk at a whisper, and balance issues. He did not receive the environmental cues that were so normal for us to process. If something was not happening directly to him or with him, he missed most of it. Like many children with special needs, Raian thrived on routine. His life fell apart if that was taken away. Without routine he had no way of knowing what might happen next.

When he was in an obsessive mode, I found it best to leave him alone. If I didn't, it triggered a stress behavior that he found hard to deal with. I saw his repetitive and sometimes destructive behavior as more than just a compulsion and tried to gauge his mood and perspective before reacting. It required finesse, grace. When he was in that state, he either constantly ran in circles, jumped, spun on his heels, turned the lights on and off in his room, or lightly banged his head against the wall. I let him air it all out to help him cope, all the while keeping a watchful eye on him. When he was done, I usually made him hot chocolate, and we sat on the couch and huddled together, sipping the warm drink. At some level I know he appreciated the space I gave him at those times. Even if his actions hurt him physically, his mental state was more important.

There was commotion on the playground when I walked in. I saw Ms. Suzanna, Raian's teacher, rush past me with an ice pack and hand it to Raian who pressed it against his bruised left knee.

"What happened?" I asked but it came out more like an accusation. I kneeled down to help Raian hold the ice pack in place. His knee looked red and swollen.

"He collided with another kid and fell against the playscape," Ms. Suzanna explained, still tending to Raian who grinned at me. "I am okay," he signed, but his nose was running and I knew that he had been crying.

No, you are not, I thought, upset at the teacher for not being watchful enough, angry at myself for being a few minutes late. Why couldn't Raian ever catch a break?

"He is okay, just a bit rattled," Ms. Suzanna offered, looking at my expression, "It's a very minor bruise."

I couldn't get over how upset I was. "Shouldn't there be more teachers outside watching eleven children?" I asked.

"Not really," Ms. Suzanna replied a bit annoyed at my reaction to what she probably considered a very small problem. "We usually have only one teacher watching them while they are on the playground."

I helped Raian wobble to the car and got him in his booster seat. As soon as I got behind the wheel, I began dissecting the situation, trying to figure out other options for Raian in my mind. I felt that the school had failed him in some way. I didn't realize that Raian was signing to me until he finally slapped his hand against his seat to catch my attention. In the rear view mirror, I saw him gesturing passionately with his arms. I pulled the car over and turned my attention to him.

"What is it?" I signed. "Are you okay?"

He nodded. "We learned about Beethoven today," he signed, brushing away the hair in his eyes.

"That's great."

"He was deaf, did you know that?"

"Uh-huh."

"He was a musician but he couldn't hear his own music." Raian's eyes shone with passion.

"He probably felt it with his heart."

Raian laid a hand against his heart and smiled.

"I feel it too."

So the music lessons at school were really helping.

"Do you enjoy music at school?" I asked.

Raian nodded. "Can I be a great musician?"

I smiled. "There's no stopping you, Raian."

He was quiet for awhile, a hand still against his chest, lost in thoughts.

"Was my father deaf?"

There was a catch in my throat. "No."

"Was he a good man?"

"He was the best."

We rode the rest of the way quietly. The school was all right for now, I decided.

I was frantically trying to meet my deadlines at work. The magazine had received another round of funding, and we were putting together a celebration issue, symbolizing our renewed commitment.

The feature I had done on a Pakistani woman politician had to be yanked at the last minute because the interviewee developed cold feet and felt that her comments and outlook would offend others in her circle.

"I feel terrible," she kept saying, "but my career is very important to me. I will be shooting myself in the foot if I let you run this interview."

Her comments would have exposed a certain colleague's financial scams.

I consented but was left with a gaping hole in a magazine that was due to hit press in less than two weeks.

"Why don't you do a story on your life?" suggested Cyma.

"Huh?"

Cyma raised an eyebrow. "Or would you rather not talk about your life?"

I thought of my child and of body parts strewn in the street, the fire, the chaos. That might be a bit much for the audience's palate. But comfort is never the goal in reporting. *You should present true and hard facts to encourage dialogue and spread information*—isn't that what Cyma always advised?

I told her I'd think about it.

And I thought about it.

What could I talk about?

The traditions I left behind?

My soul mate and his unfinished work in life?

Or the son who made me whole again?

In the end, I wrote about Faizan and our life together. Memories of times spent together washed over me as I wrote—mistyping every now and then, in my rush to get it all on paper. My hand left my mind behind as my pain took over and poured over the pages—agony, crushed youth, fallen dreams, a life wronged. Then I went in to chop and prune, stripping out all emotion. When I started working on draft three, I noticed I was weeding out important facts. I stopped and decided to follow an important rule of writing: let someone else edit your work. I took out the first draft and handed it to Tareeqa, another editor at *Chamak*, to review the next morning.

A few minutes later when I came out of my cubicle to grab some coffee, I found her at her desk, head bowed over my article.

"Arissa, is this all you?" Her eyes looked pink and puffy as if she had been crying. I didn't want to believe that it was the result of reading my work. That would be sheer vanity. I nodded and stood by her to peek in closer. She was on page ten. Four more to go, I calculated.

"It's amazing," Tareeqa said. "You never talk about it."

"It is said that if you don't talk about loss, you heal faster."

Tareeqa shook her head. "I don't believe that."

"Neither do I."

"We meet again."

I turned around at the sound and smiled at Zaki. Strange place to meet, the waiting room of a hospital. He was standing there with an arm around his son, who was looking for an escape route. "This is Safiy."

"Hi," the teenager mumbled as his father released his hold on him.

"Hello," I said briefly and turned to get Raian settled into the chair next to me with the little toy sedan that he had been screaming for on the drive over. It had fallen on the floor in the car and caused major chaos during our commute. I still felt nervous driving, and it usually took all of my concentration just to keep myself and my passenger alive.

Safiy settled across the room with a few auto magazines while Zaki plopped down beside me. "We have to stop meeting like this," he whispered in my ear, and I jumped.

"Excuse me." My voice came out a bit sharper than I intended.

Zaki looked flustered. "I am sorry, I didn't mean to—"

His voice trailed off, and I hastened to put him at ease. I wasn't blessed with *savoir-faire* either, that uncanny ability to act right in any situation. "Oh no, I didn't understand—"

We both laughed simultaneously, overlapping each other's sounds. He reached over to grab a magazine to soften the awkwardness and leafed through an edition of *Newsweek.*

"I just realized that I don't know your name," he said after awhile. " I am Zaki, by the way."

"Arissa."

"Please don't mind my asking, but I don't see a ring on your finger," he said matter-of-factly. His directness caught me totally off-guard.

"Yes, that." I looked down at my ring finger. My wedding ring had never fit my finger after the pregnancy. My body had outgrown that symbol of my marriage, and I had stopped fretting about it. In time, I retired it to my little jewelry box at home instead of getting it resized. It also made for a lot less explaining at work. When you don't have a ring but you do have a kid, I found that it shut people up pretty quickly.

"My husband passed away." I dreaded the words as soon as they came out of my mouth. Did I really want sympathy from a virtual stranger?

"Oh, I am so—"

"Please don't." I held up my hand. "It was a long time ago."

We sat in silence for awhile, looking at Raian, who had moved to the floor and was turning his toy car in a semicircle on the carpet.

"Your son," Zaki began. "Does he come here often?"

"Every four to six weeks. These are easy appointments to check his hearing. He has multiple problems, and we do many doctor visits. Sadly, this hospital is Raian's home away from home."

Why am I telling all this to a stranger? I wondered. Maybe deep down that was my tactic to keep likely suitors at bay. I liked my little cocoon, my comfort zone, where Raian and I formed a perfect circle, leaving no room for anyone else to enter. Abu had dropped several hints, and Ma and Baba had said in no uncertain terms that they would welcome any man who took their son's place in my life and yet would still remain as involved in our lives as we wanted.

"That sounds tough. Safiy and I are here for a follow-up," Zaki said. He called out to Raian. "Hello, Raian, are you enjoying your little car?"

Raian didn't respond.

"He can't hear you," I said, smiling at Raian. "He can't see very well either. We are working on speech but haven't made giant leaps. The progress is slow and far in between."

"Oh." Zaki seemed a trifle shocked. "How do you—?"

"We sign," I answered hurriedly. "He has peripheral vision."

Zaki seemed to not comprehend.

I tried to explain by making a few sign gestures. "Signs, you know." I demonstrated an eating sign. "This is for eating." I showed him another sign. "This is for more."

"Wow."

The silence afterward was so long that I figured our small talk was over and picked up a copy of *Health Wise* magazine from the side table and started reading. I had a strange habit of starting magazines from the back, like reading in Urdu—a language that is written right to left.

When I heard Raian's squeal of laughter a short while later, I was surprised to find Zaki on the floor with him, helping him grind the wheels of the car while backing it up so that it sprung forward and gathered speed. I had no idea his little car could do that, and I watched them for awhile, amazed at their silent connection.

"Would you like to have coffee after their appointments are done?" Zaki looked up at me. His eyes were the purest brown, stroked at the top by thick lashes. It was my turn to be flustered at getting caught staring at him. Raian went behind Zaki and enveloped him in a bear hug.

"Sure," I stammered just as the nurse called Raian's name. I felt I was not left with a choice in the matter.

I was right. History can be altered—but did I really want that?

Bouillons Café across from the hospital was crowded at midday, bursting with an energy that took many forms and sizes. Sullen teens tried to serve coffee amid debates and vigorous conversations, even some heated exchanges. I looked at the couple sitting across from Zaki and me. From the tensed shoulders of the woman and their gestures, they seemed to be in the middle of some kind of argument. The woman was using her fork to punctuate her sentences while with the other hand she kept sliding back the strap of her dress that kept slipping off her shoulder. At one point, the fork ricocheted off her hand and came to rest on the floor. The man jerked back in his chair as if she had aimed it at him. She glared at him as if he were a moron and bent to pick it up. Our eyes met briefly. She looked away and resumed her animated conversation with her companion.

I tried to bring my attention back to my company.

"We're having pizza night at our house on Saturday," Zaki was saying as Raian swiped his dunked cookie and put it in his mouth.

Of course, I had to say yes.

Zaki's house in River Oaks was just short of a palace. It was one of the few neighborhoods with only one thousand properties, predominately inhabited by successful professionals. Zaki's house, built on six acres, had its own private lake that could be seen from the covered porch. The huge two-story Colonial had five bedrooms, a tennis court, an indoor swimming pool, and two giant columns that seemed to hold the house erect. The house overlooked a wooded lot with hiking trails. Zaki had mentioned that he was an engineer by profession, electrical, he had emphasized, but had done well in real estate. Clearly an understatement!

His sons were twelve and fourteen and were both taller than him. They seemed nice, although in the classic teenage behavior they didn't have much to say and answered mostly in monosyllables. After dinner they plopped in front of the TV to watch football. Raian sat with us and got busy wolfing down what I had brought from home for him.

"What is that?" Zaki asked, a little grossed out.

I laughed. The semi-liquid yellow broth did look uninviting, but Raian loved it.

"Lentil, rice, and potatoes pureed up."

"No pizza for him, huh?"

"No." I ruffled Raian's head. He gave me a thumbs-up. "Maybe in a few years." I tried to sound hopeful. I took it slow. Do not expect miracles, I constantly told myself.

While the boys swam after dinner, I rolled up my jeans and dangled my feet at the shallow end of the pool, keeping a watchful eye on Raian, who had recently developed a love for pools. He was doing great and came up to me at one point, interlocking his fingers in mine. *Don't worry about me, Mama,* he said with his touch.

How can I not?

We communicated this way often, needing neither signs nor words.

A warm smile flirted with the corner of Raian's lips before he pulled away, a gesture that reminded me of Faizan. My heart stopped briefly. Our world was so different from the rest. Inside our little bubble, the space was concave, pliable; to those outside, it seemed convex. Perhaps we were oddballs to others, but put together we were an enigma.

TWENTY-TWO

"Your eyes are like roadmaps," Zaki said to me once when we were still getting to know each other, me hesitantly, him excitedly, accelerating the relationship at every chance. "It seems like there is hope, there is refuge in them."

There is no future in them, I wanted to remind him. Now they were a canvas that was stripped of its colors although I didn't feel the plainness within.

"I mean that in a good way," Zaki was quick to point out. "It's almost as if your emotions live within them and define the depth and the passion that drives you."

Does white come in shades? I wondered. *Technically, is white even a color?* At some point in my life, I had grown to accept my colorless life. I accepted that knowing Faizan was like meeting a king for the first time—you take that memory to the grave, even if you never see him again. You die happy. You saw joy once. You were lucky enough. Some never get to meet the king. The luckier ones end up with little princes who follow them around all their lives, a constant reminder of the monarch himself. Who said I was alone?

Zaki and I had fallen into a routine of meeting for coffee every Tuesday at the café across from my office. We had a very unsurprising kind of arrangement. He knew what to order for me. I knew what he would be wearing that day. I knew what made him smile. He knew the topics that irritated me. I knew not to mention the old culture to him, as it didn't have a big presence in his life. He understood that the numbers in his business baffled me. I looked at our meetings as a chance for two friends to connect who shared a few common interests. Books were not one of them, I had quickly discovered, and neither was art. Coffee and pleasant dialogue were. He was a good listener and very articulate in conversation.

"You know what else is in there?" Zaki continued, looking deep in my eyes, making me feel at once self-conscious and exposed. "A glimpse of all you carry in your heart—your burden that you carry with grace."

I was touched by his words.

"Too bad the weight has not caused my eyelids to permanently shut," I joked, sipping my chai latte.

"Don't talk like that," Zaki chided, pushing his muffin away. "I admire you. You know exactly what you want in life, and you go after it. There is no indecisiveness in your soul, no regrets."

That part wasn't true. What I wanted in life I would never get while I lived, and I preferred to keep my regrets to myself.

"Tell me about yourself." I was eager to shift the focus of the discussion away from me. "What drives you?"

"Necessity, for the most part." He laughed and then paused. His face grew a bit serious. "Some days, you!"

That caught me off-guard, and I looked away in a hurry. I was uncertain about Zaki, but I enjoyed his company. In his mind's eye, Zaki had already laid the foundation of our relationship. What he was doing now was building the house. I was still wary of the groundwork itself. To me, it did not hold much concrete and was pretty shaky. His urgency in taking the liaison to the next level made me very anxious since I was uncertain that there would ever be a connection beyond a platonic friendship. I asked myself a million times why I was so unaccepting of new relationships. Over the years, there were many who had tried to set me up with friends, brothers, distant cousins. They all had one argument: *You are young; how will you go through life without a companion?* I didn't blame them. For the longest time, I, too, had thought of the world as both my grave and my existence, a vertical tombstone. I considered myself dead by association, knowing that I belonged to a society where women lose more than half of themselves when they lose a mate and nearly all of their worth.

I had loved and felt incapable of ever loving again. Raian filled my life to the brim; any more and my cup would no doubt spill over. I cradled my two worlds—one with a degree of confidence and one that I was less vested in, hesitantly.

"Arissa, I want to be in your life," Zaki was saying. "I want us to have a life together."

What did I want?

Not that. Never that.

Although I promised him that day that I'd think about it.

I did for ten days.

And finally, I went over to his place and told him it was too soon. He suggested we take the arrangement up a notch and feel it out. Perhaps it might feel right.

I suggested we take a walk.

The evening was breezy yet warm. After a walk of half a block, I felt my thin red shirt cling to me from sweat. Zaki glanced over at me and put his arm around my waist. For once, I let him. We walked around the lake near his house, where sprinklers were sloshing water around the landscaping, leaving the air refreshingly misty. He was wearing a white hooded sweater. I tried to rest my head against his chest, but it wasn't quite comfortable and I moved away. He caught my hand and brought me closer to him again. I almost stepped on his toe and murmured an apology that somehow got lost in the siren of a fire truck in the distance.

"You need to make some decisions in your life, Arissa," I heard him say. "You can't keep running away. It's your life, but do you really want to go at it alone?"

Yes, my mind said. I didn't think I could, but lately I had started to accept the idea. I didn't answer him though, and he sighed.

"I need you, Arissa," he said softly without meeting my eyes.

Yes, but do you really? I willed his brain to answer. *Can you accept me with all of my crazy obligations, my tattered life? My son? Especially him?* I sat down on a rock, suddenly tired. I looked at the fountain shaped like a unicorn shooting out water. I threw a rock in the lake and watched it create a few imperfect semicircles that faded away quickly.

"Trust me, you **don't** want me in your life," I finally said. "My life is complicated. Yours **is not**."

The meaning of **my** words was not lost on him. He crouched near me, and I felt his gaze **burn** my face.

"Do you know **how** different your life is when your child is not normal?" I continued. "There are challenges on a daily basis. Allowances you make, things you let go off so you can devote more energy to your child." I looked at him wearily. "Why would you want us in your life? Why us? Why now after all these years? You have two wonderful children. You raised them very well by yourself."

He came closer. "But then you came along and life for me will never be the same again."

I breathed in his cologne. Our noses touched, and I stood up to resume walking, spoiling the moment.

"It's not as simple as that, Zaki. My life isn't my own—"

He cut me short. "Do you feel anything?"

"About what?"

"About me? For me? For God's sake, do you feel anything?" His voice rose in pitch. I didn't hesitate.

"I care for you, but only as a good friend." I was in no position to lie.

His face grew grim and withdrawn. "Let's head back."

"Zaki!"

He laughed a hollow laugh. "It's not enough. I'll always want more."

Dead leaves crackled under his feet as he turned back. He pushed a forgotten bicycle out of his way, almost flinging it in impatience. I stood like a waif, an orphaned soul, and then followed him.

"It's too soon," I pleaded.

"Six years." His voice thundered around me. "Six full years! How much time in hell do you need?"

I was speechless.

"It's useless." He shook his head. "I can't compete with a ghost."

I stopped in my tracks. He was right, I thought, as I watched his receding back and his hunched shoulders. No one can fight with the memory of a ghost. I had raised Faizan to the pedestal of perfection. No one will ever match up, and the sad thing is I didn't want anyone to.

I was scared of losing a friend, though, so I did something I should not have.

"I need some more time," I pleaded again. "Maybe I will be able to see things differently in time." The words spilled from me like an overturned bowl of beans, together and in a hurry—a last-ditch attempt to save a doomed friendship. The suggestion lent a false sense of hope when I knew there was none.

He turned around sharply in disbelief, eyebrows raised, and then nodded with a sigh. I stumbled over a rock, and he held out a hand to steady me.

In the next few days we each receded within ourselves to the corner of our own sanities, knowing that whatever we did or said would widen the rift between us. We held on, unable to let go. We met for coffee at our usual time but weren't sure how long we could do that without answering the inevitable question. Somehow we were both reluctant to disturb the arrangement.

In a burst of creative appreciation, Zaki bought some of my paintings that I had wanted to get rid of for awhile.

There was not adequate storage room in the little apartment, and two of those paintings reminded me too much of my life with Faizan. The memories were sealed so deeply in the colors and composition that I couldn't bear to look at them without the context and history. One was of kissing figures and the other was the painting of the white roses against a fuchsia backdrop, the one I'd painted the year I got married. The other two were my least favorite: A twisted torso of a woman with a child around her ankle and the dreaded one of red magnolias oozing blood.

I had painted the kissing figures the day Faizan and I finished decorating the den—actually the second bedroom of our Jackson Heights apartment—in our second year of marriage. Painting was a hobby that offered me release, ruled and driven as it was by an extremely crude and undisciplined obsession that you couldn't make a living from. That is why I chose business writing as a career. I can be balanced and objective in words. I paint only when I am seeking a release. When I see a blank canvas, something inside me twists, like a demon rising from sleep.

Faizan had partitioned the den into two parts: one that contained the tools of my trade—easel, paints, brushes, smock, rags, bundles of newspapers to spread on the floor—and the other where he had his tower of books. It literally was a monument. He had run out of space on the bookshelf and started building a tower of books alongside it on the hardwood floor. It amused me that he always wanted to be near me when we were home. The partitioned den was his idea so that we could be together. That day, while I painted, he had his eyes glued to *Madman* by Kahlil Gibran as he sat cross-legged on the floor. Notes from Ustad Amanat Ali's ghazals carried through the den from the stereo in the living room: *Inshaa Ji utho, ab kuch karo, is shehr main ji ko lagana kya.* Rise up, Inshaji, and leave, there is no sense lingering in this town where there is no fulfillment.

Before he had created that space for me, he always got a bit frustrated when my half-day art projects ended up being five days long. He loved and respected my work but wanted his wife by his side when he came home. Although we both knew that when the fiery inspiration took hold, we shut the other person out and disappeared for hours at end, him in his writing, me in my painting. During those moments when the muse struck, even when we were together, we were elsewhere, dream dancing our projects in our minds, carving new lines and waves of color into a canvas, writing inspiring dialogues in a chapter. The midnight muse was the worst, and we always laughed about how our thoughts escaped from us like fleeting fireflies even before we opened our eyes—our most brilliant ideas lost to the night.

I paused briefly and wiped my brush on a baby-oil-soaked rag hanging on the easel and went to the kitchen to attend to my cooking. Being a bachelor who had been on his own for so long, Faizan was the one with the culinary skills. In my own house back home, our many helpers had reigned supreme, rendering the other members of the family virtually useless in the kitchen. For Zoha back home the tradition had continued, but I had made the mistake of moving abroad. In the beginning, I learned many recipes from Faizan, but somehow in preparing them, we discovered another hidden talent of mine: the rare gift of burning even scrambled eggs. There was either too much spice in the vegetables I prepared, or too much oil. Or both. Kabobs hardened to the point that a hammer was required to break them, cakes were too crumbly, bread pudding reeked of eggs, chicken curry had too much turmeric and not enough flavor. Often I made a desperate effort to fix some dishes by pouring in ketchup or any other condiments I could find in the fridge. Faizan would have been the perfect candidate for *Fear Factor*. He consumed those experiments without complaint and often with a knowing smile on his face, perhaps realizing that one day it wouldn't be so bad, that there are only so many bad meals a woman could cook. I often felt like smacking him. I would've liked it if even once he had said, "It's awful, Arissa. How can you even expect a human to consume it?" By the second day, the leftovers almost always ended up in the trash can.

Over time, my cooking skills started to improve. The project of the day I started my painting in the remodeled den was *karahi* chicken. I poured in a tablespoon of oil and slowly sautéed green chilies and ginger.

Next I added the diced tomatoes and chicken to the sizzling combo, feeling more confident by the minute. I turned around and nearly jumped when I saw Faizan standing there, arms crossed over his chest, looking at me intently.

"You look so beautiful when you are engrossed," he remarked, glancing inside the pot and nodding his approval at the sight.

"You scared me." I frowned at him, mildly irritated. He didn't realize what an effort cooking was to me and how seriously I took it. I didn't have lofty goals of perfection, only a desire to create edible meals. "Don't you have anything better to do?"

He came near and stroked my cheek with the back of his hand. His eyes penetrated mine, but it seemed that they went much further. My breasts breathed into his chest as he came closer. The aroma, the spices from my cooking, had settled on our hair, our clothes. "Yes," he whispered against my shaky lips. "I am doing it right now. Watching you."

I still remember what I painted much later that day—a figure sitting in a wicker chaise. But when examined closely, you could see that the figure was actually two figures entwined—half of a woman's body, joined by half of a man's body. Their hands clasped each other, their lips fused in rapture.

It was one of Faizan's favorites and spent a long time in the den, hanging over his desk, enclosed in a cherrywood frame.

The burnt karahi ended up in the garbage that day.

In retrospect, I wasn't certain which one of us made the first move.

I was helping Zaki figure out where to hang the paintings he had bought from me in his living area. The room had unusual and hard-to-work-with elements. Its pale yellow arches at the entrance were split in the middle and oddly reminded me of the openness of labia, I thought with a rush of blood to my face. As soon as you entered the room, the dark walls sucked you in.

"If you move the pedestal with the jade stone bowl on one side of the entry way, maybe you can make your fireplace area the focal point of the room by dressing up the mantel?" I suggested, moving the pedestal to demonstrate my thought. "Perhaps the painting of the kissing figures can go up there since the colors are so rich in that composition. The white roses can then replace the oriental rug on the wall next to the window."

I paused to gauge Zaki's reaction. He stood next to me, nodding and reflective, the soft scent of his aftershave lingering in the room. He took my breath away when he suddenly turned to me and enveloped me in a hug. Against his chest, I felt the uncertain thudding of our hearts. I wanted to move away but my body wouldn't let me. We didn't speak; words had never resolved anything between us in the past. I let him lead me gently to the couch across the room.

It had been a long time for both of us. I had forgotten what a man's touch could do to a woman. I was shaky in his embrace; he was clumsy from having been without a woman for a while. The anticipation was more joyous and prolonged than the union itself, and it was over far too quickly for us. I felt invaded, violated by my own accord, but the arrow had left the bow.

Afterward, I was trembling and quiet when I went to get a glass of water from the kitchen, the sheet wrapped around me dragging on the floor in my hurry to get away. He didn't stop me and turned his head the other way on the couch. In the kitchen, I held the glass with both hands, wanting to crush it and make myself bleed. I looked over at the sky outside and tried to wrap my head around my emotions. I would always compare the two men, I decided, on good days or bad. There was no way out of it.

After shedding the veil, it was interesting for me to see how easily I crossed the cultural barrier to accept another man in my arms. I somehow felt more connected with Ami in that moment than I ever had.

Zaki wasn't an unattractive man. Yes, he did have a receding hairline, but that made him look even more attractive, mysterious even. His ex-wife was from Lahore, and they'd divorced when the children were four and six. Zaki had raised them single-handedly. It was most admirable and was an important factor in bringing us closer.

When we embraced, I always opened my eyes wide to look just once at the triangle formed between his head on the pillow and his shoulder on the bed by a patch of light from the lamp. To me, it was an escape route—a ray of light that brought back images of Faizan, a slow-moving film unreeling in real time where the players were switched. And then I shut my eyes.

"Open your eyes, Arissa," Zaki would beg in the throes of passion. "Look at me." And I stubbornly kept them closed, refusing to acknowledge the person making love to me, returning to my first love. From death, he rose and filled my arms. That's how I kept my sanity. That's how I lived, day to day.

I liked Zaki; I just didn't enjoy sex with him. He was a good person, a compassionate friend. In any other lifetime, I am certain, he could rock worlds. But not here and not mine. His tenderness violated the core of my being. When I was with him, I could never shake the feeling that I was cheating on Faizan—never, not even on days when I was relaxed and actually enjoyed some of it. On cynical days, I likened Zaki to a nocturnal barn owl, oddly displaced in the light of the morning.

Ma stirred in a few strands of saffron to the rice pudding on the stove and stood back in satisfaction. I came into the kitchen carrying two teacups and lingered in the doorway. The voices of Baba and Zaki carried in from the living room. They were conversing on politics in America and the war on terror. Ma smiled at me and asked me to taste the *kheer*. I shook my head. The meeting was Zaki's idea, and Ma and Baba were thrilled to learn about him. I led them to believe that we were so far just friends, although their hopeful eyes wished for more.

"He seems nice," Ma offered.

I forced myself into a benign smile and lined up small chocolate-colored bowls on a tray. Next I scooped some pudding into each and looked down at the browns, whites, and saffrons in my life.

"He is a good father and a great listener, but is that good enough?" I said more for my sake than Ma's.

"Maybe it's time you listened to your heart as well," Ma said with a hug, "It can't lead you wrong."

With that she left the kitchen. How could I tell her that I had been silencing that voice for quite awhile? It had repeatedly told me to turn and walk away. I couldn't understand what brought me back to Zaki over and over again—my own weakness and antiquated thinking of needing a man in my life, or an acute apprehension of losing a friend?

Zaki touched my upper back lightly as I walked him to his car after dinner, and I felt the square inch just below my shoulder blades burn as if touched by fire. I recoiled, and he stepped away, embarrassed. He knew and I knew without saying a word that publicly, I was not at that point yet. He was not one to back off easily, although he did for the time being. I was thankful for that but fearful of what lay ahead for me. For us.

Zaki didn't understand my obsession with finishing *Soul Searcher*. To him, it wasn't my project to end or begin. I had agreed with that thought once, but not anymore. I was far too vested in it to bow out this late. Loved ones depended on that work for their own healing, for the comfort of their passing days. Zaki felt that the world was already brimming with literature that already said everything that could ever be said. He wasn't an avid reader, so his thoughts didn't hold much weight in my opinion.

In all fairness to him, he operated with the best of intentions. But along the way, he unknowingly lost pieces of me because of his judgmental attitude. I felt offended at having to defend my project to Zaki, especially when my focus was what had initially drawn him in.

"I don't get it," he often said when our schedules collided because of that work, a hint of sarcasm in his voice. "It's a book, like a million others. I'm sorry, but what would this one do for the world that others haven't done already?"

"It is not just another work. It's a legacy," I tried to explain patiently once. "And it's not for others. It's for him. I am trying to give it life so—"

"So he can live on," Zaki finished for me. "Yes, you have told me that a million times before, but how can he?"

He saw my dark expression and perhaps realized that he had ventured too far into restricted territory and fell silent. I didn't think my journey was tithable. I didn't owe any of it to anyone. Not even to the person who had access to my body.

Ann Marie and I communicated often. Since that day at the coffee shop, I frequently consulted her on matters of importance to me and found her opinions extremely helpful. Our talks had a soothing, comfortable quality and in time, evolved into a great friendship. Her new job as an event management coordinator required her to fly to Dallas many weekends. At least once every two months, she drove in to Houston to see me. Our conversations often drifted to Zaki.

"I feel he doesn't get me," I wailed to her. "He doesn't touch my soul like Faizan did."

Ann Marie smiled. "We never stop comparing, do we?"

"What about you?" I asked. "You never remarried."

"No, I didn't," she laughed out loud. "Who would have an opinionated menopausal woman who thinks love only comes to you once in a lifetime?"

"So what are you saying, Ann Marie? That I shouldn't bother with new relationships because love doesn't happen twice in a lifetime?"

"I am not saying that." Her tone grew serious. "We each have to look within ourselves for that. The question you should ask of yourself is whether you are a person who dooms new relationships at the onset or are you someone who is more open to them? Clearly you're in a relationship but has your heart really accepted that new association? What does this person and his presence in your life mean to you?"

It surprised me how clear the answers were in my head. I was just not ready to say them out loud yet.

Raian's fears were the hardest to deal with.

Everything scared him—dogs, cats, Elmo. The list kept growing: his own shadow, the night shadows, cartoons, happy faces. Especially happy faces. If he saw one of those, he would go berserk. I had to personally take an inventory of the whole apartment and get rid of every item that had a smiley face on it. I didn't know how else to help him. Once a fear found its way in, it wouldn't leave.

One afternoon when we were visiting Zaki, Raian took out a doodle pad and started scribbling. Safiy joined him and drew some characters for him. I watched them together and felt happy that they were bonding. Zaki and I decided to go for a short hike. When we came back, Raian was in a corner of the room, huddled like a ball, bawling, and Safiy was hovering over him, trying to calm him down.

"I was just drawing stuff for him," Safiy said in his defense. He held up the doodle pad with a happy face drawn on it. I cringed and gripped the edge of the table.

"We need to leave, now," I told Zaki. "I am sorry."

I took Raian's hand and led him away. We left the doodle pad behind. Raian would not have anything to do with it anyway.

"Why is it so hard?" I said to Uncle Rizvi. I had stormed into his office, where he was behind his desk looking over some patient files. He understood my question as only a loving relative would. He gestured me toward a chair.

"Who said it was going to be easy?" He smiled, looking at me above the glasses on his nose.

"No one did," I persisted, not having any form of reference to compare the statement against. "But does it ever get easier?"

Uncle Rizvi pondered his thoughts before responding. "It might, but there will always be issues to contend with. You have to realize that Raian will continue to process information in a different way than us." He laid down his glasses on the desk. "Many of his problems won't correct themselves, but as he grows up, he'll be better able to live with them through our assistance."

I knew that part, but it saddened me to have it confirmed with such finality.

"There will always be small accomplishments that you can celebrate," Uncle Rizvi continued. "Through it all, you have to remember that this isn't easy for him either."

That made me think. My question to Uncle Rizvi probably had selfish overtones, seeking normalcy for myself rather than my son. I realized that the answer wouldn't change no matter how I asked or whom I asked.

Short-term planning, Arissa, I reminded myself as I headed out with Uncle Rizvi to get burgers for lunch. *Don't think too far ahead. There's a very good reason why the future is hidden from us.*

TWENTY-THREE

I knew the day would come, but I just didn't want my mind to think about it.

It came one afternoon when I turned the stereo on in the house after a long time. Yes, my flaws do make me unique. They also make me lose people.

Ma and I were cleaning the apartment, me less industriously than her. I lifted a stack of books off the coffee table and turned around to carry them into the den when something caught my eye—the little stereo that Faizan had bought the year before the towers fell. It had cost a small fortune, but Faizan was passionate about music, and I hated to stand in his way. He said that listening to great music inspired him, formed his characters, and moved his plot along better. He loved old classical *ghazals* and listened for hours to Mehdi Hassan, Ghulam Ali, and especially Amanat Ali Khan. He appreciated the smooth, riveting songs, nodding his head in tune like an ardent member of the audience, caught in rapture by the haunting notes.

I had not used the stereo all these years. At first it seemed like an inappropriate thing to do soon after losing a spouse, and then there was never a time when I thought I was past the point of grieving. Gradually I lost interest, but like other items of our household, it moved with us to Texas and became a part of the furniture. The forgotten stereo sat on the corner entertainment deck, waiting for someone to blow off the dust and turn it on.

I paused and acknowledged it like I would an old friend I hadn't met in ages, slightly guilt-ridden at losing touch. From a distant corner of the past, melodies came flooding in and filled the corners of my mind. I gyrated in rhythm to the music that only I heard, nodding my head in approval as Faizan had years ago. I tried to get in his mind to feel what he felt, to sense what he sensed. I always made it to a certain point and then faced a brick wall, stubborn, unyielding; it stood in the way of our mingling of senses. I realized faintly that that tactic would never work. He simply didn't exist anymore.

"Give me a sign, a real sign, something tangible that tells me that you see me, you know I suffer," I had pleaded to the night shadows for a long time. "Not the gentle caress of a wind or the slight fluttering of the light. Show me something concrete like a storm or a tornado that jolts you, like a monsoon that catches you unaware and soaks you."

Silence.

"I won't be frightened. I promise," I begged again.

The wind outside rustled the leaves, but a storm did not ensue.

"If you show me a sign now, I swear I'll never ask again."

The candle in the kitchen flickered slightly.

"Please."

Silence.

In time, I gave up. Some returned from the grave to visit their loved ones. Faizan seemed to be at peace wherever he was. Or perhaps my love was not strong enough to entice him for one final appearance.

I tapped the stereo lightly and brushed off a few flecks of dust from its surface. I saw an unopened CD on the shelf. The cover had faded, and I could not read the label. I tore off the wrapper, opened the case, and slid the disc inside the player. Ma walked in with a dust cloth and glanced over at me. I nodded the silent acknowledgement of my domain, and she continued dusting the rest of the furniture in the room.

The stereo came to life. With the duster in my hand, I attacked the tiny areas of the stereo, the buttons. Play and rewind. What if there was a rewind button in real life? Could we turn back time? If life was as simple as the Undo command on PCs, what would it be like? Could we Ctrl-X all our dreadful moments away? Press Ctrl-S before dreams fled?

Where are you? Stop this game of constant hide and seek. The woman's voice reached my ears from the speaker. Sweet, passionate, brimming with longing in poetic Hindi.

Don't you know that dusk has fallen? Your mother has grown tired now. My eyes are blurry from waiting up for you.

At that I turned sharply to where Ma stood. Her back was facing me, and I saw her frame tremble slightly. Her hands stopped dusting, and she held on to the arm of the couch nearby for support.

How can I tell you where I am, Ma? The voice turned to a man's in the song. *The expanse of sky at my disposal. My kite flies freely; its string cannot be cut. Not anymore.*

Ma turned around and walked over to where I stood as if in a trance. She cranked up the volume and sank down on the couch. I sat down next to her, watching the pain surface on her face, her eyes brimming with tears she refused to shed.

Here, I can drink straight from the river. On my tiptoes, touch dreams in bunches.

Should I turn it off? I wondered. I decided against it. Ma needed to hear it. Of all of us, she had had the least time to grieve, busy as she was in healing our souls, helping us move on.

There is only one thing missing. The man's voice full of sadness reached a higher pitch.

I held my breath.

You, Ma!

And that's when Ma lost it. Tears finally streamed from her eyes and rolled down her face. I had mended; how had I not suspected that she hadn't? I had seen occasional tears in her eyes but never anything this intense. Like a child, she cried until she was overcome, in fits, her body heaving, healing at last. I put my arms around her to offer her some comfort, and it was an odd sensation to soothe someone who seemed to have always held it together better than us. How had she managed to carry that sorrow inside her all these years? *It seems like cleansing,* I thought as I watched her.

"Women's hearts hold on to so much," she'd once said to me. "Some secrets you take to your grave because telling them might mean offending someone. That is our lot. The uglier truths get filtered within us; we wash those away, creating something beautiful out of dreadful, delicious out of distasteful."

For days Ma cooked vigorously, freezing curries and dal, ginger garlic paste, non-fried *samosas* and kabobs. She filled big jars with dry snacks such as *chewra,* the spicy Rice Krispies with slow-roasted peanuts, pistachio, raisins and curry leaves, rusks made from scratch, and five anise jars. She spent an entire day slivering mangoes, jalapenos, and carrots and then pickled them with oil and split mustard seeds. I looked at her activity and considered it therapeutic for her. *We grieve differently,* I thought. I did not realize that she was preparing to exit my life.

Even before I entered the apartment at the end of the day, I knew something was not right. The air had a sad quality to it, a passive acquiescence. Raian! My thoughts immediately went to him, and I raced in, leaving the door ajar. He was sprawled out in front of the TV, eyes fixed on *Blue's Clues,* all limbs intact. He sensed the motion and looked at me sideways, signing hello.

"What is it?" he signed again, looking at my distressed expression.

For once, I didn't answer. Instead, I raced toward Ma's room. She was writing at the desk. The diagonal rays of the sunlight were falling on her fingers as she wrote furiously, right to left in Urdu, paper angled on one side. Her lips were mouthing the words she penned. Then I saw it, the suitcase beside her, and my heart sank. Ma looked up and smiled.

"You are back, Arissa!"

I dropped my handbag and stood as still as a statue.

"Where are you going?" My words did not sound mine; I heard them through a haze. I was certain some life-altering adjustment was underway.

"Back home," Ma said, folding the paper in front of her.

"I don't understand."

"We still have a home back in Karachi and a handful of relatives. *Masha Allah*, you are doing quite well now, Arissa. I think it's time we said our goodbyes and left you in peace."

I didn't want to be left in peace. I was at peace with them present.

Ma came around to where I stood and led me to her chair. "We always thought we'd stay as long as it took for you to stand on your own two feet."

I didn't answer, just sat there feeling like a crushed can.

"And now that you are, we think it's time for us to go," she concluded. "You enjoy your work, Raian loves his school—"

She stopped and sighed. I knew what was coming next. "Your Baba and I think you should marry Zaki. He seems to be a fine man."

"But I don't want to marry him."

"Arissa, you have to look out for your own future, too. Do you want to be alone for the rest of your life?"

That dreadful question again. What was wrong with my life the way it was? "I am not alone." I pushed back the cuticle on my left thumbnail and frowned, my head bent low. "I have Raian and you."

"All the more reason you need some support," Ma said, standing up and walking over to the closet. "How long will these frail bones be your anchor?"

She paused and then pulled out a polished wooden box from a shelf at eye-level. She carried it back and opened it on the desk in front of me. It was hinged at the top with black velvet inside, filled to the brim with letters. Unsent, unstamped envelopes with just dates on them.

"I write to Faizan," she said with a passion in her eyes. "Every two weeks. I always have. When he was—" she faltered. "I used to mail the letters before. I just couldn't stop writing when he passed away."

I remembered Faizan reading those when they came, his expression an interesting collage of emotions. He'd never shared them with me.

She thrust the box in my lap. "I want you to keep them. You appreciate the worth of words and will treasure these, I know."

I had the weight of words in my care. Again. It seemed like dejá vu.

They were packing some more. I heard it through the walls of my bedroom when I was finished going through the letters in the box. Ma was poetic in words just like her son, I soon found out when piece by piece I read a mother's messages to her son. They contained uplifting thoughts, gems of truth, words of hope. Reading them somehow strengthened me. *She would have been an ideal person to finish Faizan's legacy,* I thought, *had he chosen to write in Urdu.*

I heard the thud of the suitcase on the floor and the sound of bags being dragged as I tried to sleep. They were leaving us; the very people who had held my hand and brought me this far would soon be gone. Restless, I stood up from the bed and headed to their room, tired of wavering between sleep and panic. I could hear the thumping of my heart as I leaned my back against the doorframe and stood amid the shadows waiting for them to spot me. But first I burped. It sounded more like a low growl—a body's rebellion at the scene before me.

"Come on in." Baba waved me in. I sat down awkwardly at the edge of the bed and looked at Ma. Overnight, her wrinkles had deepened.

"Why can't you stay?" My voice sounded afraid, like a little girl's. Even as I asked that, I realized that they were fearful of decisions I would not make in their presence. They knew as long as they were with me, I would commit to no one.

"Think about what I said," Ma said, not responding directly to my question but giving me the answer nonetheless. "Life waits for no one. If an opportunity is available today, do give it a sincere thought."

She heaved a long sigh as if her own words had sucked the life force out of her. I nodded and hugged her.

They left a few days later.

I had a hard time explaining to Raian what had happened although Baba had painstakingly tried to prepare him for days. *They're gone,* I kept signing. Raian was puzzled and asked over and over again if they left because they were mad at him. Was it because he didn't drink his milk to the last drop and didn't keep his room clean? My hands ached from signing *No, it's not your fault.* It didn't seem like he believed me.

I cradled him in my arms and let him rock for hours on my feet to calm him. He spent the rest of the day lying on his back, rocking forward to a sitting position and then back again as he tried to regulate the air around him, wanting to find his balance. I knew he was seeking out the constants in his life, the parts that were unchanged. I let him deal with it privately but came often to check on him, assuring him of my presence, the factor in his life that would remain unchanged, I hoped.

In the days afterward we shifted roles as he found his equilibrium and I fell apart. I was grateful for his presence as he became my coach, my teacher. When I cried, he hugged and comforted me in his heroic but silent effort.

TWENTY-FOUR

The first thing I heard as I opened the door to the apartment, the groceries in my arms, was a sharp shriek followed by uncontrollable sobbing. I ran inside the living room to see Zaki in a tussle on the floor with Raian, who was fighting him off, kicking and swatting at him. His face was bathed in sweat.

"What is going on?" I demanded.

"Raian, that's enough," Zaki said breathlessly as he caught Raian's hand in mid-air and then addressed me. "He was banging his fist on the wall. When I tried to stop him, he got upset and started scratching my face and wouldn't stop."

Oh, no.

I put the groceries down on the floor and looked at Raian in absolute calm.

"Please stop," I signed, slowly. "I love you. Please come here."

Raian struggled for a few minutes to release his hands from Zaki's grasp and then stopped. Zaki loosened his hold on him.

"I don't like him," Raian signed.

I sighed. I regretted leaving them alone to go out for groceries. I had run out of Pediasure, and that would have meant one meal that Raian wouldn't eat. He strictly followed his routine. At lunch, he expected Pediasure; if it wasn't there, he refused to eat.

He came to me and sat down on my lap.

"I let him do it," I said in an even tone to Zaki.

"What?" His tone was almost accusing.

"The doctors say that the repeated behavior helps him deal with anxiety."

"But he was hurting himself," Zaki argued.

"I know," I replied calmly. "I still let him do it for his own sanity."

Zaki got up from the floor and shrugged his shirt straight and then stuffed it back in his trousers. "He is your child, but one day he might seriously injure himself."

I feared that too, but I didn't want to be judged. Not after what Raian and I had been through together.

"That is how I…we deal with it, Zaki." To my own ears, my strident words sounded final, almost damaging, like I was past the point of caring.

"Fine."

I didn't walk Zaki to the door that day, and he didn't wish us goodbye.

"I don't want to be judged, by him or anyone else," I complained to Ann Marie over coffee. "No one's in my shoes."

"Then shake him free," said Ann Marie. "Why be in a dead end relationship?"

Am I that afraid of being alone? I wondered. It troubled me how clearly the woman saw through me. It was as if instead of ribcage and skin protecting my heart, I held it exposed, just for her, separated by a see-through curtain.

"He talks well," I offered, lamely. Ann Marie did a thumbs-down gesture.

"That fact alone wouldn't win me over," she said. "How is he in bed?"

"Ann Marie," I punched her in the arm.

"Okay, then tell me why is it that he does not complete you, does not make you feel good about yourself or the work you are doing and yet you hang on. Clearly he has some quality you admire."

I mulled over her words but could not come up with a decent answer.

"I think that if a relationship isn't naturally growing, it has no chance of survival," Ann Marie continued. "You just can't force it."

Why was it so hard for me to admit that my life, my son fulfilled me and there was room for little else in my life?

"I have to go," I said to Ann Marie. I had to think some more, by myself. I had to be with Raian, near my reality.

At home, Raian sat cross-legged on the floor, keyboard on lap. His eyes were closed as he played imperfect notes to nothing in particular. To my ears, however, it was beautiful melody. The three fingers of his left hand rested on the speaker. I sat down next to him as he opened his eyes and lifted his fingers from the speaker to my heart.

"Do you feel that?" he asked in his silent way. His eyes were bright with excitement.

I nodded. It was time for me to find my own rhythm.

There was no denying it. The plateau had come and gone, and now Zaki and I were on the downward slope of our short union. The disturbing thing was that neither he nor I was willing to do a thing about it.

Our words brought the distance between us in perspective. We threw in useless conversation as filler, sweetened like jelly on bread to hide the blandness of our relationship. The gap between us widened, and when I finally saw it, it was a big relief to me. I realized it in a second when I had missed nearly all the cues for the longest time.

We were at Souper Salad for lunch. My attention had already wandered off from Zaki's conversation to Raian, who had disappeared under the table where he sat munching on a slice of cheese. I still monitored him closely when he ate, and his unique placement was making it hard for me to see him. I tried to reason with him to come out, both of us signing furiously, him shaking the table with his irritated gestures. From the corner of my eye, I saw Zaki glancing around in a state of frustration to see if anyone else was noticing the silent commotion at our table, and a realization struck with the intensity that made me tremble with rage. *He is embarrassed by us,* I thought. The clarity blew me away. It was so obvious, so in-my-face. How could I have missed it? The signs were all there: the first time in the waiting room when he'd turned his head around to check the reaction of others noticing Raian; the bored looks he wore when I patiently did the ritualistic signing for my son a hundred million times; the faraway expressions he got when I talked about Raian's appointments, Faizan's book; and how he almost always steered the conversation back to the present when so much of what I did and said was a product of the past. I lived among ghosts and I liked that arrangement.

"We would like to leave," I declared to Zaki. It wasn't presented as a request. He looked at his half-eaten Asian salad and pushed it away, nodding. I opened my purse, took out a twenty-dollar bill, and flung it on the table. He raised an eyebrow but knew that gesture meant his exclusion from the word "we." Without a word, I dragged my screaming, convulsing boy out the door without looking back.

I avoided Zaki's calls for days, not because I didn't want closure but because I was just so angry—at him, and even at myself for letting someone who was actually ashamed of my child get that close. I cuddled Raian a little longer at night and made extra special treats for him, trying to make up for what I imagined I had put him though. He seemed unharmed, although he thrived on the extra attention.

Zaki showed up at my work. I was startled to see him in the lobby. We never met at the office. I tried to steal away, but it was too late. He had seen me. His face was ashen, his anger like a pierced boil. In two strides, he was beside me and grabbed my elbow.

"If you want this to end, have the decency to say it to my face," he said, his rage spewing all over me.

I released my arm from his grasp and faced him calmly. "I have nothing to say to you."

"Sure you do." His voice was trembling with fury. "You're too weak-willed to admit it."

"Is that what you think?"

"It's what I know. Ever since…that one event in your life, you have lived like a sacrificial victim. I am sick of the emotional baggage you carry around. You behave like some sort of a martyr. You still compare me with…with him. I can never match up, no matter how hard I try."

I was furious at how much a dead man got under his skin.

"How hard have you actually tried?" I asked, crossing my arms across my chest. "You can't even stand having a disabled child by your side in public."

The shock on Zaki's face astounded me. Had he not been truthful to himself either?

"So that is what this is about," he finally said.

"Is it not true?"

He didn't meet my eyes and seemed at a loss of words. It dismayed me to learn that what I suspected was indeed true. I saw Cyma dodge around us and head toward her office, realizing something monumental was unfolding between me and Zaki. I started to walk toward the lobby door, not wanting to prolong the spectacle we had created.

"What do you want to hear?" he asked, impatience softened by sorrow, "I am not ashamed of Raian, but it's not easy being around a child who is so different. I admit I find it a bit overwhelming at times, but it's not something I can't work on."

It *could* work except that I didn't have a lifetime to wait.

"And you, what about the way you clam up when a conflict arises?" he started again. "Shouldn't you be willing to work on some of those issues, too?"

I took a few steps closer to Zaki and looked into his unsure eyes. "I would if we had a future, but what's the point?" My voice was unusually steady. "The truth is, Zaki, we are misfits. We're two booties with totally different colors and sizes." I ignored his clueless look. "We were never meant to be together. We forced the relationship. There never was one."

Zaki stepped back as if slapped.

"I did love you, Arissa," he said at last. Past tense had crept in at the mention of our relationship. It had finally expired. The fact was strangely consoling to me.

"It was not enough. I would have always wanted more."

That night I put Raian to bed and pulled out the two blue booties from my bureau drawer. I cupped them in my palms and kissed them. They had acquired a little aroma from being nestled under my clothes— the heady fragrance of Pleasures with a hint of Amarige D'amour. I set the socks on the bed and looked at them closely for a long time. They were not mirror images of each other; one was slightly plumper than the other, the other a trifle longer—perhaps the one that Baba had created with his limited knitting skills. They were imperfect, but they worked well together. No one could say they weren't a pair. I saw a thread coming out of the longer one and tugged at it lightly. The booty unraveled in my palm.

I dropped the blue thread that was once a sock and stepped back in horror.

Now there was only one. One sock to do the job of two.

It wasn't the call I was expecting but in my hurry to answer, I forgot to check the caller ID. I winced at the familiarity of the voice at the other end.

"Arissa, bayta, how have you been?" It was Ami.

For awhile I forgot to breathe. I pictured her at the other end, twisting the cord around her index finger, a nervous gesture of hers. For an instant, I was tempted to hang up but something stopped me.

"I've missed you." There was a pause. "Terribly."

I stayed silent, watching the clock ticking away, minutes growing awkward as they lengthened devoid of words.

"There is no easy way for me to start over," Ami was saying. "There is always the fear of failing the second time around as well."

Her words searched for mine. I realized with a start that for once there was no pain in my heart, no sorrow of missed opportunities. Over the past few months, I had developed a greater tolerance for people's failings as well as a need for letting go of unimportant associations in my life. Clearly this was one.

"I always loved you but could never become closer," she said. "I regret that in many ways."

Ma's words from the past came to mind and I said them out loud. "You need to leave the guilt behind, Ami. It has no room in your life. Yours or mine."

"What does that mean?"

I inhaled deeply and plunged right in. I had rehearsed this forever in my mind. It was important to my sanity that we stop this cat and mouse game with our relationship.

"You will realize the true worth of these words some day and it's not very easy for me to say this," I began, "but you need to let me go. We can't mend the past and I don't think it's fair for us to repair something that has such a low probability for survival."

There was a gasp at the other end. "What are you saying?"

"That I free you of all obligations toward me." Somehow my own voice sounded strangely foreign to me.

"What? Are you insane? Have you completely lost your mind? I am your mother...you can't—" There was horror in her voice, obviously slated by fear of losing her firstborn. "I'll always be your mother You just can't...that's impossible."

"It's really not, Ami. It's a relationship that has never been nurtured and now we are just picking at straws. You know that and I know that."

"I am family, you can't just cut me loose," she was screaming now, hyperventilating. "You can't discard me like day-old trash. I deserve better than that."

She fell silent and I could hear heavy, jerky breathing. I waited for her to compose herself, feeling sorry for her but yet surprised by my own self-control.

"How can you want something like that?" she asked at last in a broken voice.

I sighed. "Ami, you know the answer to that."

I didn't put down the phone until I heard the soft click at the other end. *She didn't fight that battle hard enough,* I thought to myself and then chased that reflection away. It was time to move on.

I was inside the plot. It thickened and thinned out. It pulsated, it throbbed. It weakened, it strengthened.

My fingers had a life of their own as they typed. I was amazed at what appeared on the screen in front of me. I was giddy with the power that words gave me.

But for the protagonist, there was no closure.

Day dawned and the sun set without a change in his circumstances. The pain subsided—for awhile—and then returned with a vengeance, gashing wounds deeper than before. No bang or a ping, no jolt or push advanced his cause. Surprisingly, the nervous energy of my failed relationship gave birth to new ideas and thoughts in my mind. The boy became a man and was reduced to a boy at times. How will he reconcile his affairs? Will he even find fulfillment in his lifetime? And what about the people in his life? Like feathers, they got further and further away the more he reached out to them—the father, the lover, the sister. They had different names and roles at various junctions in the novel—the adversary, the naysayer, the demon. Perhaps they should all meet a similar fate, I decided finally, wearing the protagonist's hat and shuddering with the weight that decision carried. I sat back as if pushed and counted the seconds. At twenty, I turned back to the screen and started typing away furiously. *Don't look back now,* I remembered thinking, and then I retained nothing of that night until morning struck me with the force of a slap. It was the day of our anniversary—Faizan's and mine. The sixth one without him. The sixth one with Raian in my life.

When Ann Marie's call came, I was halfway out the door, late for a meeting with a 35-year-old Pakistani-American entrepreneur whose two-year-old ad agency had a growth revenue of $9 million a year. The company had partnered with an art organization in Pakistan to promote its cultural heritage by showcasing music, art, theater, and film all across the United States. The agency pledged $20,000 to *Chamak* over a period of two years, and the magazine had decided to run a profile on the company in its summer issue.

I was delighted to hear Ann Marie's voice. I hadn't spoken to her in three weeks.

"I thought you fell off the face of the earth."

"Not quite."

I told her about Zaki and she seemed relieved that it had ended.

"There never was a future in that arrangement, I was always certain."

I couldn't bring myself to talk to her about Ami.

As the minutes ticked away, I stole a few glances at the flashing light on my cell phone that meant I had a message from someone. I didn't have to take many guesses to know who it was—the appointment I had stood up.

"How's the book coming along?" Ann Marie finally asked.

"Oh, I am just finishing up," I replied. I paused as I felt a sudden rush of anxiety. That would mean the end of a very significant part of my life. What was next? A relationship that was dead and a legacy that was almost complete. That left just Raian.

"Arissa?"

I realized I had been quiet and had tuned out the last few sentences of Ann Marie.

"I know you. You are already obsessing about the future, aren't you?"

"What is it you have?" I laughed. "A mind-reading radar that relays all information to you?"

"Arissa, you have to understand that we live in a world of lies," Ann Marie's tone was serious. "We are all taught to live for the next minute. As if the turning of time can bring us perpetual happiness. Doesn't living for future rob us in some way of what we have now, at this minute? Why don't you allow yourself to savor this instant?"

I pondered over her words as I hung up.

My *now* was pretty packed, I realized as I went through some mail. I pulled out a letter from a bank and ripped it open. It was a credit card application addressed to Raian. Despite myself, I began laughing.

I was outside a bookstore, staring in a disassociated way at the poster in the window. I was aware of everything but it. The stop sign at a distance where a biker had braced himself on the handle of his bike to open a candy bar, the strong smell of coffee from within the store, the steady line of marching ants at my feet.

I jumped at the sound of a horn and looked at a woman who was entering the store with a reluctant child in tow. I turned to the warm inviting eyes of my husband in the poster, feeling strangely uplifted as if on a sunbeam. My sense of perfection was bothered by the fact that the poster was a tad lopsided. You would think they would be a bit more careful in handling a dream.

I sighed. So this was it, the end of my expedition. It scared me to have moved past that goal. I started to move as the store clerk came up behind the poster to straighten it. She looked briefly at me and nodded. She did not recognize me. She and I had met for two hours a few weeks ago. Many authors, many books ago. The veil would have made her remember me easier. The thought amused me.

I walked away carrying a sense of pride tinged by loss. This moment that has come after a million agonizing moments was mine. After that day, it will never be mine again.

That night I dreamt that my home was ablaze.

There was heat and darkness all around me, flames licking my body. I heard a chant of *Al Mani* echo around me, that verse again; there seemed to be many voices but only one that I could actually place. I saw Ma run in and out of the flaming walls of fire, her haunted eyes looking for something dear. I tried to follow her but stopped as I saw the entryway shudder and collapse before me. A moving ball of fire spun past it and headed my way. I stood paralyzed as it ricocheted off the walls, bounced off the ceiling and set the hallway drapes on fire. It was only when it reached me that I saw that the burning sphere was actually a suitcase. I sensed that there was something precious inside and tried to pry open the lock, flames scorching my impatient fingers. Inside there was an inert little body covered in a maroon blanket. I hastily pulled it out, warding off the fire. The baby wriggled in my arms, now awake, and then turned to me. It was my son as a baby. My breast tingled and cramped at the sight of him, and then milk flowed from me freely, drenching my shirt. I stood for a long time at the center of the inferno, letting my son suckle. I didn't notice at what point the flames finally lost their strength and the warmth seeped into the floor. I felt my feet burn. Then there was nothing, only light and the smile of a mother who stood at a distance and watched us in silent pride.

My Firedancer is gone, I remember thinking. *Now only fillers remain.* Somehow that didn't panic me. The fillers were my life now.

TWENTY-FIVE

July 2007

"Dearest Faizan,

I completed *Soul Searcher*!

It took me six years to complete your legacy. I have no more goals, only a little gift left by you, our son and your parting gift that gave me the gift of hope and survival!

He smiles like you. And knows the exact time to cheer me up when I am down. The other day when I came through the door, he took the groceries from me and carried them through the house. It took my breath away. He has your lopsided grin and the same shock of hair, more at the front, a few curls on the sides, straight down his back. He hates having his nails clipped. I sometimes wonder if he isn't an incarnate of you, not that I ever believed in those things. But I didn't believe in a lot of things until you left. I still believe that love lives forever. But I learned that loved ones don't."

I stopped and studied the tip of my pen. The night air brought in the scent of my freshly planted moghras from the yard. The first thing I did after buying my own home was to plant Arabian and night-blooming jasmines. The curtains danced to the rhythm of the breeze. The news said they had found more bone fragments while clearing a derelict building in New York. The authorities believed they belonged to victims of the World Trade Center attacks. It had kept me awake at nights. How would I react if the call came? It had taken years to piece my life together. How would I explain the situation to Raian?

I looked down again at the letter in front of me.

"Is it possible that through Raian, you have come to fulfill the vow of being with me forever?

I have discovered that there is a simple way of looking at life. One breath, one second at a time. You followed that routine. I never agreed, and I now see the worth in it. Our lives are not ours. The breaths we breathe are on loan; your mother taught me that. When your grief is uncontrollable, wipe away someone else's tears. It helps you heal quicker, she said. I was not always an eager pupil. I was even hurtful at times, yet she understood and stood by me in her nonjudgmental way. It surprises me how easily love comes to her, as if her heart came in ready-made compartments for all of us. She made me a better parent.

Had you lived, you would have seen that I did many things differently, not always in the manner you'd have liked to see them done, but I did what I could and hope I made the right choices. I hope you will hover over us and laugh and cry with us. Even touch us at times. I always imagined you near me, a dimension away but still closely linked. For me, you will always exist as a wonderful memory, a silent companion. I love you, Faizan.

Arissa"

I opened the wooden box and slid the letter in and looked at the stack of four orange books beside me with a sense of gratification. The wooden statue, Zarek, a gift from Juhi, lay at the top of the pile, still asleep in his steadfast perseverance. Faizan's legacy had taken many years to finish but it was finally done. *Soul Searcher*, it said on the cover, inscribed in a giant Zapfino font. At the bottom were two bedraggled children shooting *phalsas*. The art wasn't my masterpiece, but it was better than any other work of mine. It stated the author's name in bold, and at the bottom, in small print, listed me as a coauthor. The photo of Faizan at the back was taken the day of our second anniversary at Green Field Churrascaria. He was wearing a navy blue Dickies knit shirt and his broad grin creased up the skin around his eyes.

It wasn't a perfect day for a picnic but Juhi and I made the best of the circumstances as we spread a blanket on the wet grass. The park overlooked the Texas Medical Center and offered a clear view of the downtown skyline. It seemed like an ideal place to meet after Raian's eye appointment. Juhi had come down from New York to visit me with her five-year-old son, Amar, a spirited and chatty child who looked almost Caucasian with his shock of blond hair and true blue eyes.

"Are you sure you're certain about who the father is?" I had teased Juhi, and she laughed.

"It doesn't matter," she assured me. "There are some who don't think he's mine either."

I admired her. She wore a beige camisole with spaghetti straps that hugged her chest and exposed her big pregnant belly. She had married the man she'd started dating a year after Amar was born and was now expecting child number two.

Amar had begged his mother for an eye patch like Raian's and was convinced that his playmate was pretending to be a pirate. Juhi finally agreed. There was no easy way to explain a whole lot to a five year old. We sprayed our wriggly pirate kids generously with bug spray. They eyed a rabbit and took off after it, leaving us yelling after them to be careful.

"They do make our lives complete, don't they?" sighed Juhi, lying on her back on the blanket.

I lay down beside her and closed my eyes. "I guess so. Sometimes not in the way we imagined. Maybe it's wrong to see perfection as the key to bliss."

A kingfisher took off in the distance, and its loud, dry rattle disturbed the calm air just as the afternoon sun decided to hide behind a veil of clouds. I breathed in the sweet scent of the fresh wet earth. It had rained earlier that day. Amidst the hummingbird's melody and the fragrance of the myrtle trees, I heard a full-throttled laugh. I looked up to see a woman in a headscarf and a tall man pass by, the woman's hands barely touching her companion's. She turned to us apologetically, embarrassed at the intensity of her joy. I saw my past in her. In my present, I am a century old. Some notions had vacated, some dreams redesigned, thoughts regrouped, new plans drawn. Moments had moved on, echoes lingered, captivated by environs. I heard the thud of the past in my heart, the jingle of the have-beens, and weaved them in deftly with the soft tinkle of the present. After all, sound is what makes life a cheerful place. The unabashed sun shed its cover and shone in its bold splendor if only for a minute as Raian emerged from the bushes and hobbled toward me. He stood directly in my line of vision and held his hand to sign.

"You're shining, Mama," he conveyed with a grin.

Signs make the world livable, I thought as I pulled him close. He might not be a product of someone's saffron dreams but he was definitely the answer to mine.

Reflections of America Series
MODERN HISTORY PRESS

The Reflections of America Series highlights autobiography, fiction, and poetry which express the quest to discover one's context within modern society.

The Stories of Devil-Girl
ANYA ACHTENBERG

How to Write a Suicide Note: Serial Essays that Saved a Woman's Life
SHERRY QUAN LEE

Chinese BlackBird
SHERRY QUAN LEE

Saffron Dreams
SHAILA ABDULLAH

My Dirty Little Secrets
TONY MANDARICH

ABOUT THE AUTHOR

 Shaila Abdullah is an award-winning Pakistani-American author whose work focuses on the strengths and weaknesses of Pakistani women and their often unconventional choices in life. Her work also deals with the Asian experience in America, the conflict between the two worlds and the culture of her adopted country.

Abdullah received a Hobson Foundation grant for *Saffron Dreams*. Her debut book, *Beyond the Cayenne Wall,* is a collection of stories about Pakistani women struggling to find their individualities despite the barriers imposed by society. The collection won the Norumbega Jury Prize for Outstanding Fiction and the DIY Festival Award, among other accolades.

Abdullah was born in Karachi, Pakistan, in 1971. She has published several short stories, articles, and essays for various publications, including *Women's Own, She, Fashion Collection, Sulekha, and Dallas Child.* She is a seasoned print, web, and multimedia designer as well. Abdullah lives with her family in Austin, Texas and is a member of the Texas Writers' League.

More information about the author and her work is available on her website at www.shailaabdullah.com.

Printed in the United States
138370LV00002B/26/P